ALEC FORBES
AND
HIS FRIEND
ANNIE

GEORGE MACDONALD

BETHANY HOUSE PUBLISHERS
MINNEAPOLIS, MINNESOTA 55438

A condensed version of George MacDonald's classic Alec Forbes of Howglen, specially adapted and edited by Michael R. Phillips

Cover illustration by Dan Thornberg,
Bethany House Publishers staff artist.

Published by Bethany House Publishers
A Ministry of Bethany Fellowship, Inc.
6820 Auto Club Road, Minneapolis, Minnesota 55438

Printed in the United States of America

Library of Congress Cataloging-in-Publication Data

MacDonald, George, 1824–1905.
    Alec Forbes and his friend Annie / George MacDonald ; edited by Michael R. Phillips.
       p.   cm.
    Rev. ed. of: Alec Forbes of Howglen. 1865.
    Summary: Orphaned as a child, Annie's special friendship with Alec is a source of strength and security that sees them both through many difficulties in nineteenth-century Scotland.

    [1. Friendship—Fiction. 2. Scotland—Fiction.]
I. Phillips, Michael R. , 1946–
II. MacDonald, George, 1824–1905. Alec Forbes of Howglen. III. Title.
PZ7.M1475A1   1990
[Fic]—dc20   90–42070
ISBN 1–55661–140–4   CIP
                                            AC

BETHANY HOUSE PUBLISHERS
Minneapolis, Minnesota 55438

The Novels of George MacDonald Edited for Today's Reader

Edited Title	Original Title
The Fisherman's Lady	*Malcolm*
The Marquis' Secret	*The Marquis of Lossie*
The Baronet's Song	*Sir Gibbie*
The Shepherd's Castle	*Donal Grant*
The Tutor's First Love	*David Elginbrod*
The Musician's Quest	*Robert Falconer*
The Maiden's Bequest	*Alec Forbes*
The Curate's Awakening	*Thomas Wingfold*
The Lady's Confession	*Paul Faber*
The Baron's Apprenticeship	*There and Back*
The Highlander's Last Song	*What's Mine's Mine*
The Gentlewoman's Choice	*Weighed and Wanting*
The Laird's Inheritance	*Warlock O'Glenwarlock*
The Minister's Restoration	*Salted with Fire*
A Daughter's Devotion	*Mary Marston*
The Peasant Girl's Dream	*Heather and Snow*
The Landlady's Master	*The Elect Lady*
The Poet's Homecoming	*Home Again*

MacDonald Classics Edited for Young Readers

Wee Sir Gibbie of the Highlands
Alec Forbes and His Friend Annie

George MacDonald: Scotland's Beloved Storyteller by Michael Phillips
Discovering the Character of God by George MacDonald
Knowing the Heart of God by George MacDonald

SUNRISE BOOKS, PUBLISHERS

Eureka, California 95501

The Sunrise Centenary Editions of the Original Works of George MacDonald in Leatherbound Collector's Editions

Novels

Alec Forbes of Howglen
Sir Gibbie
Thomas Wingfold, Curate
Malcolm
Salted with Fire
The Elect Lady

Sermons

Unspoken Sermons I
The Hope of the Gospel

Poems

A Hidden Life & Other Poems
The Disciple and Other Poems

The Masterline Series of Studies and Essays About George MacDonald

From a Northern Window: A Personal Remembrance of George MacDonald by his son Ronald MacDonald

The Harmony Within: The Spiritual Vision of George MacDonald by Rolland Hein

George MacDonald's Fiction: A Twentieth-Century View by Richard Reis

God's Fiction: Symbolism and Allegory in the Works of George MacDonald by David Robb

CONTENTS

INTRODUCTION

One of the favorites of all George MacDonald's novels was originally called *Alec Forbes of Howglen* and was first published in 1865. It is a wonderful story of childhood, of growing up, of the seasons, of friendship, of fear and faith and loyalty, and of love. It has always been one of MacDonald's stories I most enjoy. I have read it three or four times, and I always discover new things in it.

So much of this book has become part of my life that I often find myself thinking about it unconsciously. Whenever I see snow, I immediately picture Alec in my mind standing beside his pile of snowballs. When I see a small boat, I think of Annie and Alec and Curly floating down the Glamour. When I think of rats, I am instantly in Annie's garret. And so many other images crowd into my brain—the schoolmaster's whip, harvest time in the fields, the flood, Juno, and, of course, the faces of Annie and Alec as I picture them in my imagination.

For most of the twentieth century, George MacDonald's books have been nearly lost, for MacDonald died in 1905 at the age of eighty. Though he had written over fifty books, most of them have been unavailable for years and years, not even to be found in libraries. One of the reasons for this is that most of them were very, very long (four hundred, five hundred, and some even six hundred pages!) A good many were also written with frequent passages in a heavy Scottish dialect, which to Americans today looks like a foreign language. *Alec Forbes of Howglen* is just such a book. When George MacDonald first wrote about Annie and Alec, the book was 450 pages long (with tiny print!) Try reading this passage from the original:

> *"Robert was servin' a bit bairnie ower the coonter wi' a pennyworth o' triacle, when, in a jiffy, there cam' sic a blast, an' a reek fit to smore ye, oot o' the bit fire, an' the shop was fu' o' reek afore ye could hae pitten the pint o' ae throom upo' the pint o' the ither. 'Preserve's a'!' cried Rob; but or he could say anither word, butt the house, scushlin in her bauchles, comes Nancy, rinnin', an' opens the door wi' a scraich: 'Preserve's a'! quo' she, 'Robert, the lum's in a low!' An' fegs! atween the twa reeks, to sunder them, there was nothing but Nancy hersel'. The hoose was as fu' as it cud haud, frae cellar to garret, o' the blackest reek 'at ever crap oot' o' coal."*

Perhaps some of you will be able to figure out what all that says. But many will be happy to be able to read about Alec Forbes in plain English. In this new edition of George MacDonald's classic, titled *Alec Forbes and His Friend Annie*, the Scottish has been "translated" and the original book edited and shortened. Hopefully, as a result, you will thus be able to enjoy MacDonald's gift for storytelling even more.

Some of you who read this might never have heard of George MacDonald before now. But if you enjoy this story as I think is likely, you will probably make a dear friend of this old Scottish author. If that happens, as it did to me, I hope you will discover and read many more of his books. There are *so* many to choose from! MacDonald wrote stories for children, stories for grown-ups, poetry, fairy tales, and collections of short stories. And they are all out there waiting for you to discover. I first discovered George MacDonald twenty years ago. I have been searching for his books ever since. And there are still some I haven't yet read.

Most of all, George MacDonald wrote about people. The characters in his books, like Alec and Annie and Curly, wee Sir Gibbie, and Robert Falconer and Shargar and Diamond and so many others—they all have a way of becoming your friends. I don't know what I'd have done if I hadn't made so many lifelong friends of the characters in MacDonald's books during these last twenty years.

I hope the characters in this book become your friends too, and that you will make many more such friends in the other MacDonald books you read.

Michael Phillips

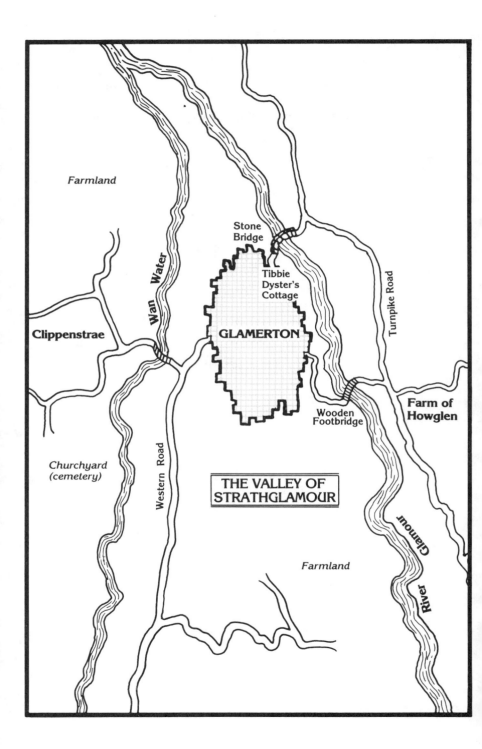

Chapter One

THE FARMYARD ON BURYING DAY

The farmyard was full of the light of a summer day at noon. Not a living creature was to be seen anywhere. Through the gate the dark forms of cattle could be seen far off in the fields. And on the road nearer by, a cart crawled along, drawn by one sleepy horse. An occasional weary moo came from some cow kept in the barn, but not even a cat crossed the yard.

Now a farmyard about noon in the summer is never the liveliest of places. But there was a particular reason why this one was exceptionally dreary and deserted.

Actually there were a good many people about the place. But they were all gathered in the nicest room of the farmhouse—a room of good size, with a clean wood floor, a black mahogany table, and chairs with high straight backs. In every one of these chairs sat a silent man whose gaze was either fixed on the floor or was lost somewhere in the air. Most were clothed in black, and each wore a black coat. Their hard, thick, brown hands were grasping their knees, or were folded in each other. No one said a word, and there was not a woman to be seen in the room.

Suddenly another man appeared at the open door of the

room. His shirtsleeves were very white against his other cloth-
ing, which like that of the rest was black.

"If any of you want to see the corpse, now's the time," he
said to the men seated there.

No one made a move to get up. After waiting a moment, the
carpenter turned around again and went back up the narrow
stairway to the upper room where the corpse lay.

"I reckon they've all seen him before," he remarked as he
rejoined his companion, a man named Thomas Crann. "Poor
fellow! His body's so worn out, there won't be much of him to
rise again."

"George, man, don't make jokes in front of the dead man,"
returned Crann. "You don't know when your own turn may
come."

"It's not disrespect to the dead, Thomas," said George
Macwha. "I was only pitying his worn face. I just don't like to
put the lid of the box over him."

"Hoot! Let the Lord look after His own. The lid of the coffin
hides nothing from His eye."

Thomas Crann was a stout, broad-shouldered man, a stonemason by trade, strong in body but asthmatic. He was regarded
in the neighborhood as a very religious man. But there were
those who did not like him because all he seemed to do was
rebuke the views of others.

Together they lifted the lid of the coffin into place and fas-
tened it down. But though there was now darkness about his
body, the dead man himself did not know it, because he was full
of light. For this man was one who all his life had been full of
goodness and truth.

In the meantime, the minister had arrived, and the usual
religious ceremony of a Scottish funeral—the reading of the
Word and prayer—was going on in the big room below. When
the prayer was over, the company of men seated themselves
again. They waited until the coffin had descended the stairs,
carried by the carpenter and mason, and was placed in the
hearse, which stood just outside the door.

Then one after another of them slowly rose and went outside,
watching in silence. At last the horse-drawn hearse began to

move, and all the men fell in behind it to move in an irregular procession out of the farmyard. They were joined by several more men in buggies and on horseback. And all of them crept as a silent black train toward the cemetery.

When the last man had disappeared down the road, the women began to come out. The first to enter the deserted room was a hard-featured woman, the sister of the dead man. In a few moments more a servant-girl appeared and began to help her put the room back in order.

"I don't need any help here," said her mistress coldly. "Go out and look for that poor, little, good-for-nothing Annie. If it had only been the Almighty's will to have taken her and left him."

"Don't say a word against the child, mem," the girl said. "The dead will hear you and not lie still."

"Go and do what I tell you this minute! What business do you have to be saying such to me? He had no drop of your blood!"

The girl made no reply but left the room in quest of Annie. When she reached the door, she stood for a moment and called "Annie!" But then she let the end of the call die away, and decided to set off to find the missing child by the use of her eyes instead of her voice.

First she went into the barn, then through it out into the field, but she could find the girl nowhere. At length she came to the door of one of the cow-houses. She looked round the corner into the stall next to the door. This stall was occupied by a favorite cow—brown with large white spots—called Brownie. There was fresh-cut grass at one end. Half-buried in the grass, with her back against the wall, sat Annie, holding one of Brownie's ears with one hand, and stroking the creature's nose with the other.

She was a delicate child, about nine years old, with blue eyes half full of tears, hair somewhere between dark and fair, and a pale face which now held a faint smile. The old cow continued to hold out her nose to be stroked.

"Isn't Brownie a fine cow, Emma?" asked Annie, as the maid went on staring at her. "Poor Brownie! Nobody paid any attention to me, and so I came to you, Brownie."

She laid her cheek—white, smooth, and thin, against the broad, flat hairy forehead of the friendly cow. Then turning again to Emma, she said, "Don't tell Auntie where I am, Emma. Let me be. I'm best here with Brownie."

Emma did not say a word but returned to her mistress.

"Where's the child, Emma? At some mischief?"

"Hoot, mem! The child's well enough. Children mustn't be followed every minute like calves."

"Where is she?"

"I can't just downright exactly take it upon me to say," answered Emma, "but I have no fear about her. She's a wise child."

"You're not the lassie's keeper, Emma. I see I must seek her out myself. You're helping her hide from me as usual."

So saying, Auntie Meg went out to look for her niece. It was some time before her search brought her to the cow-stall. By that time Annie was almost asleep in the grass, though the cow was gradually pulling it away from under her. Through the open door the child could see the sunlight lying heavy upon the hot stones that paved the yard. But where she was it was so cool and dark, and the cow was such good, kindly company, and she was so safe hidden from Auntie. Or so she thought—for no one had ever found her there before and she knew Emma would not tell. Therefore, as I say, she was nearly asleep with comfort, half buried in Brownie's dinner.

But she was roused all at once to a sense of danger. She looked up, and at that moment the hawk nose of her aunt came round the door. Auntie's temper was no better than usual. After all, it had pleased the Almighty to take the brother she loved and leave behind this child whom she regarded as a painful responsibility. The woman's small, fierce eyes, and her big, thin nose—both red with secret crying—did not appear to Annie to contain the mother love of the universe.

"You plaguesome brat!" she cried. "Emma has been looking for you and I have been looking for you far and near, in the very rat holes, and here you are on your own father's burying day taking up with a cow!"

It would not be hard to find the causes of Annie's preference for the company of Brownie to that of her aunt. For to Annie and her needs there was comfort in Brownie's large, mild eyes and her hairy, featureless face, which was all nose and no nose.

Indeed, she found more of God in Brownie than in the human form of Auntie Meg.

Without a word of reply, Annie rose, flung her arms around Brownie's head, and kissed the white star on her forehead. Auntie seized her hand with a rough but not altogether ungentle action, and led her away to the house.

The stones felt very hot to her little bare feet.

CHAPTER
TWO

A CONVERSATION

By this time the funeral was approaching the churchyard. All along the way the procession had been silently joined by others. All stopped at the gate to the little cemetery, and from there the hands of friends and neighbors carried the dead man to his grave. Then, after uncovering their heads as a last token of respect and farewell, the company left, going their separate ways.

In one of the buggies leaving the place of the tombs, a conversation was going on. One of the two, Robert Bruce[1], was a cousin of James Anderson, the deceased. The other was called Andrew Constable, a worthy elder of the church.

"Well, Robert," began Mr. Constable after they had gone on in silence for about a mile or so, "what's to be done with little Annie Anderson and her Auntie Meg, now that the poor man's gone? You must be their nearest living relative."

"They can't have much left after the doctor's paid."

"I'm sure you're right there. He's been sick so long, I can't

---

[1]This Robert Bruce had been named after one of Scotland's greatest heroes, King Robert Bruce, who defeated the English in 1314 at Bannockburn and was king of Scotland from 1306 to 1329. The cousin of Annie's father liked to call the ancient king his "namesake", and liked to make people think he was related to the king.

remember the last time he was able to do a day's work."

"James Dow looked well after the farm though, during the illness."

"No doubt. He's a good man. But there can't be much money left."

A pause followed.

"What do you think, Andrew?" began Bruce again. "You're well known as an honest and levelheaded man. Do you think that folk would expect anything of me if the worst came to the worst and they had no where else to turn?"

"Well, Robert, I don't think much good can come of looking to what people might expect of you."

"That's just what I was thinking myself. For you see, I have my own family to provide for, and a difficult enough time already. I could hardly afford to be helping them with money so hard to come by."

"No doubt. No doubt. But—"

"I know what you're going to say. Because of my shop I have to be a little careful about what people say. If I once got—not to say a bad name—but just the wind of not being so considerate as I ought to have been to my relatives, then folk might starting walking on past my door and cross over to Jamie Mitchell's shop across the street."

"Do what's right, Robert Bruce."

"But a man's got to take care of his own family first."

"Well," said Andrew with a smile, for he understood well enough that Bruce meant only his immediate children, although he pretended to have mistaken his meaning, "then if the girl falls to your hands, no doubt you must take charge of her."

"I didn't mean James Anderson's little Annie—I mean my own."

"Whatever your decision, I hope you will cast your care upon *Him*."

"I know all about that, Andrew. But my opinion on that particular scripture is this—that every man has to hold what he can by himself, and what runs over may be committed to Him, for you can hold it no longer. Them that won't take care of what they have will be destroyed. It's lazy and thoughtless to be running to God with every little thing. You know the story about my namesake and the spider?"[2]

"Well enough," answered Andrew.

He did not add that he could see nothing that the old story had to do with what they were talking about. But Bruce's remark did not take him by surprise. Bruce was in the habit of bringing up his namesake of ancient Scotland whenever he could. He wanted everybody to think, though he never actually *said* it, that he was descended from the king.

Andrew Constable knew well that it would be a bad day for poor little Annie Anderson if she had to go live under Bruce's roof, for the merchant had quite a reputation for meanness and selfishness. As they rode along, therefore, he silently hoped that Auntie Meg might find some way of managing financially without having to part with the child. For he knew too that though her aunt was fierce and hard, she had yet a warm spot somewhere about her heart.

Margaret Anderson had known perfectly well for some time that she and Annie would have to part before long. The lease of the farm would run out at the close of the autumn of next year. It had been losing money anyway, so she had no desire to renew it, especially alone. When her brother's debts were paid, even after the sale of the animals, there would not remain more than a hundred and fifty pounds.

For herself, having no other home to go to, she planned to get a job as a maid. But what was to become of Annie she could not yet see.

In the meantime they would remain on the farm for another year. Auntie Meg made sure she prepared her by telling her of the coming change. But it seemed to Annie so long in coming that it never would arrive. So for the whole next year she enjoyed the pleasures of the farm life, without thinking much of the ap-

---

[2]A famous tale is told of a time when the original Robert Bruce lay imprisoned and discouraged, and watched a spider in his cell working hard, against the odds, to construct his web. From his persistent efforts it is said the future king of Scotland gained courage to continue the battle against his enemies. This legend had nothing at all to do with the scripture verse the modern Robert Bruce was talking about.

proaching time when she would have to go away.

And why should Annie think of the future when the present was full of such delights?

Even with Auntie's temper, there were numberless pleasures around Annie. She could ride out into the fields perched aloft on the foreman's shoulders, Dowie as he was called. And if she was late for one of her meals and Auntie scolded her and told her she would have to go to bed without supper, rosy-faced Emma always managed to bring the child the best of everything, even cream in her milk and butter on her oatcake. And Brownie was always friendly, ever ready to let Annie share a corner of her stall as a refuge. And she would ride the horses to water, sitting sideways on their broad backs like a barefooted lady.

And then there were the great delights of the harvest season. She would stay out in the fields with the reapers from morning till night. She shared in their meals and made their labor easier with her gentle frolic. Every day after the noon meal she would go to sleep on the shady side of a stook of straw, on two or three sheaves which Dowie would lay down for her in a choice spot.

Indeed, the little mistress was very fond of sleep. She would go to sleep anywhere. In fact, this habit was one of her aunt's chief grounds of complaint. Before time to cut the hay, when the grass in the fields was long, if she came upon any place that took her fancy, she would tumble down at once and fall asleep on it. At such times it was not easy to find her. But in the harvest field, at least, no harm could come of this habit, for Dowie always watched over her like a mother. The only discomfort of the harvest field was that the sharp stubble forced her to wear shoes. But when the grain had all been carried home and the potatoes had been dug up and heaped in warm pits for the winter, and the mornings and evenings began to grow cold again, then she had to put on both shoes *and* socks, which she did not like at all.

So through a whole winter of ice and snow, through a whole spring of promises, through a summer of glory, and another autumn of harvest joy, the day grew nearer when Annie and her Aunt Margaret would have to leave the farm.

And still to Annie it seemed as far off as ever.

CHAPTER
THREE

ROBERT BRUCE

O ne lovely evening in October, when the shadows were falling from the western sun, and a keen little wind was just getting ready to come out the moment the sun was out of sight, Annie saw a long shadow coming in at the yard. She continued to fasten up the cows for the night, drawing iron chains around their soft necks.

In a few moments the shadow stopped in front of her. It was none other than her father's cousin, Robert Bruce. He spoke to her in the smoothest voice he could find, fumbling at the same time in his coat pocket.

"How are you tonight, Annie? Are you well? And how's your auntie?" He waited for no reply to any of these questions, but went on, "See what I have brought you from the shop."

He put into her hand about a half dozen pieces of candy wrapped up in a bit of paper. With this gift he left her and walked on to the open door of the house. As a cousin, he considered himself privileged to enter without so much as even a knock. He found the mistress in the kitchen overseeing the cooking of dinner.

"How are you tonight, Margaret?" he said, again in a smooth tone. "You're busy as usual, I see. Well, the hand of the diligent maketh rich, you know."

"That portion of the Word must be of limited application," returned Margaret. "No man would dare say that my hand hasn't been diligent. But God knows I'm no richer for all my hard work."

"We mustn't complain, Margaret. Right or wrong, it's the Lord's will."

"It's easy for you to say, Robert Bruce, with all your money in the bank. But I'm a poor, lonely body that has to work for her bread. And I'm not so young as I might be. Not that I'm about to die of old age either."

"I haven't as much in the bank as some people think, though what's there is safe enough. But I have a good business, and it might be better yet if I had more money to put into it. But tell me, Margaret, what are you going to do with yourself?"

"I'm going to my uncle and aunt—old John Peterson and his wife. They're old and frail now and need someone to look after them."

"Then you're well provided for. Praise be thanked, Margaret."

"Oh, no doubt!" replied Margaret with bitterness. But Bruce took no notice of her sarcasm about his wealth and her poverty.

"And what's to become of the child?" he asked.

"I'll just have to find some decent person in the town to take her in and let her go to school."

"What'll that cost you, Margaret, to pay someone to take her in?"

"I don't know, but the lassie's able to pay for her own upbringing."

"Oh, I know about the hundred and fifty pounds she inherits from her father. But it's not far that will go these days. Why don't you lend the money out at five percent interest, and then there would be something coming in from it? The child might almost—not easily, I grant—be brought up on the interest."

Margaret lifted her head and stared at him.

"And who would give five percent for her money when he can get almost as much from the bank?"

"I would, Margaret. The poor orphan has nobody but you and me to look to. And I would willingly do that much for her.

I'll tell you what—I'll give her five percent for her money, and for the little interest I'll take her in with my own children. She can live with us and eat and go to school with them. And then—after a while—we'll see what comes next."

This seemed like a very fair offer to Margaret. It was known around town that the Bruce children were well enough dressed and looked well fed. Robert did have the reputation of being somewhat mean. But Margaret did not regard that as the worst possible fault, or one that would hurt the child. So she told her cousin she would think about it, which was all he had expected. He left feeling certain she would agree in the end.

Bruce rode back into town feeling quite pleased with himself! To get both the money and its owner into his hands was a wonderful prospect. He did not actually intend to be dishonest to Annie. He was only glad to think that in the public's eye he would have done his duty by his relative, and at the same time he would have all that money to put to use in his business! He was sure he could feed and clothe Annie for much less than the interest would amount to.

And then, if anything should happen to her—she had always been rather delicate—like a serious illness, or even a premature death, well, perhaps he would end up with the money at *no* interest at all! If she did well, he had three sons growing up. One of them might marry the young heiress. Grocer Robert was as scheming about his plans as had been old King Robert of time past.

But the foreman of the farm, James Dow, was not at all pleased when he heard of the arrangement Margaret had made.

"I can't stand that Bruce," he said. "He wouldn't fling a bone to a dog before he'd looked it over himself to see if anything was left on it."

James agreed with Margaret, however, that it would be better to keep Annie unaware of her destiny as long as possible. The reason for this was because now that she was about to part with Annie, Margaret was feeling a growth of tenderness toward her for the first time.

But also they did not want to say anything to Annie because they doubted whether she would be entirely comfortable in her new home.

CHAPTER
FOUR

THE LITTLE GRAY
TOWN OF GLAMERTON

A day that is fifty years off comes as certainly as if it were next week. Annie's feeling that things would continue on happily at the farm forever did not stop the sandglass of Old Time.

At last the day arrived when she and her Aunt Margaret had to leave the farm. Everything they had was to be sold at a public auction. A great crowd of friends, neighbors, and acquaintances gathered at the farm.

Little Annie now understood what all the bustle meant. The day of desolation her aunt had been telling her about for so long had actually arrived. All the things she had known so well were vanishing from her sight forever.

She was in the barn when the sing-song of the auctioneer's voice made her look outside and listen. Suddenly the truth dawned on her. She burst into tears over an old rake that had just been sold. She had always called it hers because she had dragged it during the harvest time.

Wiping her eyes after a moment, she fled to Brownie's stall. She buried herself in the straw and hay and began crying again.

27

After a while she stopped crying and gazed sadly at the old cow feeding away as if food were everything and an auction nothing at all. Soon footsteps approached the stable, and to her further dismay, two men she did not know untied Brownie and actually led her away before her eyes.

She continued to stare at the empty space where Brownie had stood. But how could she sit there without Brownie!

She jumped up, sobbing so hard that she could scarcely breathe, and rushed across the yard into the crowded house, and up the stairs to her own little room. There she threw herself on the bed, buried her eyes in the pillow, and, overcome with grief, fell fast asleep.

When she awoke in the morning, she didn't remember Emma's undressing her and putting her to bed. Yesterday now seemed only like a dreadful dream. But when she went outside she found that yesterday would not stay among her dreams.

Brownie's stall was *empty*.

The horses were all gone and most of the cattle. The pigs were gone too, and most of the chickens and ducks. Two or three favorite hens were left, which Auntie was going to take with her. But all the living creatures Annie had loved were gone. Not one had been kept for her.

Her life seemed bitter with the bitterness of death.

In the afternoon her aunt came up to her room where she sat in tearful silence. Auntie told her that she was going to take her into the town. Then without further explanation, she began to put Annie's few personal belongings into an old trunk. Along with some trifles that lay about the room, she threw into the bottom of the box about a dozen old books which had been on the chest of drawers since long before Annie could remember. Annie sat in silence and asked no questions. Her life had grown all dark, and she did not care what came next.

For an hour the box stood on the floor like a coffin.

Then Emma came up, with red eyes and red nose, and carried it downstairs. Auntie came up again, dressed in her Sunday clothes. She dressed Annie in her best dress and bonnet and led her down to the door. There stood a horse and cart. As Annie was getting into the cart, Emma rushed out from somewhere, grabbed her up, kissed her several times, and before Margaret could turn around in the cart to see what was the commotion, handed her into James Dow's arms and vanished again.

Dowie was going to put her into the cart with a kiss, for he dared not speak. But before he knew it, Annie's arms went round his neck and she clung to him sobbing. This roused Auntie's anger. She spoke harshly. Annie let go, Dowie was free, and Annie fell into the cart with her face buried. Dowie then got up in front. The horse started off gently, and Annie was helplessly borne away to meet the unknown.

She had often been along this road before. But it had never looked as it did now. The first half mile went through fields whose crops were gone. The stubble was sticking through the grass. The potato stalks, which ought to have been gathered and burned, lay scattered about the brown earth.

Then came two miles of moorland country, high and bleak and barren, with small hills of peat. Next came some scattered, ragged fields, till after two miles more they began to pass the first houses of the gray market town.

By this time it was night, and the stars were shining in the cold, frosty sky. A few faces were pressed close to the window-panes as the cart passed, and some rather untidy women came to their doors to look.

By and by the cart stopped at Robert Bruce's shop door.

Dowie got down and went into the shop. The house was a low one, although of two stories, built of gray stone with thatched roof. Inside the window burned a single candle. Annie could see what to her looked like treasures—calico and sugar and all the many items in the combined store of a dry goods dealer and grocer. But Robert Bruce also sold penny toys and halfpenny picture books, and every kind of candy. It was indeed a place of delight for the younger generation of Glamerton!

But Annie did not have long to look at these wonders through the window. Bruce came to the door, greeted his cousin and helped her down, and then turned to take Annie. Dowie was there before him, however, and took the silent child in his arms. He carried her into the shop and set her down on a sack in front of the counter. From her perch, Annie drearily looked at her surroundings.

Auntie was standing in the middle of the shop. Bruce was holding the counter open and inviting her to enter into the back room with him.

"You'll come in and take a cup of tea after your journey, Margaret?" he said.

"No, thank you, Robert. James and I must turn right around and go back home. There's still a lot to look after, and we mustn't neglect our work. The household things are all to be picked up in the morning."

Turning to Annie, she continued, "Now, Annie, lass, you'll be a good child and do as you're told. And mind you don't disturb things in the shop."

A peculiar smile passed over Bruce's face. Annie made no reply but stared at Mr. Bruce.

"Good bye, Annie!" said her aunt, rousing the girl a little from her stupor.

She then gave her a kiss. As far as Annie knew it was the first kiss she had ever given her. Then she left. Bruce followed Auntie out and Dowie came in. He took her up in his arms and whispered, "Goodbye to ye, my bonnie bairn. Be a good lass and ye'll be taken care of. Don't forget that. And remember to say yer prayers."

Annie kissed him with all her heart, but she could say nothing back. He set her down again and went out. She heard the harness rattle and the cart roll off. She was left sitting on the sack.

Presently Mr. Bruce came in again. He passed behind his counter and made an entry in his business ledger book. It recorded the day and hour when Annie was put down on that very sack. He was so detailed! And yet it was some time before he seemed to remember she was even there. Suddenly he looked up at the pale, weary thing as she sat with her legs hanging lifelessly down the side of the sack.

"Oh child, are you still there?" he asked, pretending to have forgotten her.

He went around to her, set her feet down on the floor, and led her by the hand through the mysterious gate of the counter and through a door behind it. Then he called in a sharp tone. "Mother!"

Immediately a tall, thin, nervous-looking woman appeared, wiping her hands in her apron.

"This is little Miss Anderson," said Bruce. "She has come to stay with us. Give her a biscuit and take her up the stairs to her bed."

It was the first, and it would also be the last time he would call her Miss Anderson, at least while she was one of the household. Mrs. Bruce took Annie by the hand in silence and led her up two narrow flights of stairs into a small room with a skylight. By nothing but the shine of the stars, she helped her unpack the box. But she forgot the biscuit, and for the first time in her life Annie went to bed without any supper.

Annie was afraid lying in a strange place without any light. For a while she tried to imagine herself in Brownie's stall among the grass and clover, for she did not like not knowing what was next to her in the dark.

But then the memory of Brownie being led off by those strange men came back to her. And with the memory everything else she had loved came back upon her. The sorrow drove away the fear, and she cried till she could cry no longer, and finally she slept.

It is by means of sorrow sometimes that God is able to give His beloved His restful sleep.

CHAPTER FIVE

THE ROBERT BRUCES

The following morning Annie woke early and dressed herself. There was no water in her room to wash with, so she crept down the stairs to look for some. But nobody else was awake.

She looked with longing out the window of the back door of the house, for she wished she could get outside into the fresh air. But seeing she could not open it, she went back up to her room. She sat on the side of her bed and gazed around the dingy room. At home she had had pretty curtains; here there were none of any kind. Everywhere she looked there were bare rafters and boards, nothing was even painted. And there were holes in the roof and floor she did not like. They were not large holes, but they were dreadful. For they were black and she did not know where they might go. She grew very cold.

At length she heard some noise in the house below. Presently came some baby screams and the sound of the shop shutters being taken down. At last footsteps approached her door.

Mrs. Bruce entered. Finding her sitting dressed on her bed, she exclaimed, "Oh! You're already dressed, are you?"

"Yes, ma'am," answered Annie as cheerfully as she could. "But," she added, "I would like some water to wash myself with."

"Come down to the pump then," said Mrs. Bruce.

Annie followed her to the pump where she washed in a tub. She ran dripping into the house for a towel, but was dried instead by the hands of Mrs. Bruce in her dirty apron.

By this time breakfast was nearly ready, and in a few minutes more Mrs. Bruce called Mr. Bruce from the shop and the children from the yard. Then they all sat around the table in the kitchen—Mr. Bruce to his tea and oatcakes and butter and Mrs. Bruce and the children to badly made oatmeal porridge and thin bluish milk.

This poor quality milk was remarkable seeing that they had cows of their own, and the milk that came from the cows was good enough. But they also sold milk in their shop. And to make more money Mrs. Bruce cheated her customers by adding water to it. Yet if any customer had accused her of selling watered milk, Mrs. Bruce's answer would have been to show them how much better it was than what she kept for her own family. She put twice as much water in what she used for hers and the children's porridge—except of course for the little saved aside for her husband's tea.

There were three children, two boys with big jaws—the elder a little older than Annie—and a very tiny baby. After Mr. Bruce had prayed for the blessing of the Holy Spirit upon their food, they gobbled down their breakfasts with a variety of strange noises.

When they finished the Bible was brought out. A psalm was sung. A chapter was read. The time of devotions ended with a prayer of fifteen minutes, in which the God of Jacob was especially invoked to bless the Bruces, His servants, in their store, and to prosper the labors of that day in particular. The prayer would have been much longer. But a click on the latch of the shop door brought it to a speedy end. Almost before the *amen* was out of his mouth, Robert Bruce was out of the kitchen. When there was money to be made, Bruce waited for no one, not even the Lord himself.

When he had taken care of the first customer, he returned, sat down, looked at Annie, and spoke to her very seriously.

"Now, Annie," he said, "you'll get today to play by yourself.

But tomorrow you must go to school. We can have no lazy folk about this house, so we must have no words about it."

Annie was not one to argue about that or anything. She was only too glad to get away from him. Indeed, the thought of school, after what she had seen of the Bruce household, sounded rather appealing. She answered, "Very well, sir."

Seeing that she was agreeable, Bruce added, "You can come into the shop today and see what's going on." He said this in the tone of someone giving another a great favor. "When you're more of a woman, you may be fit to stand behind the counter yourself—who knows?"

Robert Bruce thought of his shop as his battleground. The customers were his enemies whom he must defeat so he could take their money. It was so interesting to him every moment that he thought it must be to everyone else too. Annie followed him into the shop and saw a wonderful wealth of things around her. But the militant eyes of Robert Bruce never stopped watching her to make sure she took nothing, even when he was trying to talk some customer into buying something she didn't need.

Long before noon Annie was sick with boredom. Bruce did not so much as take a picture book down from the window for her to look at.

"Nasty trash of lies," he said as he hung the fresh bait up in his window, "fit only for dirty laddies and lassies." Though he regarded such books as trash, Bruce minded not at all the money they brought into his cash register.

He stood always watching in his shop like a great spider that ate children, with his windows full of allurements like a web.

They ate at noon on salt herrings and potatoes—much more wholesome food than bad porridge and watered milk. Robert Bruce the younger, who inherited both his father's name and bad temper, made faces at Annie across the table as often as he thought he could do so without being seen by his parents. But Annie was too delighted with the change of menu to mind. Indeed, she ate so fast that it was all she could do to stop the herring bones on the way to her throat.

After dinner, business went on in the shop. In the afternoon Mrs. Bruce went behind the counter and Mr. Bruce sat down at the desk to do paperwork. Not that there was much of that sort of thing necessary, but Bruce was so fond of business that he liked to seem busier than he was. As it happened to be a half holiday, the two boys were home from school in the afternoon, and Annie was sent with them into the yard to play.

"And keep away from the dog," said Bruce.

Outside, Annie soon found herself at the mercy of those who had none. It is amazing what a hidden amount of torment there is in boys, ready to come out the minute someone weaker than themselves is present. Children, even ordinarily good children, are ready to tease any child who simply looks teasable.

Now the two Bruce boys, as one would naturally expect, were not good children. And they hated Annie because she was a girl and appeared to them weak. If she had been aggressive or disagreeable, they would have made some attempt to be friendly with her. But as it was, she at once became the object of whatever they could think of to torment her with.

At one time they satisfied themselves with making faces at her. Then at other times they rubbed her face with dirt. She took it as long as she could, but at last could stand it no longer. She had been really hurt when one of the boys had tripped her, and she ran crying into the shop, where she sobbed out, "Please, sir, they won't let me be."

"Don't come into the shop with your stories. Make it up among yourselves."

"But they won't make it up."

Robert Bruce turned angrily from such an interruption of his high calling, and strode outside. He was instantly greeted with a flood of assurances from his sons that Annie had fallen and then tried to blame them. He turned sternly to her and said, "Annie, if you tell lies, you'll go to hell."

But he was not so prejudiced toward his own that he did not give them a lesson too, though it was of quite a different tone.

"Remember, boys," he said, "that poor Annie has no father or mother, and you must be kind to her."

He then turned and left them for the more important matter of making money. The persecution began again immediately, though not quite so bad. The little wretches abstained from their intense pleasures until a time, perhaps, when their father was not so close.

Somehow the day passed.

After lengthy and boring evening prayers, the two boys went off to bed, but Annie stayed behind.

"Can't you take off your own clothes, as well as put them on, Annie?" asked Mrs. Bruce.

"Yes, well enough. Only I would like a little candle," came Annie's trembling reply. "It's so dark in my room."

"Candle! No, no child," proclaimed Mrs. Bruce. "You'll get no candles. You would burn the house down around our ears. I can't afford candles. You can just feel your way up the stairs. There's thirteen steps to the first landing, and twelve to the next."

With a choking heart, Annie left.

She groped her way up the steep stairs and found her room. It was again a clear starlit night and she was able to find everything she wanted. She soon got into bed and, to be on the safe side, buried her head under the covers before she began to say her prayers. But her prayers were suddenly interrupted by a terrible noise of scrambling and scratching and scampering in the very room beside her.

Annie's fear of rats amounted to a frenzied horror.

She dared not move a finger! To get out of bed with those creatures running about the room was as impossible as it was for her to cry out.

But Annie's heart did what her tongue could not do. It cried out with a great cry to One who was more ready to hear than Robert or Nancy Bruce. And what her heart cried was simply this: "Oh God, save me from the rats!"

There was no need for God to send an angel from heaven to answer this little one's prayer: the cat would do. Annie heard a scratch and a mew at the door. The rats made one frantic scramble and were still.

"It's pussy!" she cried, recovering her voice in joy.

Given strength by the cat's arrival, and certain that God had sent it in direct answer to her prayer, Annie sprang out of bed, darted across the room, and opened the door to let it in. A few minutes later and Annie was fast asleep, guarded by God's angel, the cat. And always after that, she took care to leave the door open a little to allow pussy to enter.

Though it is always ready to shut, there are also ways of keeping the door of the mind open.

CHAPTER
SIX

SCHOOL

N ow, Annie, put on your bonnet and go to the school with
the rest, and be a good girl."

This was Robert Bruce's statement of goodbye to Annie before
he left the kitchen for the shop, after breakfast and prayers had
been observed. It was quarter to ten, and the school was about
five minutes away.

Fearful yet full of hope, Annie obeyed. She ran upstairs,
made herself as tidy as she could, smoothed her hair, put on her
bonnet, and went back down to wait at the door for her companions. She was very excited, and looked forward to something
which might not be so bad. She hoped the teacher was nice!

As they walked off, the boys got one on each side of her.
Nobody said a word for about half the distance. Suddenly Robert
Bruce junior opened the conversation abruptly.

"You'll get it!" he declared, as if he had been thinking about
it all the while.

"What'll I get?" asked Annie timidly, for his voice made her
afraid.

"Such lickings," he answered, apparently enjoying the
thought. "Won't she, Johnny?"

"Ay, she will," answered his younger brother Johnny, following his leader with confidence.

Annie's heart sank within her. The poor little heart was used to sinking now. But she said nothing, and determined to try to avoid all occasions for "getting it."

Not another word was spoken before they reached the school, the door of which was not yet open. Many of the boys and girls had already assembled, filling the street with the musical sound of children's voices while they waited for the schoolmaster. None of them paid any attention to Annie. So she stood about looking at the school. It was a long, low building with thatched roof. There were five windows facing the street and some in the back. The melting night's frost was dripping from the thatch in slow, clear drops.

Suddenly a small boy cried out: "The master's coming!" and instantly the noise sank to a low murmur.

Annie looked up the street and saw the figure of the approaching teacher. He was dressed in what seemed to be black but was really dark gray. He came down the hill of the street swinging his arms and marching at a rapid pace. He already had the door key in his hand, and now he extended his arm with the key pointing straight toward the keyhole. He swept through the little crowd of boys and girls, which cleared a wide path for him, without a word or gesture of greeting either from him or from them.

He strode into the building, followed by the troop of boys, and lastly by the girls. At the very last of all, a short distance back, came Annie, like a lamb without a mother that followed the flock because she did not know what else to do. She went down a step into a sunken hallway and then up another step, through a door on the left and into the schoolroom. There she saw a double row of desks, with a clear space down the middle between the rows. Each scholar was hurrying to his place at one of the desks, where they then stood silently.

The teacher, Murdoch Malison, had already taken his position as master at the front of the class, where he waited solemnly to begin the daily prayer. Annie had barely managed to reach a vacant desk among the girls when he began. The boys were silent as death while the master prayed. Silent but not still. Their restraint was limited only to their vocal chords. But since their tongues were unable to carry out their normal function, they were stuck out of mouths everywhere, sending telegraphic messages to all parts of the room throughout the ceremony of the prayer, along with winking eyes, contorted features, and a wild use of hands. Since he was afraid of being discovered in the attempt to watch the class while he prayed, the master kept his eyelids tight. He played the spy with his ears alone. The boys and girls understood this perfectly, and so in utter silence carried out their signs and signals and movements with delight, and without fear of being found out.

As soon as the prayer was over, they dropped with noise and bustle into their seats. Annie was soon pushed out of her seat by a girl who arrived late. Some younger ones on the opposite side, however, liking the look of her, made room beside them. The desks were double, so that the two rows at each desk faced each other.

"Bible class, come to the front," were the first words of the master that rang through the room.

A moment of chaos followed, while all the boys and girls considered capable of reading the Bible arranged themselves across the room in front of the master's desk. Each read a verse, often leaving half a sentence to be taken up by another. In this way, what was originally intended as a help to *find* the truth was changed into a means of hiding it.

Not knowing what to do, Annie had not dared to stand up with the class, although she could read fairly well. A few moments after the readers were dismissed, she felt a huge shadow standing before her. She looked up, and there was the master bending down over her!

He began to question her, but for a few minutes she was too frightened to say much about her learning. The best of her education was certainly of a different kind than Mr. Malison could have understood. Thus he concluded that she was less intelligent than she was, and she was put into the spelling book instead of the Bible class. She was made to copy letters and various strokes with the quill over and over again. It was dreadfully dreary, and in the middle of it she fell fast asleep. Her head dropped on her outstretched arm and the quill dropped from her sleeping fingers.

But she was soon roused by the voice of the master.

"Ann Anderson!" called the loud voice in a burst of thunder, and Annie awoke to shame and confusion, amid the laughter of those around her.

Before the morning was over she was called up to the front of the class, along with some children considerably younger than herself, to read and spell. The master stood before them, holding a long, thick whip of horsehide. The end had been cut into strips and then hardened in the fire.

Now there was a little pale-faced, delicate-looking boy in the class who blundered a good deal, and was slow to give out his answers. Every time he did not answer quickly, or give the right answer, the cruel serpent of leather went at him, coiling around his legs with a sudden hissing sound. This made him cry and his tears blinded him so badly that he could not even see the words which he had been unable to read before. He kept trying to read, however, and still the whip of torture went snapping at his thin little legs, raising upon his skin many welts and sores.

Finally the master passed on to the next, who was Annie.

It was no wonder that the trembling child, who could read pretty well, should completely fail in reading the sentence in front of her. If she had been left to herself, she would have taken the little boy in her arms and cried with him. As it was, she struggled mightily with her tears, but did not succeed in reading much better than the poor boy who was still busy wiping his eyes with his sleeve. Since she was a newcomer as well as a girl, and since she was wearing a long dress, she escaped the whip for the time.

That first day at school was a dreadful experience. Well might the children have prayed with David: "Let us fall into the hands of the Lord, for his mercies are great, and not into the hands of men."

At one o'clock they were dismissed and went home to midday dinner, to return again at three.

In the afternoon Annie was made to write figures on a slate. She wrote till her back ached. The boredom was broken only by the punishment of the master upon various offending boys. He had a severe temper and a savage sense of obedience, and would deliver a full swing of the *tawse*, as his whip was called, down on the outstretched hand of the culprit who had not done his work to the master's expectation.

Annie shivered and quaked every time. Once she burst out crying but managed to choke her sobs, even if she could not hide her tears.

Late in the afternoon a fine-looking boy, three or four years older than her, was called up to receive punishment, deserving or undeserving as the case might be. The master was fond of justice, and justice was to him the same as punishment. He did not particularly want to punish the innocent. But he did not spend a great deal of time worrying about whether a given punishment was merited in every case. Punishment was higher to him than truth.

Without a word of defense the boy held out his hand with his arm at full length, received four stinging blows upon it, grew very red in the face, and returned to his seat with the suffering hand sent into retirement in his pocket. Annie admired his courage so much that she made up her mind to bear her own persecutions more patiently. And if ever her turn should come to be punished, she resolved to take the whipping as she had seen Alec Forbes take it.

At five the school was dismissed for the day, but not without another prayer. Jubilant shouts arose as the boys rushed out into the street. Every day to them was a cycle of strife, suffering, and deliverance—birth and death and the struggle of life in between. And the stone-hearted god that ruled the world was the schoolmaster, Murdoch Malison. Most of the children, after the burdens of the day, were now going home to heaven for the night.

But Annie, having no home, was one of the exceptions. She walked away slowly, dispirited and hopeless—a terrible condition for a child—and wondered how Alec Forbes could be so merry.

Poor Annie had but one comfort left. She hoped no one would prevent her from creeping up to her own desolate attic room, which was now the dreary substitute for Brownie's stall. The mean Bruce boys were not likely to follow her there. And if the rats were in the attic, so was the cat—or at least the cat knew the way to it.

There in her room by herself she might think in peace about some things she had never had to think about before.

Chapter Seven

A NEW FRIEND

In such a way Annie's days continued to go by.

Gradually, she became used to the sight of the punishment of her schoolfellows. But none of it yet came upon her. It would have been hard even for a savage man like Mr. Malison to punish the nervous, delicate, anxious little orphan who worked so hard at her studies and was quiet as a mouse.

However, the loss of human companionship, with no green fields and country sounds and smells, was making Annie very sad. The little color she used to have in her cheeks slowly died away. Her face grew even more thin and her blue eyes looked wistful and large. There were not tears to be seen in them often now, and yet they looked well acquainted with tears—like fountains that had once been full of water and were now dried up. She never smiled anymore, for there was nothing to make her smile.

But there was one good thing about this time of desolation: the thought of her dead father came to her often, and she began to love him more deeply than ever before. Her mother had died when Annie was born and she had been her father's treasure. But during the period of his illness, she had seen so little of him that for a while she almost forgot him. In the minds of children the grass grows very quickly over their buried dead. But now Annie began to remember, and learned a little what death meant. It was not with an added sadness, for it comforted her to remember how her father had loved her. And she said her prayers oftener because they seemed to go somewhere near the place where her father was. She did not think of her father being where God was, but of God being where her father was.

The winter was drawing nearer and the days were now short and cold. A watery time began, and for many days in a row the rain kept falling steadily. I almost think Annie would have died without her dead father to think about.

On one of those rainy days, however, she discovered that good things are often revealed in odd ways. It had rained the whole day, not just a drizzle but a hard rain. Now and then the school became silent, just to listen to the great noise made by the thunderous torrent of the heavens. But the boys thought only of the fun of dabbling in the puddles as they went home, or of the delights of fishing in the swollen and muddy rivers.

The afternoon went on. It was nearly time to go, and still the rain was pouring. In the dreary gloom there had been more than the usual amount of wandering from one part of the school to another, and the elder of the Bruce boys had stolen toward a group of little boys next to Annie, who was sitting with her back to them. As he passed her, young Robert gave Annie a spiteful dig with his elbow, and she let out a little cry.

Now the master occasionally threw his tawse, not so much to hurt the offender—though that happened as well—but mostly to embarrass them. For the culprit had to take the whip of torture back up to the hands of the evil schoolmaster. He threw the tawse at Annie, and it struck her hard, even before she had recovered her breath after the blow Bruce had given her. In pain and terror she rose, and pale as death staggered up to the master, carrying the whip with the horror she would have felt if it had been a snake. With a grim smile he sent her back to her seat, and she sobbed, while some of the girls laughed at her, for the short remaining time until the class was dismissed for the day.

There could be no better fun for most of the boys and some of the girls than to wade through the dirty water running between the schoolhouse and the street. Many of them dashed through it at once, shoes and all. But as it was too wide to cross in a single jump, some of the boys and almost all of the girls took off their shoes and socks and carried them across the steadily rising little stream. But the splashing dirty water looked so ugly that Annie just stood standing looking at it in dismay, the forgotten tears still creeping down her cheeks. All of a sudden she was caught up from behind by a boy who was carrying his shoes and socks in his other hand.

She glanced timidly around to see who it was, and the brave, brown eyes of Alec Forbes met hers with a smile. In that smile the cloudy sky of the universe gently opened and the face of God looked out upon Annie. For that brief moment, it gave her all the love and understanding she had been dying for during the last weeks—weeks that seemed as long as years. She could not help herself—she threw her arms around Alec Forbes' neck and sobbed as if her heart would break. She did not care about the Bruces or the rats or even the schoolmaster now!

Alec clasped her tighter, and vowed in his heart that if ever that brute Malison lifted his hand against her again, he would protect her himself. He carried her across the street, set her down, then bid her goodbye and turned and ran home barefoot through the flooding town.

The two Bruces had gone on ahead with the only two umbrellas, one of which Annie had shared with one of them in coming to school. By the time she got home she was soaking wet. But no one took any notice of her condition, and as a result she had a severe cold and cough the next day.

That night she lay awake for a long time, and when at last she fell asleep, she dreamed she took Alec Forbes home to see her father. And her father had put his hand on Alec's head, and said: "Thank you, Alec, for being kind to my poor Annie." And then she cried, and woke up crying—strange tears out of dreamland, half of sorrow and half of joy.

How her feelings about school were changed the next day! After the prayer, she glanced around to catch a glimpse of her new friend. There he was, cheerful as usual. He took no notice of her and she had not expected he would. But now that he had befriended her, it was not long before Alec found out that Annie's two Bruce cousins were very unkind to her.

In the afternoon, while she was busy over an unusually difficult addition sum, Robert came up quietly behind her, licked his finger, and then the moment she had figured out the answer rubbed it from her slate. The same moment he received a box on the ear. He yelled with pain and rage, caught sight of who had struck him, and cried out, "Sanny Forbes hit me!"

"Alexander Forbes! Come up," called out the voice of the master.

Forbes was not the most first-rate of scholars, and thus was not a favorite with him. For Mr. Malison did not understand what was fine in character. If the name reaching his ears had been one of his better Latin students, he probably would have let Bruce's cry go without taking any action.

"Hold up your hand," he said sternly.

Alec obeyed. Annie gave a smothered shriek, jumped out of her seat, and rushed up to the master. When she found herself face to face with the tyrant, however, she could not speak a single word in Alec's defense. She opened her mouth, but her tongue refused to do what she wanted, and she stood gasping. The master stared at her, his arm stopped in mid-air ready to strike Alec's hand. All the blackness of his anger at Forbes he now turned upon Annie.

He stood thus for one awful moment. Then he motioned her aside with a sweep of his head, and brought down the tawse on Alec's hand. Annie gave a choking cry. So awful was the pain that Alec could not help withdrawing his hand. But almost the same instant, ashamed of his weakness, he presented it again and received the remaining blows of his punishment. The master then turned to Annie. Finding her still speechless he gave her a push and said: "Go to your seat, Ann Anderson. The next time you do that I will punish you severely."

Annie sat down and neither sobbed nor cried. But it was several days before she recovered from the shock.

Chapter Eight

STOLEN CANDY AND A FALSE ERRAND

For some time neither of the young Bruces ventured even to make a mean face at her at school, but their behavior to her at home was only so much the worse.

Two days after a rainstorm, as Annie was leaving the kitchen after family worship to go to bed, Mr. Bruce called her.

"Annie Anderson," he said, "I want to speak to you." Annie turned toward him trembling.

"I see you are frightened because you know what it's about," he went on, staring sternly into her pale face. "You can't even look me in the eye, can you? Where are the sugar candies, Annie?"

Annie continued to stare, bewildered. Bruce added, "I know well enough where they are, and so do you!"

"I know nothing about it," answered Annie finally.

"Don't lie, Annie. It's enough to steal, without lying."

"I'm not lying," she protested, starting to cry. "Who said I took any candies?"

"That's not the point. You wouldn't cry that way if you were innocent. I never missed anything before. And you know well enough that God's eye sees all things, and you can't hide from Him."

Bruce could hardly have intended her to believe he had been inspired from on high to discover the thief of his sweets. But he thought it better not to mention that the informer was his own son. Johnnie, on his part, had thought it better not to mention that he had been incited to the act by his brother Robert. And Robert had thought it better not to mention that he did so partly to cover up his own crime and partly to get revenge on Annie for the box on the ear which Alec Forbes had given him.

Bruce spoke the truth when he said that he had never missed anything before. But I suspect that the two boys had long ago begun to take things so small and so cautiously that it had not been noticed. This time, however, the candies taken were too many not to be noticed by the keen eyes of the boys' father.

"I don't want to hide from it!" cried Annie. "If God does see, then *He* knows," she went on in desperation. "I wouldn't touch a grain of salt without permission."

"It's a pity, Annie, that you don't get your share of Mr. Malison's discipline. I don't want to give you a lickin' myself, because you're someone else's child. But now to add lying to your stealing, Annie, I don't know what else I ought to do but whip you!"

In spite of his statement, Robert Bruce never so much as laid a hand on his own children. He was too much afraid of their mother. She was ordinarily perfectly submissive. But she would have flown into the rage of a hen with chicks if even her own husband had dared to punish one of *her* children. The shop might be more Robert's than hers, but the children were more hers than Robert's.

Overcome with shame and righteous anger, Annie burst out in the midst of fresh tears.

"I wish Auntie would come and take me away! It's an awful house to be in!"

These words had a visible effect upon Bruce. He had been expecting a visit from Margaret Anderson, Annie's aunt, within a day or two. He shuddered to think what she might do if Annie told her terrible stories about life under his roof. The use of

Annie's money had not been given to him for any specific period of time. Dowie did not especially like Bruce and had consulted a lawyer to take precautions for his little mistress and to make sure she would not be left defenseless in the hands of a selfish man like Bruce. Thus, if things went badly for Annie, both Auntie Margaret and James Dow would no doubt have used Annie's money to make some other living arrangements for her.

The sale of the farm and its assets had turned out better than expected, and Annie's inheritance was two hundred pounds. This had been committed to Bruce, for him to use the interest to pay for the added expense of having Annie live with him. In reality, however, the interest he received from the bank where he put most of Annie's money was three or four times whatever small amount Annie's food and other scant provisions might cost. He was not anxious to lose so profitable a boarder! To lose the two hundred pounds now would seem to a money-possessed man like Bruce nothing short of ruin.

He was convinced Annie was the guilty person. But he thought it better to lose a few pieces of candy than to quarrel about it and run the risk of upsetting her. So with the selfish cunning so common to his kind of person, he went to the shop, brought back a piece of sugar candy about the size of a pigeon's egg, and said to the still-crying child: "Don't cry, Annie. I can't stand to see you crying. If you want a bit of candy any time, just tell me and don't take it yourself. That's all. Here."

He thrust the lump of candy into Annie's hand. But she dropped it on the floor and rushed upstairs as fast as the darkness would let her. In spite of her anger, she was soon sound asleep.

Bruce searched about the floor for the piece of candy until he found it. He then put it back in the drawer he had taken it from, and made up his mind to be more careful in the future not to offend little Annie Anderson.

In a few days the Saturday arrived upon which he expected Margaret's visit. Bruce was on the watch the whole afternoon. He had not told Annie that her Aunt was coming to town, and he did not want her to see her. He thought it best that Auntie Margaret should hear nothing from the girl's lips about her new life as one of the Bruces.

From his shop door he could see all along the street a long way. Being very quick sighted, he recognized Margaret when she was still a great distance away as she sat in an approaching buggy.

"Annie!" he called, opening the inner door to the house. Annie immediately came downstairs from her room.

"Annie," he said, "run out the back door and through the yard and over to Logan Lumley's and tell him to come over to see me directly. Don't come back without him. That's a good child!"

He sent her off with this message, knowing well enough that the man had gone to the country that day and there was no one at his house who was likely to know where he had gone. He hoped that Annie would go and look for him about the town, for he knew she would be afraid to return and tell him she had failed to deliver his message. Thus she should remain gone during her aunt's visit.

"Well, Margaret," he said with his customary greeting, "how are you today?"

"Oh, not that bad," answered Margaret with a sigh.

"And your aunt, Mistress Peterson?"

"Well enough. How's Annie getting on?"

"Not that bad. But she's a bit wild and unruly."

He thought to please her with the remark because she had always been in the habit of saying the same thing herself. But distance had made Annie dearer in her aunt's memory, and her nose took fire with anger as she replied: "The lassie's well-mannered enough. I saw nothing of the sort in her all her life! If you can't manage her, that's *your* fault!"

A little perplexed, Bruce showed nothing on his face, and was ready to answer her back in a moment.

"Would you like to see her?"

"Why else do you think I came?"

"Well, I'll go and look for her."

He went to the back door and called aloud, "Annie, your auntie's here and wants to see you."

"She'll be here in a minute," he said to Margaret as he re-entered the shop.

After a little more conversation, he pretended to be surprised that Annie did not make her appearance, and went once more to the door and called her name several times. He then pretended to search for her in the yard and all over the house and returned with the news that she was nowhere to be seen.

"She's afraid that you've come to take her with you and she's run away somewhere. I'll send the laddies to look for her."

"No, never mind. If she doesn't want to see me, I'm sure I don't need to see her. She knew I was coming?"

"I told her myself," lied Bruce.

"Well then, I'll just be off to the town," said Margaret, her face growing red as she spoke.

She bustled out of the shop, too angry with Annie to say good bye to Bruce. She had not gone far, however, before Annie came running out of a narrow alley, almost right into her aunt's arms.

"You little limmer!" cried Margaret, seizing her by the shoulder, "what made you run away. I don't want you, you brat!"

"I didn't run away, Auntie."

"Robert Bruce called you to come in himself."

"It was him that sent me off to Logan Lumley's to tell him to come to the shop."

Margaret could not make heads or tails of the mystery. But as Annie had never told her a lie, she could hardly doubt what she said. She took a moment to think about it, then gave her some rough advice and a smooth penny and went away on her errands. It did not take her long to realize that Bruce was behind the affair, and wanted to part her and the child. This made her so angry at Bruce that she did not go near the shop again for a long time. Therefore Annie was left alone and Bruce had what he wanted.

He would not have needed to be so full of scheming. Annie never said a word to her aunt about his treatment of her. It is one of the marvels about children how much they can bear without complaining. Parents have no right to suppose that all is well among playmates or in a schoolroom merely from the fact that their children do not complain. Teachers and other children may be cruel, and yet children will be silent about it.

Vengeance of a sort soon came upon Robert Bruce the younger. For the evil spirit in him—inherited from no such remote ancestor as the king—would not allow him to keep from evildoing too long, even in school. He knew Annie better than his father did, that she was not likely to complain of anything. The only danger, he thought, lay in the chance of being discovered red-handed in the deed.

One day when the schoolmaster had left the room to talk with some visitor at the door, Robert saw Annie stooped over tying her shoe. Thinking that Alec Forbes was looking in the other direction, he gave Annie a strong push. She fell on her face in the middle of the floor.

But Alec had caught sight of the deed and was down upon him in a moment. He already knew that a simple box on the ear was of no lasting value, so this time Alec gave him a downright good thrashing. Robert howled vigorously, partly from pain, but partly in the hope that the same consequences as before would come to Forbes. He was still howling when Mr. Malison came back into the room.

"Robert Bruce, come up," he commanded the moment he opened the door. And Robert Bruce went up. Despite all his protests and accusations of Alec Forbes, he received an even more painful punishment from the master than Alec had given him. For the master there was no particular principle as to the person on whom the punishment should fall. In his eyes, punishment was enough in itself. He was not capable of seeing how unjust it was for punishment to fall on the wrong person. This time, however, his punishment landed on him that deserved it.

If young Bruce howled before, he howled ten times worse now, and went home still howling. Annie was sorry for him, and tried to say a word of comfort. But he replied by hitting her several times with hatred.

As soon as he reached the shop, he told his father that Forbes had beaten him without his even saying a word to him. This was as correct as it was untrue. Then he said that the master had sided with Forbes and had licked him soundly. Robert the elder was instantly filled with smoldering wrath, and from that moment on he hated Alec Forbes. For like many others of similar nature, he was completely unaware of the sinfulness in his own children, and was prejudiced in their favor no matter what the circumstances.

CHAPTER
NINE

THE SHORTER
CATECHISM

In her innermost heart Annie now dedicated herself to the service of Alec Forbes. And it was not long before she had an opportunity to help him.

One Saturday the master made his appearance in black socks instead of his usual white, a bad sign in the eyes of his scholars. And on this day their worries were justified. The joy of having all Saturday afternoon off was almost outweighed by the terrible weight of having to study the Shorter Catechism all morning. This of course made them hate the Catechism, a book of questions and answers about God.

Every Saturday Murdoch Malison's pupils had to learn a certain number of questions and answers from the Shorter Catechism, with their corresponding Scripture verses to prove the answers. Whoever failed in the task had to be imprisoned in the schoolroom for the rest of the day. On one Saturday each month, the students were given a test on all the questions and proofs that had been covered during the previous month.

The day in question was a test day, and the only proofs Alec Forbes had been able to display was proof that he did not know

the answers to the master's questions. As a result he was condemned to be kept in all afternoon—a hard trial indeed for an
active boy like him, whose chief delight was the open air and
the active exertion of his growing body.

Seeing his sad expression, Annie was filled with concern and
lost track of the class and did not know when her turn came.
Suddenly the master was standing before her silently. He had
approached without making a sound, and then stood until Annie
finally realized he was there. Then with a smile on his thin lips,
but a thundercloud on his brow, he repeated the question: "What
doth every sin deserve?"

Bewildered and embarrassed to find herself the reason for
the silence, Annie could not remember a single word of the answer as given in the Catechism. So in her confusion she fell back
on her common sense and experience.

"What doth every sin deserve?" repeated the tyrant.

"A lickin'," whispered Annie, her eyes filling with tears.

For a moment the master thought about punishing her by her
own words and giving her a whipping at once. But instead he
gave a side wave of his head, indicating the culprit's doom to be
kept in for the afternoon. Annie got up and took her place on
the other side of the room with the condemned, with a flutter
of joy in her heart that Alec Forbes would not be left without a
friend. A few more boys made up the unfortunate party of those
who had failed, but they were younger ones. The hour arrived
and the school was dismissed. The master strode out, locking
the door behind him, and the defaulters were left inside.

For some time there was dreary silence in the room. Alec sat
with his elbow on his desk, biting his nails. Annie divided her
silent attention between her book and Alec. The other boys
seemed to be busy with their catechism books, in the hope of
getting out as soon as the master returned. At length Alec took
out his knife, and out of sheer boredom, began to whittle away
on the desk in front of him. When Annie saw that, she crept
across the floor and sat down at the opposite desk. Alec looked
up at her, smiled, and went on with his whittling. Annie slid a
little nearer and then asked him to listen to her say her Catechism. He agreed and she repeated the lesson perfectly.

"Now let me hear you, Alec," she said.

"No, Annie. I can't say it. And I won't say it for all the teachers in the world."

"But he'll lick you, Alec, and I can't stand it," said Annie, tears rising in her eyes.

"Well, I'll try then—to please you, Annie."

Her heart bounded with delight! The great boy, so strong and brave, learning a lesson just to please her!

But it would not work.

"I can't remember a word of it, Annie. I'm dreadfully hungry besides. I was in too big a hurry with my breakfast. If I had known what was coming I would have eaten more," he added, laughing drearily.

As he spoke he looked up and his eyes wandered from one window to another for a few moments.

"No, it's no use," he resumed at last. "I've grown too much to escape that way."

Annie was as sad over Alec's hunger as any mother over her child's. She felt it pure injustice that he should ever be hungry. But she was unable to think of any way to help him, and she could only answer, "I don't know what you mean, Alec."

"When I was your size I could squeeze out of a smaller hole than that," he said, pointing to the open windowpane in an upper corner of the wall, "but I'm too big now."

Annie sprang to her feet.

"I could get through it, Alec. Just hold me up a bit. You can lift me, you know."

"But what'll you do when you *are* out, Annie?"

"Run home and get a loaf of bread to bring back with me."

"But Rob Bruce'll box your ears before he'll give you a loaf of bread, and it's too far to run to my mother's. Malison would be back long before that."

"Just help me out and leave the rest to me," said Annie confidently. "If I don't fetch a loaf of white bread, you don't ever have to trust me again."

The idea of bread, a rare delicacy to Scottish country boys, was too much a delight for Alec's imagination. He jumped up and put his head out of one of the open panes to see if the coast was clear. He saw a woman approaching that he knew.

"I say, Lizzie," he called.

The woman stopped.

"What do you want, Master Alec?"

"Just stand there and pull this lassie out. We're kept in together and nearly starving."

"He's a bad man, that master of yours."

"Never mind ol' 'Murder' Malison. Just pull out the lassie, will you?"

"Where is she?"

Alec jumped down and held Annie up to the open window, less than a foot square. He told her to put her arms through first. Then they got her head through, at which point Lizzie caught hold of her—the school building was so low to the ground—and dragged her out and set her on her feet. But a windowpane was broken in the process.

"Go, Annie," cried Alec. "Never mind the window. Run!"

She was off like a live bullet.

She scampered home prepared to encounter whatever dangers were necessary in order to bring Alec back something to eat. She had sixpence of her own in coppers in her box. But how was she to get into the house and out again without being seen?

With the greatest care she managed to get in the back door unnoticed, and then up to her room. In a moment more the six pennies were in her hand and she was back in the street. She dashed straight for the baker's shop.

"A six-penny loaf," she panted out.

"Who wants it?" asked the baker's wife.

"There's the coins," answered Annie, laying them on the counter.

The baker's wife gave her the loaf with a biscuit, which had traditionally always gone along with a sixpence purchase, and Annie sped back to the school like a runaway horse to his stable.

As she approached, out popped the head of Alec Forbes. He had been listening for the sound of her feet. She held up the loaf as high as she could and he stretched down as low as he could and so their hands met on the loaf.

"Thank you, Annie," said Alec. "I won't forget this. How did you get it?"

"Never mind that. But I didn't steal it," answered Annie. "But how am I to get in again?" she added, suddenly realizing the difficulty as she looked up to the window above her head.

"I am an idiot!" said Alec, scratching his head. "I never thought of that." The window was so high above Annie's reach, the thing was clearly impossible. "You'll catch it," said one of the urchins to Annie, with his nose flattened against the window.

Annie's face turned pale. By this time Alec had made up his mind what was to be done.

"Run home, Annie," he said. "And if Murder tries to lay a finger on you Monday, I'll murder *him*. Now run home before he comes and catches you at the window."

"No, Alec," pleaded Annie.

"Hold your tongue," interrupted Alec, "and run, will you?"

She did not want to leave him, but Annie saw that he was determined. Therefore she obeyed, and turned to walk slowly home, avoiding the places where there might be a chance of meeting her jailor.

She found that no one had seen her former visit, and the only remarks made were those concerned with the disgrace of being kept in. When Mr. Malison returned to the school about four o'clock, he found the room quiet as death. The boys appeared totally absorbed in studying their catechism books. But to his additional surprise the girl was nowhere to be seen.

"Where is Ann Anderson?" he demanded.

"Gone home," cried two of the little prisoners.

"Gone home!" shouted the schoolmaster in a tone of savage incredulity. It was plain enough she was gone, and from former experience he probably knew well enough how her escape had been made.

"Yes," said Alec. "It was me who made her go. I put her out at the window, and I broke the pane," he added, knowing it would be found out sooner or later, "but I'll get it fixed on Monday."

Malison turned white as a sheet with rage. Indeed, the situation was so hopeless that Alec had spoken with too much carelessness.

Anxious to butter up the teacher, the third youngster called out, "Sanny Forbes made her go and fetch him a loaf of white bread."

The little informer still had some of the crumbs sticking to his jacket. But how corrupting is a reign of terror! The bread was eaten, and now the giver was being betrayed by the urchin in the hope of gaining a little favor with the tyrant.

"Alexander Forbes, come up!"

I will not carry the description beyond this point.

After he had vented his anger on young Forbes, the master allowed them all to leave without further reference to the Shorter Catechism.

Chapter Ten

ALEC AND MR. MALISON

The next day, Sunday, was anything but a day of rest for Annie, for she looked forward with dread to the coming Monday.

The awful morning dawned. When she woke and the thought of what she had to face came back into her mind, she turned sick. Breakfast time came, worship followed, and then to school she had to go.

Everything went on as usual for some time. The Bible class was called up. The master listened to their readings, then dismissed them. Annie was beginning to hope that the whole affair was somehow or other going to pass by. She had heard nothing of Alec's fate after she had left him imprisoned, and his face gave no sign of what had happened. She dared not lift her eyes from the spelling book in front of her to look in the direction of the master.

Suddenly without warning the awful voice resounded through the school with the terrible words: "Ann Anderson, come up."

For a moment she went blank. When she recovered herself

she was standing before the master. She vaguely remembered being asked two or three questions. What they were she had no idea. He spoke again.

"Did you, or did you not, go out at the window on Saturday?"

She did not see that Alec Forbes had left his seat and was slowly making his way toward the front of the classroom.

"Yes," she answered, trembling from head to foot.

"Did you, or did you not, bring a loaf of bread to those who were kept in?"

"Yes, sir."

"Where did you get it?"

"I bought it, sir."

"Where did you get the money?"

Every eye in the school was fixed upon her. Those of her two cousins were sparkling with delight.

"I got it out of my own chest, sir."

"Hold up your hand."

Annie obeyed, her face pleading with a silent terror.

"Don't touch her," said Alec Forbes, stepping between the executioner and his victim. "You know well enough it was my fault. I told you so on Saturday."

Murder Malison, as the boys called him, answered him with a hissing blow of the tawse over his head, followed by a series of furious blows all over his body as the boy twisted and writhed. Alec made no attempt to resist and was finally knocked down by the storm. He lay on the floor and the master continued to lash him, holding him down with one foot. Finally Malison stopped, exhausted, and turned white with rage toward Annie, who was in agony, and repeated the order: "Hold up your hand."

But as Malison turned, Alec bounded to his feet, his face red and his eyes flashing. He jumped at the master. Malison threw him off, lifted the whip and sent a stinging lash around his head and face. Realizing it was no longer a fair fight, Alec lowered his head like a ram and rushed full tilt against the pit of Malison's stomach. The tall man doubled up and crashed backward into the peat fire. In his attempt to keep himself from falling, he thrust his right hand into the coals.

Alec rushed forward to drag him off the fire, but he was up

before Alec could reach him, doing his best to hide his intense pain.

"Go home!" he shouted to the scholars throughout the room, and sat down at his desk to hide his suffering.

For one brief moment there was silence. Then a shouting arose and the whole school rushed to the door, as if the devil had been after them to catch whoever was last through it. What a strange uproar it was that invaded the ears of the town of Glamerton—the uproar of jubilant freedom from all its children at eleven o'clock on a Monday morning.

But the culprits, Annie and Alec, stood and stared at the master, whose face was covered with his left hand, while the other hung helpless at his side.

At length Mr. Malison lifted his head and made a movement to get his hat. He saw the two still standing there and gave a little jump. But the moment he looked at them their courage failed.

"Run, Annie!" said Alec.

Away she bolted, and he was after her as well as he could, which was not with his usual speed by any means. When Annie had rounded a corner, she stopped and looked back for Alec. He was a good distance behind her, and for the first time she realized the condition of her champion. Now that the excitement was over, he could scarcely walk. He was a mass of bruises and welts from the whip from head to foot.

Annie went back to him, and he put his hand on her shoulder to help steady himself. She went with him as far as the gate to his mother's garden, which was nearly a mile from the town on the other side of one of the rivers which watered the valley plain. Then she went slowly home, taking with her the memory of the smile which, in spite of his pain, had shown on his face as he said goodbye to her.

When she got home she saw at once, from the black looks of the Bruces, that the story—whether in its true form or not—had arrived before her.

Nothing was said, however, till after worship that evening. Then Bruce gave her a long lecture on the wickedness and certain punishment of "taking up with loons like Sanny Forbes." But he came to the conclusion, as he told his wife later, that the lassie was already growing hardened against spiritual things, for she had not shed even a single tear as a result of his lecture.

The moment Annie lay down on the bed she fell to weeping over the sufferings of Alec. She was asleep a moment later. If it had not been for the power of sleep in the child, she undoubtedly would have died before now from sheer sadness.

There was considerable excitement around the fires of Glamerton that night from the news carried home by the children of the master's defeat. The religious persons of the community seemed to side with the master. The worldly—namely those who did not profess to be particularly religious—all sided with Alec Forbes.

Among the religious there was at least one exception. He had no children of his own, but he liked Alec Forbes. That man was Thomas Crann, the strong, stern stonemason.

CHAPTER
ELEVEN

ANNIE VISITS
HOWGLEN

Thomas Crann was building a house, for he was both a contractor and a day laborer. He had arrived at a point where he needed the help of a more skilled carpenter. Therefore, he went to see George Macwha, whom he found planing a piece of wood at his workbench. His workshop had two or three more workbenches in it, some pine boards leaning against the wall, and the tools and materials of the carpenter's trade all about. The floor was covered with wood shavings.

Crann, as he usually did with most people, gave Macwha a gruff greeting and they began to discuss the business at hand. Once that had been taken care of, their conversation got around to what had happened at the school.

"A terrible laddie, that Sanny Forbes!" remarked the carpenter. "They say he gave the teacher such a licking it almost killed him."

"I've known worse laddies than Sanny Forbes," was Thomas Crann's brief reply.

"Oh, I've nothing against the laddie. Him and our Willie's always together."

Thomas's only answer was a grunt and a silence of a few seconds. But after a moment he spoke again.

"I'm not sure thrashing the schoolmaster is such a bad sin. He's a dour creature that Murdoch Malison. And for Alec, I have great hopes for him. His father was an honest man and one of the Lord's own. And if his mother's been a little too soft on him and given the lad too much rope, he'll come right before long."

"Well, I dare say you're right, Thomas."

"And besides, they say he took his own licks without saying a word, and attacked the master only when he was going to lick the poor orphan lassie—James Anderson's lassie, you know."

"It's the same tale they're telling all over town. I have no doubt that's just the way it happened."

"Well let Malison take it then, and be thankful! For it's no more than was well spent on him."

With these conclusive words Thomas Crann left the workshop. No sooner was he gone than out from behind the stack of boards standing against the wall came Willie, the eldest of the Macwha children. He was a dark-skinned, black-eyed, curly-headed, roguish-looking boy, Alec Forbes' companion and occasional partner. He was more mischievous than Alec which sometimes led him into small scrapes. But whenever anything extensive had to be done, Alec was always the leader.

"What are you hiding for, you rascal?" said his father. "What mischief are you up to now?"

"Nothing," was Willie's cool reply.

"Why were you hiding then?"

"Thomas Crann never sets an eye on me without accusing me of something."

"You get no more than you deserve, I don't doubt," returned George. "Here, take the chisel and cut that beading into lengths for me, will you?"

"I'm going over the river to ask about Alec," replied Willie, hoping to get out of the work.

"Ay! there's always something! What's the matter with Alec now?"

"Mr. Malison nearly killed him. He hasn't been to school for two days."

With these words Willie bolted from the shop and set off at full speed. And though the first part had been a slight exaggeration, the last part of his statement was perfectly true.

The day after the fight, Mr. Malison came to the school as usual, but with his arm in a sling. To Annie's dismay, Alec did not appear all day.

It had been impossible for Alec to hide his physical condition from his mother. The heart of the widow was so sad over the sufferings of her son, though Alec did not utter a word of complaint, that she vowed angrily that he should never go to that school again. For three days she held to her resolution and would not let him go. This worried Mr. Malison who feared he had now made two enemies in both son and mother. He had reasons for wanting to be well-liked by as many parents as possible, for he hoped someday to be made pastor of the church in Glamerton. The present clergyman was getting old, and though the people themselves did not decide who filled the pulpit, it was helpful if a man were highly thought of.

Mr. Malison said nothing whatever about the events of Monday, and things went on as usual in the school. There was just one exception: for a whole week his whip did not make its appearance.

As soon as school was over on that first day of Alec's absence, Annie darted off on the road to Howglen where he lived. She never slowed to a walk until she reached the garden gate. She went straight to the kitchen door and knocked. The servant who answered it saw a girl with shabby dress and a dirty bonnet over a disorderly mass of hair. Annie was not kept so tidy on the interest of her money as she had been by her aunt at the farm. The servant girl took her for a beggar, returned to the kitchen and brought her a piece of oatcake. But Annie said: "No thank you. I'm no beggar. I only wanted to know how Alec was today."

"Come in," said the girl, "and I'll tell the mistress."

Annie followed the maid into the kitchen and sat down on the edge of a wooden chair.

"There's a lassie wanting to know how Master Alec is," said the maid through the parlor door.

"That must be little Annie Anderson, Mama," said Alec, who was lying on the sofa.

Alec had told his mother all about the affair. Some of her friends from Glamerton had called as well and given their versions of the story, in which Alec's bravery was made greater than in the way he told it. Indeed, everyone except the young Bruces sang Alec's praises, for every one of them hated the master. So Mrs. Forbes was proud of her boy—though she did not want him to know it. Therefore, she could not help being interested in Annie. She had known James Anderson, her father, and he had been to her home more than once on business. Everybody had liked him, for he was of good character and had a genuinely kind heart.

"Tell her to come up, Mary," she said.

So Annie was shown into Mrs. Forbes' dining room.

To Annie's eyes the place seemed magnificent, for carpet and curtains and an oak sideboard and a sofa were all luxuries she was not familiar with. She entered very timidly and stood close by the door. But Alec scrambled from the sofa, took hold of her by both hands, and pulled her to his mother.

"Here she is, Mama," he said.

Mrs. Forbes, though wondering why her son was so familiar with a girl dressed so shabbily, received her kindly and shook hands with her.

"How do you do, Annie?" she said.

"Quite well, I thank you, mem," answered Annie.

"What's going on at school today, Annie?" asked Alec.

"Not much unusual," answered Annie. "The master's a bit quieter than most days. He must be better behaved for his burnt fingers. But, oh, Alec!"

The little maiden burst into a fit of crying.

"What's the matter, Annie?" said Mrs. Forbes, drawing near and genuinely concerned at the child's tears.

"Oh, mem! You didn't see how the master whipped him!"

Tears from some mysterious source came into Mrs. Forbes' eyes. But at that moment Mary opened the door and said, "Mister Bruce is here, mem, wanting to see you."

"Tell him to come upstairs, Mary."

"Oh no, mem! Don't let him come till I'm gone. He'll take me home with him," cried Annie.

Mary stood waiting.

"But you must go home, you know, Annie," said Mrs. Forbes kindly.

"Ay, but not with *him*," pleaded Annie.

From what Mrs. Forbes knew of the manners and character of Bruce, she was not altogether surprised at Annie's reluctance. So turning to the maid, she asked, "Have you told Mr. Bruce that Miss Anderson is here?"

"Me tell him! No, mem."

"Then take the child into my room till he is gone." Turning to Annie she said, "But perhaps he knows you are here, Annie."

"He can't know that, mem, though he is sharp enough."

"Well, we shall see."

So Mary led Annie away to the sanctuary of Mrs. Forbes' bedroom.

Chapter Twelve

ROBERT BRUCE
VISITS HOWGLEN

B ruce was not following Annie at all. But his visit will need a few words of explanation.

Bruce's father had been a faithful servant to Mrs. Forbes' father-in-law, who had held the same farm at Howglen before his son. They were both what are called gentleman-farmers. The younger Bruce had been anxious to go into business and set up a shop for himself. For his father's sake, Alec's grandfather had loaned him the money to do so. Bruce had paid the money all back before the death of the old man, who had never asked any interest on it. Before many more years had passed, Bruce was known to have prospered so well with his shop that he had accumulated some savings in the bank.

Now Alec's father had spent a great deal on improvements about the farm—draining, fencing, and the like. Just then his younger brother came to him in an emergency. He had no cash of his own, but he thought of Bruce. So he went to him to ask for a loan for his brother.

Bruce carried out a thorough investigation of the financial condition of Mr. Forbes, and finally loaned him a hundred pounds, at the usual rate of interest, secured by the farm if payment should not be made, for a certain number of years. But Mr. Forbes died shortly afterwards, leaving his wife in a difficult position financially. Mrs. Forbes had paid the interest of the hundred-pound debt now for the two years since the death of her husband. But as the rent of the farm was heavy, this extra interest was a burden. She kept hoping for better times for the farm.

Mr. Bruce very much doubted whether the widow would be able to pay him back his hundred pounds when the day arrived when the note came due. This made him all the more concerned that he always receive his interest from her on time. So he was neither in pursuit of Annie nor curious about the welfare of Alec. Indeed, if Malison had killed the boy outright, Bruce would have been more pleased than otherwise. But he was in the habit of reminding the widow of his existence by an occasional call, especially when the time approached for the half-yearly payment of the interest. And now the report of Alec's condition offered him an excuse to look in upon her without seeming to be too greedy after his money.

"Well, mem, how are you today?" he said as he entered, rubbing his hands.

"Quite well, thank you, Mr. Bruce. Take a seat."

"And how's Mr. Alec?"

"There he is to answer for himself," said Mrs. Forbes, looking toward the sofa.

"How are you, Alec, after all this?" said Bruce.

"Quite well, thank you," answered Alec, in a tone that did not altogether satisfy either of his listeners.

"I thought you had been rather injured."

"I got a bruise or two, that's all," said Alec.

"Well, I hope it'll be a lesson to you."

"To Mr. Malison, you should say, Mr. Bruce. I am perfectly satisfied I did no wrong."

His mother was surprised to hear him speak like a grown man. She was also annoyed by his behavior to Bruce. She feared they might one day be in his power because of the debt. But she said nothing. Bruce grinned and was silent.

"I hear you have taken James Anderson's daughter into your family now, Mr. Bruce."

"Oh, ay, mem. There was no one to look after the little lassie. So though I could hardly afford it, with my own small family growing up, I was in a manner obliged to take her. James Anderson was a cousin of mine, you know, mem."

"Well, I'm sure it was very kind of you and Mrs. Bruce. How is the child getting on?"

"Oh, fair, mem . . . only fair. She's a little the worse for taking up with loons."

He glanced at Alec with an expression of spite.

Alec held back the expression that rushed to his lips. A little small talk followed, and the visitor left with a laugh from between his teeth as he took one last look at Alec with satisfaction at his plight.

Almost as soon as he was out of the house, the parlor door opened and Mary brought in Annie. Mrs. Forbes' eyes looked at her with astonishment, and something of a mother's tenderness awoke in her heart toward the child. During Bruce's call Mary had been busy with the child. She had combed and brushed Annie's thick brown hair, washed her face and hands and neck, made the best she could of her poor, dingy dress, and put one of her own Sunday collars about her.

Annie had let her do everything without question, and now Mrs. Forbes was captivated by the pale, patient face, and the longing blue eyes that looked at her as if the child felt that she ought to have been her mother but somehow they had missed each other. They gazed out of the shadows of the mass of dark wavy hair that fell to her waist.

"What have you been about, Mary?"

Thinking she was being made fun of, silent tears rose in Annie's eyes. When Annie cried, the tears always rose and flowed without any sound. Rarely did she sob. This completed the conquest of Mrs. Forbes' heart. She drew the little one to her and kissed her, and Annie's tears stopped instantly. Mrs. Forbes wiped away those still lingering on her face. Mary then went to get the tea, and Mrs. Forbes left the room for a moment, leaving Annie seated on a footstool in front of the bright fire while Alec lay on the sofa looking at her.

"I wouldn't want to be rich folk," said Annie aloud, forgetting that she was not alone.

"We're not rich folk, Annie," said Alec.

"Ay, you are," returned Annie.

"Well, why wouldn't you like it?"

"You must always be afraid of spoiling things."

"Mama would tell you a different story," laughed Alec. "There's nothing here to spoil."

Mrs. Forbes returned. Tea was brought in. Annie behaved herself like a lady, and after tea ran home with mingled feelings of pleasure and pain. For no matter what she had said to Alec, the Bruce's kitchen fire, small and dull smelling shop, and her own dreary attic room did not seem so attractive after her brief visit to the warmth and comfort of the house at Howglen.

She was immediately questioned about why she had been so long in coming home from school. She told the truth—she had gone to ask about Alec Forbes, and they had kept her to tea.

"Did I not tell them just today that you ran after the loons!" said Bruce with a smile of triumph. Then suddenly he realized that they had not asked him to stay to tea. "It's not decent for a poor girl like you, Annie, to go to well-to-do folk's houses where you're not wanted," he added. "So don't let me hear of it again."

But Bruce's influence over Annie, an influence of rebuke and criticism and meanness, was gradually growing weaker. He could still make her uncomfortable. But she had almost reached the point where she no longer cared a straw for his opinion of her. And she had faith enough in Alec to hope that he would defend her from whatever Bruce might have said against her.

Apparently, Mary had been talking in the town about little Annie Anderson's visit to her mistress. And so the story of what a beautiful head of curly hair she had came to be known. Having never thought about Annie's hair before, Mrs. Bruce now had occasion to reflect, and a few days later she came to the back door with a great pair of scissors in her hand.

"Come here, Annie," she called. "Your hair's too long. It's time I cut it. It's giving you sore eyes."

"There's nothing the matter with my eyes," said Annie.

"Don't talk back. Sit down," returned Mrs. Bruce, leading her into the kitchen.

Annie cared very little for her hair, and thus submitted to the haircut without another sound. Mrs. Bruce cut it short all the way around, so that it now fell about her face.

Later that night the wavy locks of rich brown were taken by the careful hands of Mrs. Bruce to Rob Guddle, the barber, for long and beautiful hair could fetch a good sum. The hands that carried the money back home were none the less careful. With a smile to her husband, half loving and half cunning, Mrs. Bruce dropped the sizeable amount into the till.

CHAPTER
THIRTEEN
—

ALEC RETURNS
TO SCHOOL

Although Alec was not a bright boy as far as books were concerned, and therefore was not a favorite with Mr. Malison, he was not by any means stupid. His own eyes could teach him more than books could. For he was very observant of things about him, both in nature and in humanity. He knew all the birds, and their habits, and all their eggs. Not a boy in Glamerton could find a nest quicker than he, nor treated a nest with such respect.

Indeed, he was rather an uncommon boy. Along with more than the usual amount of activity even for a boy, he had a tenderness of heart altogether rare in those his age. He was as familiar with farm animals and their ways of feeling and acting as Annie herself. He hated cruelty in any form. And yet, if it became necessary, he could carry out stern justice.

He was equally at home with the world of men around him. He knew the simple people of the town wonderfully well, and took to Thomas Crann more than anyone else, even though Thomas would often give him long religious lectures. Alec would listen seriously enough, believing Thomas to be right, though he could never make up his mind to give any attention to what was required of him as a result.

At last his mother gave in to his desire to return to school, and on the fourth day Alec made his appearance. He did his best to try to stay out of mischief, and the master seemed to appreciate his efforts.

It would be an injustice to judge Mr. Malison too harshly by the customs of his day. Throughout the whole country, it was the feeling of parents and teachers everywhere that the tawse should be used at the least sign of trouble. *Law* was the highest idea most ordinary people had of God, and still is. And this law had to be supported by means of the leather strap to instill the great truth in the young children of the land. If a wise and even-tempered man used it, no harm could result. But in the hands of a fierce, changeable man like Malison, with a bad temper and no great sense of truth, it became the means of great injury to those children under his care.

Mr. Malison had nothing of the childlike in him. Thus he never saw the mind of the child when he beat the bodies of his students with his cruel blows. It is a good thing for such masters that in the end they will ultimately be judged by the heart of a great and loving Father, not by one such as themselves.

Annie began to be regarded as the friend of Alec Forbes. And since Alec was a favorite with most of his classmates, and since even those who did not like him feared him, even her cousins began to look upon her with something like respect and to lessen their teasing and hurting of her. But this did not make life for her any better at home, where everything remained distasteful and miserable. And how could it have been anything but miserable in a house where the entire aim was first of all to make money, and second not to spend it.

Mr. and Mrs. Bruce had not the slightest idea they were unkind to Annie. On the contrary, Bruce thought himself the most generous and unselfish of men in the whole town if he gave her a scrap of string. And if the neighbors asked about Annie, and Mrs. Bruce replied, "The child's just like other children—she's good enough," she thought she was being more just and kind than nearly any other woman in the land.

But neither cared for her or showed her half the consideration they showered on their own two angelic older children. When Alec's mother sent for her one Saturday, soon after her first visit, they could hardly hide their irritation at the preference shown her. Especially as Mrs. Forbes was so indebted to them, the parents of two boys in every possible way superior to Annie.

CHAPTER
FOURTEEN

WINTER

The winter drew on. In northern places like Scotland, that season is as different from summer as if it belonged to another solar system. Cold and stormy, it is yet full of delight for all beings who can either romp, sleep, or think it through. But alas for the old and sickly, in poor cold homes, with scanty food and provisions for fire! For them the winter is horrid indeed.

The winter came.

One morning all awoke and saw a white world around them. Alec jumped out of bed in delight. It was a sunny, frosty morning. The snow had fallen all night, and no wind had interfered with the gracious alighting of the feathery water. Every branch, every twig was laden with its sparkling burden of flakes. Away across the countryside stretched the outspread glory, the only darkness in it being the line of the winding river. All the snow that fell on it vanished, as death and hell shall one day vanish in the fire of God. It flowed on, black, through the banks of white to the town, where every roof had the sheet that was let down from heaven spread over it. The streets lay a foot deep in the yet unspoiled snow. Soon, like the story of history itself, it would be trampled, dirtied, and driven with human feet, till at last God's strong sun would wipe it all away.

From the door opening into this fairyland, Alec sprang into the untrodden space. He had discovered a world without even the print of human foot upon it. The keen air made him happy, and the peaceful face of nature filled him with jubilation. He was at the school door before a human being had appeared in the streets of Glamerton. Its dwellers all lay still under those sheets of snow, which seemed to hold them asleep in its cold enchantment.

Before any of his fellows made their appearance, he had kneaded and piled a great heap of snowballs and stood by his pyramid prepared for a joyous fight. He attacked the first that came, and soon there was a great troop of boys pelting away at him. But with his store of balls at his feet, he was able to hold off ten or twelve pretty evenly.

By and by the little ones gathered, but they kept away for fear of the flying snowballs. By now the boys had divided into two equal teams and were pelting away at each other. At length the woman who was in charge of the schoolroom finished lighting the fire and opened the door. Annie and several others of the smaller ones made a run for it during a lull in the fury of the battle.

"Stop!" cried Alec, and the flurry ceased.

But one boy, just as Annie was entering the room, threw a snowball at her. He missed, but Alec did not miss him; for hardly was the ball out of his hands when the attacker received Alec's right between the eyes and toppled over on his back.

When the master appeared at the top of the lane, the fight came to an end. As he entered the school, the group around the fire broke up and went to their seats. Alec had entered close behind the master and caught up with Annie, for he had observed her limping as she ran into the school.

"What's the matter with you, Annie?" he said.

"Juno bit me," she answered.

"Ay! Very well!" returned Alec in a tone that had more meaning in it than just the words themselves.

Soon after the Bible class was over and they had all taken their seats, a strange quiet stir of excitement gradually arose. The master became aware of more than the usual flitting to and fro among the boys, like the coming and going of a swarm of bees. "John Morison, go to your seat!" he cried. John went. "Robert Rennie, go to your seat."

Robert went. And this continued till he had shouted out orders to six, and then finally could stand it no longer. The unruliness persisted. At last the *tawse* was thrown, and a couple of lickings followed, but still he was not able to put a complete end to the movings about.

The reason was simple: The General was gathering his troops.

As soon as he was seated, Alec had said in a low voice across the double desk to one of the boys on the opposite side, calling him by his nickname, "I say, Divot, do you know Juno?"

"Maybe not," answered Divot. "But if I don't, my left leg does."

"I thought you knew the shape of her teeth. Just give Scrumpie there a dig in the ribs."

"What are you after, Divot? I'll give you a clout on your ear!" growled Scrumpie.

"Hoot, man! The General wants you." *General* was Alec's nickname.

"What is it, General?"

"Do you know Juno?"

"Hang the beast! I know her too well. She took her dinner off one of my hips last year."

"Just creep over to Cadger there and ask if he knows Juno. Maybe he's forgotten her."

Cadger's reply was interrupted by the interference of the master, but he signalled his answer, conveying to the General that he remembered Juno well enough. Such messages and replies, despite more than one licking in the meantime, kept passing all morning.

Juno was Robert Bruce's dog.

She had the nose and legs of a bulldog, but was not by any means purebred. Her behavior was worse than her breed. She was a great favorite with her master, who said he kept her chained in his back yard to protect the house and store. But she was highly unpopular with the growing generation of boys and girls in Glamerton, for she was fond of biting and often got loose. Bruce had received many complaints, without doing a thing about them. Certain of the boys had from time to time vowed various words of vengeance. But now Alec Forbes had taken up the cause of humanity and justice, for the brute had bitten Annie.

It was soon understood throughout the school that war was to be made upon Juno. Every able-bodied boy must be ready when the General called. The minute they were dismissed the boys gathered in a knot at the door.

"What are you going to do, General?" asked one.

"Kill her," answered Alec.

"How?"

"Stone her to death, like the man who broke the Sabbath."

"Broken bones for broken bones, eh?"

"Ay."

"But there's no stones to be gotten in the snow, General," argued Cadger.

"You simpleton! We'll get more stones than we can carry from the side of the road up yonder."

A confused chorus of suggestions and exclamations now arose, in the midst of which Willie Macwha, whose obvious nickname was Curly, came up.

"Here's Curly."

"Well, is it all settled?" he asked.

"She's condemned but not executed yet," said Grumpie.

"How will we get at her?" asked Cadger.

"That's just the problem," said Divot.

"We can't kill her in her own yard," said Houghie.

"No, we'll just have to wait for the right time and take her when she's out and about," said the General.

"But who's to know that? And how are we to gather?" asked Cadger, who seemed both too practical and too worried for such activities.

"Just hold your tongues and listen to me," retorted Alec.

The excited assembly was instantly silent.

"The first thing is to store plenty of ammunition."

"Ay, ay, General."

"Where should we stow the stones, Curly?"

"In our yard. They'll never be noticed there."

"That'll do. Sometime tonight, you'll all carry what stones you can—and make sure they're the kind that'll do the job—to Curly's yard. He'll be watching for you. And, I say, Curly, you have an old gun, don't you?"

"Ay, but she's an old one."

"Load her up. But stand well back when you fire if you can. It will be our signal to come."

"I'll be careful, General."

"Scrumpie, you don't live that far from the dragon's den. You just keep your eye on her comings and goings. As soon as you see her loose in the yard, you be off to Willie Macwha. Then, Curly, you fire your gun, and if I hear the signal I'll be over in seven minutes and a half. Every one of you that hears must look after the rest, and we'll gather at Curly's. Bring your bags for the stones, them that has bags."

"But what if you don't hear, for it's a long road to your house, General," asked Cadger.

"If I'm not at your yard in seven and a half minutes, Curly, sent Linkum after me. He's the only one that can run. It's all that he can do, but he does it well. Once Juno's out, she's not in a hurry to get back in again."

The boys separated and went home in a state of excitement to their dinners.

CHAPTER
FIFTEEN

———

JUNO

At this time of year in Scotland, the sun now set between two and three o'clock in the afternoon, because it was so far north. Therefore there were no long evenings to favor the plot against Juno.

Probably their hatred of the dog would not have driven the boys of Glamerton to such extreme measures—even though she had bitten Annie Anderson—if her master had been a favorite, or even a man who was generally respected. But Alec knew well enough that the townspeople did not like either Bruce or his beast of a dog and were not likely to sympathize with him if the brute were punished.

When dinner was over and the blazing fire had filled the room with warmth and comfort, Alec rose to leave the house again.

"Where are you going, Alec?" asked his mother.

"Into the yard, Mama."

"What can you do in the yard? It's full of snow."

"It's just the snow I want, Mama."

And in another moment he was under the clear blue night-heaven, with the keen, frosty air blowing on his warm cheeks. He immediately got busy with a shovel and a wheelbarrow, slicing and shoveling in the snow. He was building a hut, in the fashion of an Eskimo house, with a very thick circular wall of snow and ice, which rounded into a top at the center. He paused often in his work and turned toward the town, but no signal came. When called in to tea later he gave one last long look townwards. Out he went again afterward, but still no news came that Juno was ranging the streets, and he was forced to go to bed at last and fall asleep with disappointment.

The next day he strictly questioned all his officers as to the manner in which they had fulfilled their duty and found no cause for complaint. Everything was ready.

"What are you so worked up about, Alec?" asked his mother that night.

"Nothing in particular, Mama," answered Alec, ashamed of himself for showing his nervousness.

"You've looked out the window twenty times in the last half hour," she went on.

"Curly promised to burn a blue gaslight, and I wanted to see if I could see it."

She suspected there was more to it, but his mother was forced to be content with his answer.

But that night also passed without sight of the light, which Curly said he would light before firing the gun. Juno kept safe in her barrel, little thinking of all the plans against her in the wide snowcovered country all around. Alec finished his Eskimo hut, and since more snow fell that night, it looked as if it had been there all winter. It seemed that a long spell of white weather had set in. Alec decided to enlarge his original ice-dwelling and was hard at work on his project on the third dark evening.

"What can that be, over at the town there?" said Mary to her mistress, as she glanced out of the window.

"What is it, Mary?"

"I don't know, mem. It's a curious kind of blue light.—And, preserve us! It's cracking as well," cried Mary, as the faint sound of a far-off explosion reached her.

But Alec was too busy in the depths of his snow-vault to see the signal or hear the roar of Curly's gun.

By and by a knock came to the kitchen door. Mary went and opened it.

"Where's Alec? Is he at home?" said a rosy boy, almost out of breath from running as fast as his legs could carry him, and from the excitement of the moment.

"He's in the yard."

The boy turned and immediately Mary shut the door.

Linkum found Alec's snow house, and as he approached he heard Alec whistling a favorite tune as he shoveled away at the snow.

"General!" cried Linkum.

"Here!" answered Alec, throwing down his shovel and bolting in the direction of the call. "Is it you, Linkum?"

"She's out, General."

"The devil have her if she ever gets in again, the brute! Did you go to Curly?"

"Ay, did I. He fired the gun and burned his light, and waited seven and a half minutes, and then he sent me for you, General."

"Confound it!" cried Alec, and tore through the shrubbery and hedge, the nearest way to the road, followed by Linkum, who even at full speed could not keep up with Alec.

Away the two boys flew like the wind, along the well-beaten path to the town, over the footbridge that crossed the Glamour, and full speed up the hill to Willie Macwha, who was anxiously awaiting the commander with a dozen or fifteen more of the troops. They all had their book bags, pockets, and arms filled with stones. One bag was filled and ready for Alec.

"Now," said the General, in the tone of Gideon of old, "if any of you are afraid of the brute, just go home now."

"Ay, ay, General."

Nobody moved a muscle.

"Who's watching her?"

"Doddles, Gapey, and Goat."

"Where was she last seen?"

"Taking up with another tyke on the town square."

"Come along then. This is what we'll do. We mustn't all go together. Some of you—you three—down the Back Wynd. You six up Lucky Hunter's Close. And the rest by Gowan Street. The first to reach the water pump, wait for the rest."

"How are we to make the attack, General?"

"I'll give my orders as it seems best, after I see the situation," replied Alec.

And away they all shot.

The muffled sounds of the feet of the various companies of the army, as they thundered past upon the snow, roused the old wives dozing over their knitting by their fires, causing various remarks: "Some mischief of the loons!" "Some devilry of the rascals from Malison's school!"

They reached the square almost together and found Doddles at the pump, who reported that Juno had gone down to the yard of the inn, and Gapey and Goat were watching her. Now she would have to come out to get back home again, for there was no back way out of the innyard. So by Alec's orders they broke up a little, to avoid looking suspicious, and gradually approached the inn and the way they knew Juno would take to go home.

The town was dark, but reflecting the brilliant moonlight over the snow.

"There she is! There she is!" cried several at once in a hissing, whispered excitement.

"Hold still!" cried Alec. "Wait till I tell you. Don't you see that there's Long Tom's dog with her, and he's done nothing. We can't punish the innocent with the guilty."

A moment later the dogs took their leaves of each other and Juno went off at a slow slouching trot in the direction of her own street.

"Close in!" cried Alec.

Juno found her way blocked in a threatening manner, and tried to pass by.

"Let at her, boys!" cried the General.

A storm of stones was their answer to the order, and a howl of rage and pain burst from the animal. She turned and tried to run, but found that she was the center of a circle of enemies.

"Let at her! Hold at her!" yelled Alec.

Thick as hail the well-aimed stones flew, though not half of them hit the dog. She darted first at one, then at another, snapping and biting wildly, and meeting with many a kick and a blow in return.

The neighbors began to look out from their doors and windows, for the boys were no longer trying to keep their cries quiet. But not one of the good folks tried to interfere. And indeed, they could not clearly make out what was going on in the moonlight.

Although cowardly enough now, the brute was infuriated with pain, and had made a determined rush at one of her antagonists, and a short hand-to-teeth struggle was now taking place. For a moment the stoning ceased.

"She has a grip of my leg!" cried Alec, "and I have a grip of her throat! Curly, get in my jacket pocket and take out a piece of twine you'll find there."

Curly did so, and drew out a yard and a half of garden line.

"Put it around her neck, and two or three of you take a hold at each end and pull for your lives!" They hauled with hearty vigor, and finally Juno's teeth relaxed their hold on Alec's calf. In another minute her tongue was hanging out of her mouth, and when they stopped pulling she lay limp on the snow. With a shout of triumph they started off at full speed, dragging the brute by the neck through the street. Alec tried to follow them, but found his leg too painful and was forced to go limping home.

When the victors had run till they were out of breath, they stopped to confer. The result was that in solemn silence they drew the dog home to the back gate. Finding all quiet in the yard, two of their company snuck into the yard to lay the dead body in its house. Curly and Linkum pulled her in, tumbled her into her barrel, which they then set up on end, and left Juno lying neck and tail together in a silent heap.

Before Alec reached home his leg had swollen very large and was so painful that he could hardly limp along. For Juno had taken no passing snap but a great, strong mouthful. He hid his condition from his mother for that night. But the next morning his leg was so bad that there was no longer any way to hide it. To tell a lie would have been too hard for Alec, so there was nothing to do but confess.

His mother scolded him far heavier than she actually thought the wrongdoing justified, telling him he would get her into disgrace in the town as the mother of a lawless son who interfered with other people's property in a way little better than stealing.

"I imagine, Mama, a loon's legs are about as much his own property as the tyke was Rob Bruce's," replied Alec. "It's not the first time she's bitten half a dozen legs that were neither her own nor her master's."

Mrs. Forbes did not have an answer to this argument.

CHAPTER
SIXTEEN

REVENGE

Alec was once more condemned to the sofa, and Annie had to miss him and wonder what had become of him. She always felt safe when Alec was there, and became timid when he was not, even though whole days would sometimes pass without either speaking to the other.

About noon, when everything was fairly quiet and orderly in the school, the door opened and the face of Robert Bruce appeared, with gleaming eyes of wrath.

"God preserve us!" said Scrumpie to his neighbor. "Such a lickin' as we're gonna get! Here's Rob Bruce! Who's gone and told him?"

Some of the gang of conspirators who were standing in a group by the door stared in horror. For following Bruce, and led by the scrap of Alec's very own twine, came an awful ghost—Juno on her own feet, a pitiable limping mass that looked like a walking corpse of a dog.

"She ain't dead after all! Devil take her, for he's in her," whispered Doddles hoarsely.

"We didn't kill her enough," murmured Curly.

And now the storm began to break. The master had gone to the door and shaken hands with his visitor, glancing with a puzzled look at the miserable animal which barely had enough shape left to show that it was a dog.

"I'm very sorry, Mr. Malison, to come to you with my complaints," said Bruce, "but just look at the poor dumb animal! She couldn't come and defend herself, so I had to bring her. Stand still, you brute!"

For Juno had caught sight of some boys' legs, and began to tug at the string feebly. She no longer, however, was looking at the legs as made for dogs to bite but as fearful instruments of vengeance, in league with stones and string. So she was straining and pulling toward the door. But her master had brought her as chief witness against the boys and she must remain.

"Eh, lass," he said, "if you could but speak you would soon point out the rascals that mistreated you.—Mr. Malison, she was one of the bonniest and friendliest animals you could ever set your eyes upon—"

Smothered laughter gurgled throughout the room.

"—till some of these loons here have just driven the soul out of her with stones."

"Where does the soul of a demon live?" asked Goat, in a whisper, to the boy next to him.

"The devil knows," answered Gapey, "if it doesn't live in the bottom of Rob Bruce's belly."

The master's wrath was always ready enough to rise against boys and all their works. And now it began to show itself in the growing redness of his face. This was not one of his worst passions—in those times he grew white—for this injury had not been done to himself.

"Can you tell me which of them did it?"

"No, sir. There must have been more than two or three at it, or she would have frightened them away. The best-natured dog in all the town!"

A decisive murmur greeted his last comment.

"William Macwha!" cried Malison.

"Here, sir."

"Come up."

Willie went. He had made up his mind that since so many already knew about it and some were already beginning to turn cowardly, it would be of no use to deny the deed.

"Do you know anything about this cruelty to the poor dog, William?" said the master.

Willie gave a Scotsman's answer. While evasive, it was fully the truth. "She bit me, sir."

"When? While you were stoning her?"

"No, sir. A month ago."

"You're a lying wretch, Willie Macwha!" cried Bruce. "She's the quietest, kindliest beast that ever was born. See, sir, just look at her. She'll let me put my hand in her mouth and take no more notice than if it were her own tongue."

Now, whether it was that the said tongue was still swollen and painful, or that Juno disapproved of the whole proceeding, I cannot tell. But the result of this proof of her good temper was that she chomped down with all her strength and caused her teeth to meet through Bruce's hand.

"Curse the she-devil!" he roared, snatching the hand away with the blood beginning to flow.

A laugh, not smothered this time, billowed and broke through the whole school. It was delightful enough that Juno had bitten her master. But the fact that Bruce, a churchman, should speak so in public, was altogether too much.

"Isn't it good we didn't kill her after all?" said Curly.

"Good doggie," said another, patting his own knee as if to entice her to come and be petted.

"At him again, Juno!" cheered a third.

Writhing in pain and mortified by more embarrassment than he had ever felt at his would-be proof that Juno would not bite, and still more embarrassed that he had reacted so and was now being laughed at by the whole school, Bruce turned away.

"It's their fault, the bad boys! She never did anything like that before. They have ruined her good temper," he said as he left the school, following Juno who was tugging away at the string as if she had been a blind man's dog.

"What do you have to say for yourself, William?" demanded Malison.

"She started it, sir."

But the best of excuses could not satisfy the master. The punishment fervor had taken renewed hold on him. But he would ask more questions first.

"Who besides you tortured the animal?"

Curly was silent.

He did not have a particularly high sense of honor, nor many ethical principles to rule his behavior. But he was devoted to his friends, which is the highest form of conscience to be found in many.

"Tell me their names!"

Curly was still silent.

But a white-haired urchin, who had received uncounted whippings at the hand of the master, and was thus corrupted by fear, cried out in a wavering voice: "Sanny Forbes was one of them, and he's not here, 'cause Juno bit him."

The poor little boy gained little by his treachery, however, for after school one of the smallest of the conspirators fell on him and gave him a thrashing, which he no doubt deserved more than one of Malison's.

But the effect of Alec's name on the master was amazing. He changed his manner at once, sent Curly to his seat without the whip, and nothing more was ever heard of Juno or her master.

The following morning, the neighbors across the street stared in astonishment at the place where the shop of Robert Bruce had been. It looked as though an avalanche had fallen from the heavens directly onto his house! It was completely buried in snow! Not a door or window was visible!

Spades and shovels in boys' hands had been busy for hours during the night, throwing snow up against the house. The first action, however, had been to block up the door with a huge snowball, which they had rolled in silence the whole length of the long street, until it was taller than any of the boys who helped push it into place.

Bruce and his wife slept in a little room immediately behind the shop, that they might watch over their treasures. Bruce's first movement in the morning was always to go into the shop to unbolt the door and take down the shutters.

His amazement when he looked out the windows upon a blank wall of snow may well be imagined! He did not question that the whole town was similarly covered. Such a giant snowstorm had never been heard of before, and he remembered uneasily the curse he had uttered in the schoolroom. For a brief moment he imagined that the whole town of Glamerton had been buried because God was punishing him for what he had said.

"Nancy! Robbie! Johnnie! We're buried alive!" he cried out.

"Preserve us, Robert! What's happened?" cried his wife, rushing from the kitchen.

"I'm not buried," said Robert the younger, entering from the backyard. His father rushed out to the back door, and to his astonishment and relief saw the whole world about him. It was a private judgment, then, upon him and his shop. And so it was—a very private judgment. It was probably because of the embarrassment and guilt he felt that he chose not to take his complaint this time to Murdoch Malison.

Alec Forbes had nothing to do with this revenge against him. But Bruce always thought he was at the bottom of it and hated him all the more. He disliked all loons but his own, but Alec Forbes he hated above the rest. For in every way Alec was the very opposite of Bruce himself. The Bruces' disapproval and dislike of Annie rose after this incident, once their sons told them that it was because Juno had bitten her that the boys of the school, with Alec for a leader, had attacked her as they had.

For the rest of Juno's existence, the moment she caught sight of a boy she fled as fast as her four bowlegs would carry her, not daring even to let her tail stick out behind her, in case one of them might use it for a handle and grab her as she ran.

When Annie heard that Alec had been bitten she was miserable. She knew that his bite must be worse than hers, or he would not be kept at home. She wanted to go see how he was, and followed the path to his house. But when she arrived she could not quite make up her mind to knock at the door. For despite the lady's kindness she was a little afraid of Mrs. Forbes. So she wandered around the side of the house until she came upon the curious heap of snow with the small round tunnel opening into it. She examined Alec's Eskimo hut all around, and then entered into the hollow little tunnel. It was dark, with a faint light from the evening glimmering through the roof. But it wasn't so cold as outside, where a light frosty wind was blowing. Annie sat down, and before long, as she often did, fell fast asleep.

In the meantime, Alec was sitting alone by the light of the fire, finishing the last of a story he was reading. His mother had gone into town. When he was through reading he got a candle and went out into the gathering darkness to see how his little snow room looked in candlelight.

As he entered he could hardly believe his eyes. A figure was there—completely still, perhaps dead! If he had not come then, Annie might indeed have slept on till her sleep took her into the next world.

Her face was pale and deathly cold. Alec had a difficult time waking her. Alec took hold of her hands, but she did not move. He sat down, took her in his arms, and spoke to her. He became frightened when she did not answer, and began shaking her. Still she would not open her eyes! But he knew she was not dead yet, for he could feel her heart beating. At length she lifted her eyelids, looked up in his face, gave a low happy laugh, like the laugh of a dreaming child, and was fast asleep again the next moment.

Alex hesitated no longer. He tugged her out of the chamber, then rose with her in his arms, and carried her into the parlor and laid her down on the rug in front of the fire, with a pillow under her head.

When Mrs. Forbes came home, she found Alec reading and Annie sleeping beside the fireside. Before his mother had recovered from her surprise, Alec said, "I found her sleeping in my snow hut outside, Mama. If I hadn't brought her in she would have been dead by now."

Poor little darling, thought Mrs. Forbes. She stooped down and drew the child a little way back from the fire. Then she made some tea, and proceeded to take off Annie's bonnet and shawl. By then Annie was beginning to move and Alec rose to go to her.

"Let her alone," said his mother. "Let her come to herself slowly. Come to the table."

Alec obeyed. They could see that Annie had opened her eyes and lay staring at the fire. What was she thinking about? She had fallen asleep in a house of snow, and now here she was by a bright fire!

"Annie, dear, come to your tea," were the first words she heard.

She rose and went, and sat down at the table with a smile, taking it all as the gift of God, or a good dream, and never asking how she had come to be so happy. She carried that happiness with her across the bridge as she went home later, through the town and up to her garret.

Pleasant dreams came naturally that evening.

CHAPTER
SEVENTEEN

BOATS AND CHIMNEYS

The spirit of mischief had never been so thoroughly aroused in the youth of Glamerton as it was this winter. The snow lay very heavy and thick. And almost every day a fresh fall added to its depth, and the cold strengthened the impulses of the boys to muscular exertion and activity.

"The loons are just growing to be perfect devils," growled Mr. Chapman, the wool carder, running into his own shop, the remains of a snowball melting down the back of his neck. "We'll have to get another constable to hold them in order."

The present representative of the law was a long-legged, short man who ran so slowly that the boys called him "Stumping Steenie." They were no more afraid of him than they were of his old cow—which, since her owner was a widower, they called *Mrs. Stephen.* So there was certainly grounds for the wool carder's remark. Though it is doubtful how much a second constable would have helped matters.

"I never saw such gallow birds," chimed in a farmer's wife who was standing in the shop. "Did you hear what they did to Rob Bruce?"

"They tell me they all but buried him alive."

"Oh, ay! Everyone knows that. But there's a later story."

Here Andrew Mellon, the clothier, dropped in and the lady turned to him. "Did you hear what the loons did to Robert Bruce the night before last?"

"No, what was that? I do believe they are out to drive the man crazy."

"Well, I was standing at the counter of his shop, and Robert was serving a little girl with a penny worth of candy, when all at once there came such a blast and a smell fit to smother you out of the fire and the shop was full of the smell and the smoke before you knew it. 'Preserve us all!' cried Rob. But before he could say another word, from inside the house comes Nancy running and opening the door with a screech: 'Preserve us all!' she yelled, 'Robert, the chimney's plugged!' And I tell you, the house and shop was as full as it could be, from cellar to attic, of the blackest smoke that ever burned from coal."

"What did Bruce do?" asked Mellon.

"We all ran outside, and it was a sight to see the creature Bruce with his long neck looking up at the chimneys. But not a spark or a wisp of smoke was coming out of them. It was easy to see what the matter was. The loons had climbed up on the roof and had flung a handful of blasting powder down each of the smoking chimneys of the house and then covered them with a big piece of turf. Not a single lad was in sight, but I doubt if any of them were far away. There was nothing to do but get a ladder and just go up and take them off. Poor Robert was just ranting with rage. Not that he said much, for he dared not open his mouth for fear of swearing, and Robert wouldn't swear, you know."

"What laddies were they, do you know?" asked Chapman.

"There's a heap of them up to tricks. There's snowballs flying wherever you go these days!" replied the woman.

"I just got one in the back of my neck!" agreed the wool carder.

"Well, as long as they keep their hand from what doesn't belong to them, I don't mind a little mischief now and then," said Andrew. "They'll not turn out the worse for a prank or two."

The fact was, none of the boys would have dreamed of interfering with Andrew Mellon. Everybody respected him, not because he was an elder in the church, but because he was a good-tempered, kindly, honest, unselfish man.

In the meantime, while Alec was confined to the house with his wounded leg, he had been busy inventing all kinds of projects to keep him busy for the period of the snow. His schoolwork never occupied much of his thoughts.

The first day of his return to society, when school was over, he set off walking, rejoicing in his freedom. He came to the Wan Water, the other river that flowed through the wide valley on the other side of Glamerton. As he stood looking at it, all at once a vision of summer arose in his mind. He thought of how delightful it would be to go sailing down the rippling river. His next thought was an idea: why shouldn't he build a boat?

He *would* build a boat! He would begin at once. Here was work that would keep him busy all the rest of the winter.

His first step must be to go home and have dinner. His next— to talk to Wille's father, who had been a ship carpenter in his younger days. He would run over to the Macwha's that very evening!

It was a still, lovely night, clear and frosty. Alec walked to the town. The street was empty. Nothing moved but an occasional shadow. As he came near to Macwha's shop, he had to pass a row of cottages, all built right next to each other, which all stood with their backs to a steep slope.

When he was about opposite the middle of the row, he heard a stifled laugh followed by the sound of hurrying steps running away. A moment later and suddenly every door of every cottage in the whole row was torn open and out ran the inhabitants— an old woman, a shoemaker with a tool still in his hand, a tailor holding a pair a scissors, and two or three whole families. Everyone rushed into the middle of the road, turned around, and looked up at their roofs. "What's up, Betty?" Alec asked an old lady, hobbling out of her cottage, nearly crippled with rheumatism.

But before she could speak, Alec saw the smoke coming out all of the houses, filling the air with a variety of scents—burning oak bark, burning leather cuttings, damp firewood and peat, the cooking of red herrings, the boiling of porridge, the baking of oatcake, etc. Luckily for all the inhabitants, the devil loons hadn't used any blasting powder here.

The old woman looked around and, seeing Alec whom she knew was one of the obnoxious schoolboys, said, "Go and take the divot off my chimney, Alec, like a good lad! You shouldn't play tricks on poor old folks like me. I'm in tears from the smoke in my eyes." She wiped her eyes with an apron.

Alec was on the roof of Mrs. Lapp's cottage before she had finished. He grabbed the divot and threw it halfway down the hillside at the back of the cottage. Then he scrambled from one chimney to the other and went on pitching the big pieces of sod down the hill. At length, two of the men who had climbed up at the other end of the row, met him. They thought he was a repentant sinner, and took him down as their prisoner, telling him it wasn't right for a gentlewoman's son to treat the poor in that way.

"I didn't do it," Alec assured them.

"Don't lie," came the sharp answer.

"I'm not lying."

"Who did it then?"

"I can guess. And it won't happen again if I can help it."

"Tell us who did it."

"I won't say names."

"He's one of them!"

"The loons and their mischief aren't to be put up with any longer!" said a burly shoemaker walking up and grabbing Alec by the arm. "I'll give him a whipping he won't soon forget!"

"I didn't do it," persisted Alec.

"Who killed Rob Bruce's dog?" asked the shoemaker, squeezing Alec's arm.

"I did, though he's not dead," answered Alec. "And I will do yours the same good turn if he bites children."

"And quite right too!" put in the shoemaker's wife. "Let him go. I'll be bound he's not one of them."

"Tell us how you came to be here then."

"I went up to take the divot off Mrs. Lapp's chimney. Ask

her. Once up there I thought I might give the rest of you a good turn."

"Well, well! Then come inside and warm yourself," said the shoemaker, convinced at last of Alec's innocence.

So Alec went, had a chat with them, and then continued on to George Macwha's. The carpenter liked Alec's idea at once. Alec was a fair hand at all sorts of work, and it was soon arranged that the vessel should be built at one end of the workshop. George would give directions, and Willie could give what help he chose, and otherwise Alec should build his boat himself.

Just as they concluded their discussion, in came Willie, wiping some traces of blood from his nose. He gave Alec an angry gesture.

"What have you been after now, laddie?" asked his father.

"Alec's just given me a bloody nose," said Willie.

"What do you mean, Curly?" asked Alec in amazement.

"That divot you flung off Mrs. Lapp's chimney," said Curly. "It came right onto the back of my head as I lay on the hillside. You pretended you didn't see me, no doubt?"

"I say, Curly," said Alec, putting his arm around his shoulders and leading him aside, "we must have no more of this kind of work. It's shameful. Don't you see the difference between choking an evil tyke of a dog and choking a poor widow's chimney?"

"It was only for fun."

"It's no fun that both sides can't laugh at, Curly."

"Rob Bruce wasn't laughing when he brought the varmit to the school, nor when he went home again."

"That wasn't for fun, Curly. That was downright earnest justice."

Curly paused a moment to think it over in his mind. "Well, Alec, I see there is a difference. Say no more about it."

"I won't. But if I was you, Curly, I would take old Betty a sack of kindling."

"I'll take it tonight, Alec. Father, do you have an old sack?"

"There's one up in the loft. What do you want with a sack?" But Curly was in the loft almost before the question had left his father's lips. A moment later he was down in the workshop on his knees filling the sack with all the shavings and chips he could find. In a few moments more Curly was off to Widow Lapp with his bag of kindling.

"He's a fine fellow, that Willie of yours, George," said Alec to Willie's father. "He only needs to have a thing well put before his mind before he acts on it directly."

"It's good for him he makes a friend of you, Alec. There's a heap of mischief in him.—Where's he off to with that bag?"

Alec told him the whole story, much to George's satisfaction, who could appreciate the repentance of his son. From that day on he thought even more of young Alec, and of Willie as well.

"Now, Curly," said Alec as soon as he reappeared with the empty sack, "your father's going to let me build a boat, and you must help me."

"What's the use of a boat in this weather?" said Curly.

"You buffoon!" returned his father. "You never look an inch past the end of your own nose! You wouldn't think of a boat before the spring. The summer would be over and the water frozen again before you had it built! But I can't attend to it just now, Alec," he added, turning to Alec, "though I'll help you get started tomorrow morning."

So the troubles of the townsfolk from the loons ended, and without having to add another constable. For since Curly was now withdrawn from the ranks of the troublemakers, there was no one else to take the lead.

Curly soon had both his hands quite occupied with boat building.

CHAPTER EIGHTEEN

BOAT BUILDING

E very afternoon now, the moment dinner was over, Alec set off to the workshop and did not return until eight o'clock or sometime later. Mrs. Forbes did not particularly like this change in his habits, but she had the good sense not to interfere.

One day he persuaded her to go with him and see how the boat was getting on. This caused her to be more appreciative of his nightly work. For there was the beginning of a boat already taking shape in the workshop, and there were Alec and Willie working away before her eyes. The quiet little chat she had with George Macwha, in which he spoke highly of Alec, also made her feel better about his leaving her every evening.

But Mrs. Forbes never noticed the little figure lying in a corner half buried in wood shavings and fast asleep. It was, of course, Annie Anderson. Having heard of the new occupation of her hero, one afternoon she had followed her feet, and before she knew where they were going she had found herself at George's shop door. Peeking in, she had watched Alec and Willie for some time at their work without showing herself. But George came up behind her, took her by the hand, and led her in, saying kindly: "Here's a new worker, Alec. She wants to learn boat building."

"Annie, is that you?" said Alec. "Come on in. There's a fine heap of spales you can sit on and see what we're about."

And so saying he seated her on the shavings and half-buried her with an armful more to keep her warm.

"Close the door, Willie," he added. "She'll be cold for she's not working."

Willie shut the door, and Annie found herself very comfortable indeed. There she sat, in perfect contentment, watching the progress of the boat. But after she had sat for a good while in silence, she looked up at Alec and said: "Is there nothing I can do to help you, Alec?"

"Nothing, Annie. Lassies can't saw or plane, you know."

Again she was silent for a long time. Then with a little sigh she looked up and said, "Alec, I'm cold."

"I'll bring my plaid blanket to wrap you in tomorrow."

Annie's heart bounded with delight. For were his words not an express invitation to return!

"But come with me," Alec went on, "and we'll soon get you warm again. Give me your hand."

Annie gave her hand to Alec, and he lifted her out of the heap of spales and led her away. She never thought of asking where he was leading her. They had not gone far down the street when a roaring sound fell upon her ear, growing louder and louder as they went on. Then they turned a sharp corner, and she saw the blacksmith's fire. The door of the smithy's shop was open, and they could see the blacksmith at work some distance off. The fire glowed with gathered rage at the impudence of the bellows blowing in its face. The huge smith, with one arm flung over the shoulder of the bellows, urged on the contest between air and fire, while he stirred up the latter by poking a piece of iron into the very middle of it.

Annie was delighted to look at it, but there was a certain fierceness about the whole affair that made her afraid of going nearer. She could not help feeling scared of the giant smith, with his muscular arms that twisted and tortured iron bars all day long—and his black, fierce-looking face.

Just then he grabbed up a great iron spoon, dipped it into a tub of water, and poured the spoonful on the fire. It hissed and sputtered at the fresh insult, like one of the fiery flying serpents she had read about in her Bible. But she showed no hesitation by the motion of her hand lying in Alec's to follow him as he led her into the shop and right up to the wrathful man.

"Peter Whaup, here's a lassie that's almost frozen to death with cold. Will you take her in and let her stand by your fire and warm herself?"

"I'll do that, Alec. Come in, my child. What do they call you?"

"Annie Anderson."

"Oh, ay! I know all about you well enough. You can leave her with me, Alec. I'll look after her."

"I must go back to my boat, Annie," said Alec in a tone of apology, "but I'll come back for you before long."

So Annie was left with the blacksmith.

Chapter Nineteen

DOWIE IN THE SMITH'S SHOP

With his leather apron, Peter Whaup swept off a space on the front of the raised hearth of the forge, out of the way of dust and cinders. Then he wiped his hands on the same apron, and lifted the girl as tenderly as if she had been a baby, and set her down on the spot he had cleared, about a yard away from the fire.

And there sat Annie in front of the smith, looking back and forth between him and the fire. She was not the least afraid of him now that she had heard him speak.

He asked her a great many questions about herself and the Bruces, and about her former life at home. And every question he asked, he seemed to put in a yet kindlier voice. Sometimes he would stop in the middle of blowing, lean forward with his arm on the handle of the bellows, and look full in the child's face till she was through answering him.

"And you say you liked it at the farm best?" he said.

"Ay. But, you see, my father died—"

"I know that, my child. A good man, your father. The Lord hold tight to you!"

"I'm thinking He holds tight to us all, Mr. Whaup."

She then told him about the rats and the cat. When she was done, the smith drew the back of his hand across both his eyes and then pressed both eyes hard with the thumb and forefinger of his right hand. But he hardly needed to do so, for Annie would never have noticed his tears and the heat from the fire would quickly have dried them. Indeed, this smith's great heart was just like his fire!

He pulled out the red-hot bar which he seemed to have forgotten ever since Annie came in. Then he stood with his back to her to protect her while the sparks flew from his blows, and put the piece of iron on his anvil and began to hammer away at it with a fury. Then just as suddenly he stopped, and put the iron once more in the fire, roused the wrath of the coals with the bellows, and said, "So you knew James Dow, then?"

"Ay! I knew Dowie as well as Brownie."

"Who was Brownie?"

"Nobody but my own cow."

"And was James kind to you?"

Annie could not even answer the question. Peter saw her lips and the muscles of her face begin quivering as if she were about to break into sobs and tears.

But the sound of approaching steps and voices interrupted their conversation. In the door two men appeared, each carrying two plows to be sharpened. The instant she saw them, Annie tumbled off her perch and ran toward the door.

"Dowie! Dowie!" she cried.

In another instant the plow was on the ground and Annie was lifted high in Dowie's arms.

"My little mistress!" he exclaimed, kissing her. "How do you come to be here?"

"I'm safe enough here, Dowie. Don't be afraid. I'll tell you all about it. Alec's in George Macwha's shop."

"And who's Alec?" asked Dowie.

Leaving them to their talk, James Dow's young companion and the blacksmith set to work sharpening the blades of the plows. In about fifteen minutes Alec returned to the shop.

Speaking to Dowie, who still held her in his arms, Annie said,

"This is Alec that I told you about. He's so good to me. Alec, here's Dowie that I like better than anybody in the whole world."

She turned and kissed the dark ruddy face. It was a clean face despite the appearance to the contrary given by three days' growth of beard, which Annie's kiss was too full of love to mind.

Later Dowie carried Annie home in his arms. On the way she told him all about the kindness of Alec and his mother. He asked her many questions about the Bruces. But Annie's patient nature caused her not to tell him how bad things were for her. However, Dowie had his own thoughts on the matter of the Bruces.

"How are you tonight, Mr. Dow?" said Robert, who treated him with oily respect because he was not only familiar with Annie's financial affairs, but was a kind of natural if not legal guardian of her and her property. "And where did you find this stray lamb of ours?"

"She's been with me all this time," answered Dow, not wanting to give an answer before he understood the drift of the question. A Scotsman would always like the last question first.

"She's a bad one for running out," said Bruce softly to Dow, and with a cutting look thrown at Annie, "without asking permission, and we never know where she is. That's not right for such small girls."

"Never you mind, Mr. Bruce," replied Dow. "I know her better than you, meaning no offense, seeing she was in my arms before she was a week old. Let her go where she likes, and if she does what she shouldn't do, I'll take all the blame for it."

There was no great worry about Annie's safety in the minds of Mr. and Mrs. Bruce. The shop and their own children—chiefly the former—occupied their thoughts almost entirely. The less trouble they had from the presence of Annie the better pleased they would be—provided no one would ever accuse them of neglecting her. For this reason they rarely asked about Annie's absences, only criticized her for them to others.

But Bruce did not like the influence that James Dow had with her, and before they went to bed for the night, he had another lecture ready for Annie.

"Annie," he told her, "it's not right for one in your position to be so familiar. You come from a father of property. You'll be a lady someday, and it's not right to take up with servants. James Dow's just a working man, and beneath your station in life altogether. It's not proper for a low man like that to take you up in his arms as if you were a child of his own."

"I like James Dow better than anybody in the whole world," said Annie, "except—"

She stopped short. She would not expose her heart to this man.

"Except who?" asked Bruce.

"I'm not going to say," returned Annie firmly.

"You're a bad-mannered lassie," said Bruce, pushing her away.

She walked off to bed, caring nothing about his rebuke. Since Alec's kindness had opened to her a well of water of life, she had almost stopped caring about the meanness of her guardians. She forgot them as soon as she was out of their sight.

And certainly they were better to forget than to remember.

Chapter Twenty

BALLADS

As soon as she was alone in her room, Annie took out of her pocket a little package which Dowie had bought for her on their way home. She undid the paper and found two or three tallow candles! She could now have a small light in her room to read by at night!

But how was she to get a light? For this was long before matches had come to Glamerton. Annie knew of only one way.

She waited on the edge of her bed in the cold and darkness, until every sound in the house had stopped. Then she stepped cautiously down the old stairs, which would creak and crack now and then, however gentle she attempted to be, down to the fire.

What a pretty study she would have made for an artist to paint! Her face was close to the grate, her mouth puckered up to act as a bellows, one hand holding a piece of twisted paper between the bars, while she blew at the reluctant fire, a glow spreading over her face at each breath, and then fading as the breath stopped, till at last the paper caught into a tiny flame.

Then she lit her candle and again with careful steps made her way back up to her own room. She set the candle in a knothole in the floor. Then she opened the box in which lay the few books her aunt had thrown into it when she left her old home. One of these contained poems of a little-known Scottish poet her father had been fond of reading. It was very cold work at midnight in winter, and in an attic too. But she feared that if she showed openly that she enjoyed such a book in the sight of any of the Bruces, it would be taken away from her as "altogether unsuitable for one so young."

When she entered George Macwha's workshop the next evening, she found the two boys already busy at their work. Without interrupting them, she took her place on the heap of shavings which had remained undisturbed since the previous night. As she sat, without thinking about it, some pieces of one of the ballads she had read several times from her father's book began to come out of her mouth. The boys did not know what to make of it at first, hearing something come all at once from Annie's lips which broke the silence in the shop like a foreign sound. But they said nothing until she had finished all she could remember:

"O lat me in, my bonny lass!
It's a lang road ower the hill;
And the flauchterin' snaw began to fa',
As I cam' by the mill."

She continued for several more stanzas until her memory failed her.

George Macwha, who was working at the other end of the shop when she began, drew near with his chisel in his hand, and joined the listeners.

"Well done, Annie!" he exclaimed as soon as she had finished. She felt very shy and awkward about what she had done.

"Say it over again, Annie," requested Alec.

This was music to her ears!

So she repeated it again, this time adding still another verse that came back to her.

"Eh, Annie! That's real bonnie. Where did you get it?" he said.

"In an old book of my father's."

"Are there any more like it?"

"Ay, several," replied the lassie.

"Learn another for us, will you?"

"I'll do that, Alec."

"Didn't you like it, Curly?" asked Alec, for Curly had said nothing.

"Ay, fegs!" was Curly's only comment.

Such a reception motivated Annie wonderfully, and now she continued her midnight reading with new enthusiasm. She dared even to carry the precious volume to and from school as well. She practiced verses the whole way, taking a roundabout road so that her cousins would not interrupt her or discover what she was doing.

A rapid thaw set in, and before long the dark colors of mire and dirt began to appear in the middle of the vanishing whiteness. But once the snow was gone, a hard black frost set in, and the surfaces of the two rivers, the Glamour and the Wan Water, froze over with ice, and grew thicker and stronger every day. Out came the troops of boys with their ironclad shoes and clumsy skates, and skimmed along the frozen floors of delight. Alec and Willie almost forgot their boat for a time, repaired their skates, and joined their schoolfellows in the fun.

For many afternoons and into the early evening, Alec and Curly skated on the icy river, and Annie was for a time left lonely. But she was not sad, for she knew they must eventually return to the boat. She still went to the shop now and then to see George Macwha, who kept on steadily at his work. If he asked she would repeat a ballad or two, and then go home to learn another.

This was becoming difficult, however, for her candles were now gone and she had no money to buy more. The last candle had come to a tragic end. As she heard footsteps approaching, before she could put it away in its usual safe place in her box, she hastily poked it into one of the holes of the floor and forgot it. When she tried to find it that night it was gone. Her first fear was that it had been discovered. But neither Mr. nor Mrs. Bruce said anything of it, and she concluded that her enemies the rats had carried it off.

But she soon faced an even greater difficulty. It was not long before she had exhausted the contents of the little book of her father's. And there was no more of that kind in her chest. She thought and thought about where she might find another, and at last decided to ask Mr. Cowie, the clergyman. Without asking anyone's permission, the very next afternoon she went to his house and knocked on the door.

"Could I see the minister?" she said to the maid.

"I don't know. What do you want?" was the maid's reply.

But Annie was Scottish too. And perhaps she realized she would probably not be let in if she revealed her request to the servant. So she only replied, "I want to see the minister himself, if you please."

"Well, come in and I will tell him. What's your name?"

"Annie Anderson."

"Where do you live?"

"At the Bruces', in the Wast Wynd."

The maid went and returned a minute later, informing her that she was to go up the stairs. She led her up to the study where the minister sat. To Annie's amazement, the room seemed to be filled with books from the top to the bottom of every wall. Mr. Cowie held out his hand to her and said, "Well, my little maiden, what do you want?"

"Please, sir, would you lend me a songbook?"

"A psalm book?" said the minister.

"No, sir, I have a psalm book at home. It's a songbook that I want, a book of poems and ballads."

Now the minister was a worthy, kindhearted man. He knew some of what the Lord's words meant, and among them certain words about little children. Besides that, he had the feeling that to be kind to little children was an important part of his job as a minister. So he drew Annie close to him as he sat in his easy chair, and said in the gentlest way, "And what do you want a songbook for, my daughter?"

"To learn poems out of it, sir. Don't you think they're the bonniest things in the world?"

For Annie had by this time learned to love ballad verse above almost everything but Alec and Dowie.

"What kind of poems do you like?" the clergyman asked instead of answering her.

112

"I like them best when they make you cry, sir."

She looked up in his face with her open, clear-blue eyes. And the minister began to love her, not merely because she was a child, but because she was this child.

"Do you sing them?" he asked.

"No. I only say them. I don't know the tunes."

"And do you say them to Mr. Bruce?"

"Mr. Bruce, sir! Mr. Bruce would say I was crazy. I wouldn't say them to him for all the sweeties in his shop."

"Then who do you say them to?"

"To Alec Forbes and Willie Macwha. They're building a boat, sir, and they like to have me by them to say poems and songs to them while they work. And I like it well."

"It'll surely be a lucky boat," declared the minister, "to rise to the sound of rhyme, like some old Viking warship."

"I don't know, sir," responded Annie, who had no idea what he meant.

He led her into the dining room to ask his daughter's assistance in finding a suitable book. There tea was all laid out. He led Annie to the table and she went without a questioning thought. It was a pleasure to her not to know what was coming next, provided someone she loved knew. So she sat down to the tea with perfect peacefulness.

The minister's daughters were very kind and friendly. In the course of the meal, Mr. Cowie told them the difficulty, and one of his daughters said that she might be able to find the sort of book the girl wanted. After tea she left the room and returned after a bit with two volumes filled with all sorts of ballads—some old, some new, some Scottish, some English.

She put the books in Annie's hands. The child eagerly opened one of the books and glanced at a page. It sparkled with just the right kind of ballad words! The color of delight grew in her face. She closed the book, "Eh, mem, but surely you won't trust me with both of them?"

"Yes, I will," answered Miss Cowie. "I am sure you will take care of them."

"That I will," returned Annie with an honesty and determination that made a great impression on Mr. Cowie. She ran home later with a feeling of richness such as she had never before experienced.

Her first business was to scamper up to her room to hide the precious treasures in her chest.

When she told Mr. Bruce that she had had tea with the minister, he held up his hands in amazement. But why he was so amazed would have to remain unrevealed, for he said not a single word to explain why he had made the gesture.

The next time Annie went to see the minister, it was on a very different quest than the loan of a songbook.

CHAPTER TWENTY-ONE

MURDOCH MALISON

One afternoon as Alec went home to dinner, he was surprised to find Mr. Malison leaning on one of the rails of the footbridge over the Glamour, standing alone looking down on its frozen surface.

There was nothing so unusual in this. But what was surprising was that the scholars seldom encountered the master anywhere except in school. Alec planned just to pass him, but the moment his foot was on the bridge the master lifted himself up from the railing and turned toward him.

"Well, Alec," he said, "and where have you been?"

"To get a new strap for my skates," answered Alec.

"You're fond of skating, are you, Alec?"

"Yes, sir."

"I used to be when I was a boy. Have you had your dinner?"

"No, sir."

"Then I suppose neither has your mother?"

"She always waits till I get home, sir."

"Then I won't intrude. I did mean to call on her this afternoon."

"She would be very glad to see you, sir. Come with me and have dinner with us today."

"I think I had better not, Alec."

"Do, sir. I know my mother would make you welcome."

Mr. Malison hesitated. Alec asked him again. He yielded, and they continued along the road together.

Mr. Malison's school life was both inwardly and outwardly very different from the rest. The moment he was out of school, the whole character and behavior of the man changed. He was now as meek and gentle in speech and action as any mother could have desired.

And the change did not mean he was a hypocrite. He was willing to accept responsibility for that part of his time spent in the classroom. But he rarely interfered with what the boys did out of school, and only did so when there was pressure brought against him—as in the case of Juno. Therefore, there was usually as little connection between the two parts of the day, as they passed through the life of the schoolmaster, as between the waking and sleeping hours of a sleepwalker.

But as he leaned over the rail of the bridge, his thoughts had turned to Alec Forbes and his hostility toward him. Out of school he could not help feeling that the boy had actually not been altogether wrong, however unpleasant his behavior toward him had been. And he had to admit that after the incident, Alec had been perfectly gentlemanly, and had done nothing to turn the other students against him. If anything, he had been more cooperative than ever.

So there was but one way to set matters right, as Mr. Malison saw it, and that was to make friends with his adversary. Indeed, in the depths of every human heart, reconciliation is the only victory which can give true satisfaction. And by no means was the master the only one to gain by the resolve toward friendliness that came into his mind the very moment he felt Alec's footsteps upon the bridge.

They walked together to Howglen, talking kindly the whole way. Alec had that very day translated a passage from Latin into English very accurately, greatly pleasing the master. However, Mr. Malison had no idea what caused the sudden success in a subject Alec had always before hated. The particular passage had to do with the setting of sails, and Alec could not rest till he had come to a full understanding of what was being said. So he had wrestled with the words and his Latin dictionary and grammar book until finally he pictured in his mind and understood the facts of the section perfectly.

Alec had never had praise from Mr. Malison before, and he found he enjoyed having his schoolwork complimented. And through the pleasure dawned the idea that perhaps he might be a good student after all, if he put his mind to it. Mrs. Forbes received Mr. Malison in a friendly manner, forgetting the former bitterness she had felt toward him.

As soon as dinner was over Alec rushed off to the river and his boat, leaving his mother and the master together.

"We'll make a man of Alec someday yet," said the schoolmaster.

"Indeed," returned Mrs. Forbes, somewhat irritated at the suggestion that anything was standing in the way of Alec's ultimate manhood. "Indeed, Mr. Malison, after the way you treated him a month ago, you would do well to try your hand at making a man of him now."

For a moment the teacher was embarrassed and began to grow red in the face. "Well, ma'am," he said with an awkward laugh, "if you had to keep seventy boys and girls quiet, and hear their lessons at the same time, perhaps you would feel yourself in danger of sometime hastily doing what you might later repent of."

"Well, well, Mr. Malison, we'll talk no more about it. My laddie's none the worse for it. And I hope you *will* make a man of him someday, as you say."

"He translated a passage of Latin today in a way that surprised me."

"Did he? He's not a dunce, I know. If it weren't for that silly boat he and William Macwha are building, he might be made a scholar. George should have more sense than to encourage such a waste of time and money. He's always wanting something or other for the boat, and I can't find it in my heart to refuse him. For whatever he may be at school, he's a good boy at home, Mr. Malison."

But the schoolmaster did not reply at once. A light had

dawned on him. So this was the secret of Alec's translation!

After a moment's pause, he answered, "I suspect, ma' am, that the boat—which I knew nothing about—was Alec's private tutor in the translating."

"I don't understand you, Mr. Malison."

"I mean, ma'am, that his interest in the boat made him take an interest in those Latin lines about ships and their rigging. So the boat taught him to translate them correctly."

"I see."

"And that makes me wonder whether we shall be able to make him learn anything well that he does not take an interest in."

"Well, what *do* you think he is fit for, Mr. Malison? I should like to see him be able to be something other than a farmer like his father."

Mrs. Forbes thought that as long as she was able to manage the farm with hired help, Alec might as well be employed in some other way. And she had ambition for her son as well.

But the master made no definite suggestion. Alec seemed to have no special qualification for any profession. So after a long talk, his mother and the schoolmaster had come no nearer than before to a determination of what he might be fit for in the future. The visit, however, restored a good relationship between them.

CHAPTER
TWENTY-TWO

HELLFIRE

The frost finally broke up on a Friday night. A day of wintry rain followed, dreary and depressing. But the two boys, Alec and Willie, had a refuge from the weather in their boat building.

In the early evening of the following Saturday, Thomas Crann, the mason, entered the shop and spent the next few minutes in close conversation with George Macwha, in which Crann mostly criticized his friend for his spiritual lack of enthusiasm.

"You ought to come to our Missionary kirk, George," said Crann. "Eh! man, then you'd be converted! That Presbyterian church where you go is full of nothing but dry bones!"

But Macwha refused to engage Crann in the sort of spiritual argument the big man thrived on, and finally he left and strode out of the shop, no doubt thinking the carpenter was on his way to hell for being such a lukewarm excuse for a Christian.

Annie was perfectly convinced that Thomas, because of his spiritual sounding words, possessed some divine secret. The stern tone of his voice had more to do with her thinking this than anything he said. As he passed out the door, she looked up reverently at him as if he were God's own spokesman. Thomas had a kind of gruff gentleness toward children which they found very attractive. He laid his hard, heavy hand kindly on her head, saying, "You'll be one of the Lord's lambs, won't you now? You'll go into the fold after Him, won't you?"

"Ay, will I," answered Annie, "if He'll let in Alec and Curly too."

"You must make no bargains with Him. But if they'll go in, He'll not hold them out."

Annie was not exactly comforted by his words, and watched as the honest stonemason strode away through the darkness to his own rather cheerless home, where he had neither wife nor child to welcome him.

By this time Alec and Curly were in full swing with their boat building. But the moment Thomas went, Alec took Annie to the blacksmith's forge to get her well dried out before he would allow her to take her place on the heap of shavings.

"Who's preaching at the Missionary kirk in the morning, Willie?" asked the boy's father. For Willie knew everything that took place in Glamerton.

"Mr. Brown," answered Curly.

"He's a good man, anyway," returned his father. "I think I'll turn Missionary myself for once, and go hear him tomorrow night."

At the same instant Annie entered the shop, her face glowing with the heat of the fire she had just left and the pleasure of rejoining her friends. No more was said about the Missionary church. In another few minutes she began to repeat to the eager listeners one of the two new poems she had gotten ready for them from the book Miss Cowie had loaned her.

However Thomas's words had effected the rest, Annie had heard enough to make her want to go to the Missionary church. It seemed plain to her that Thomas knew something she did not know. And where could he have learned it but at church?

So without knowing that George Macwha was going to be there, not expecting to see Alec or Curly, and without consulting any of the Bruce family, Annie found herself peering through the inner door of the church a few minutes after the service had started.

Shy and in awe from the huge solemness of the place, she

went upstairs into the balcony, and stole to a seat as a dog might creep across a room and under the master's table. When she finally got up the courage to lift her head, she found herself in the middle of a sea of heads. The minister was reading from the Bible in a stern voice, and Annie's awe grew even greater. The harshness of the chapter, however, was softened by the gentleness of an old lady sitting next to her who put into her hand a Bible, smelling sweetly of dried leaves.

For his sermon, Mr. Brown preached on the following text: "The wicked shall be turned into hell, and all the nations that forget God." His message consisted of two parts: "Who are the wicked?" and "What is their fate?" The answer to the first question was, "The wicked are those that forget God." The answer to the second was, "The torments of everlasting fire."

Knowing that she forgot about God a good deal of the time, the sermon immediately convinced Annie that she was one of the wicked and that she was in danger of hellfire. The fear caused by the sermon, however, like that brought on by the Bible reading, was considerably lessened by the kindness of the unknown hand, which kept up a contrasting ministry of peppermint candies.

But the preacher's explanations grew so horrifying, that by the time the sermon was over, Annie became aware that the piece of candy which had been given her fifteen minutes earlier was still lying undissolved in her mouth.

When everything had come to an end—the prayer, the singing, and the final benediction—Annie crept out into the dark street as if it were the outer darkness of eternity itself. She felt the rain falling on something hot, but she hardly knew that it was her own cheeks being wet by the heavy drops.

Her first impulse was to run to Alec and Curly, put her arms around them, and beg them to flee from the wrath to come. But she did not have time to look for them tonight. She must go home. She was not too much afraid for herself, for there was a place where she knew her prayers were heard as certainly as in any old Jewish temple—namely, her own little garret room, with holes in the floors out of which came rats, but with a door as well, in through which came the prayed-for cat.

121

But alas for Annie! Going to church had not helped her feel close to God at all. For as she was creeping from step to step up to her room in the dark, the thought came to her that maybe she didn't need to pray against the rats at all. A spiritual terror was seated on the throne of the universe, and was called God. Whom could she pray to against *Him*? A great darkness fell over her soul.

She knelt by her bedside. But she could not pray. For wasn't she one of them that forgot God? Didn't that mean she was wicked? And wasn't God therefore angry with her every day?

What about Jesus Christ? Maybe she could cry out to Him! But did she believe in Him? She tried hard to convince herself that she did. But at last she laid her weary head on the bed and groaned in despair.

At that moment a rustling in the darkness broke the sad silence with a throb of terror.

The rats! She jumped to her feet. All the rats in the universe could attack her now, for God was angry with her because she was wicked and forgot Him! And she could not pray. The cat would not help now!

With a stifled scream she darted to the door and half tumbled down the stairs in an agony of fear.

"What makes you make such a dreadful racket in the house on the Sabbath night?" shouted Mrs. Bruce. "Keep quiet, you little urchin!"

But Annie hardly felt the criticism. She was forced to creep back upstairs in dread, and at length to go to bed, where God made her sleep and forget Him. The rats did not come near her again that night.

Curly and Alec had been in the chapel too. But they were not of a temperament to be worried by Mr. Brown's sermon.

CHAPTER
TWENTY-THREE

TRUFFEY

Murdoch Malison knew nothing of the worlds of thoughts and feelings which lay within the young faces assembled in the school as usual the next day. He knew almost as little of the mysteries that lay within himself.

All day Annie was haunted with the thought of the wrath of God. Before school was over she had made up her mind what to do. And before school was over, Malison's own deed had opened his eyes to a horrifying vision of his own character.

Despite the humanity and even kindness he could demonstrate outside the classroom, it would have been hard to find a harsher Scottish schoolmaster of the rough, old-fashioned type. Independent of right or wrong, his whole method was based on law. He had his favorite students in various degrees. These found it easy to please him. Those he did not like found it impossible to please him no matter how hard they tried.

Now there had come to the school about two weeks before, two unhappy looking little twin orphans, with thin white faces and bones in their clothes instead of arms and legs. They had been given to the care of Mr. Malison by their grandfather. The old man was bent into all the angles of a grasshopper. As he went tottering away with his stick in one hand, he said in a quivering, croaking voice, "Now you just give them the whip well, Mr. Malison, for you know that he that spareth the rod spoileth the child."

Given permission so clearly, Malison certainly did give them the whip well. Before that day was over, they had both lain shrieking on the floor under the torture of the lash more than once.

The schoolmaster's old habits of severity now returned upon him, and this day Annie was to be one of the victims. Although he would still not dare to whip her, he was about to make this day—following so closely upon the sermon she had heard the night before—the most wretched day that Annie's sad life had yet seen. The very spirits of the pit seemed to have broken loose and filled Murdoch Malison's classroom with the fire and brimstone of hell itself.

About halfway through the day Annie fell fast asleep. She was roused by a stinging blow from the tawse, thrown with accurate aim at the back of her bare neck. She jumped up with a cry, and tottered up between sleep and terror to take the leather snake back to the master. Halfway there she would have fallen had not Alec caught her in his arms. He sat her back down, took the tawse from her trembling hand, and carried it himself to the tyrant. Malison's fury broke loose in a dozen blows on the right hand which Alec held up without flinching. As he walked to his seat, burning with pain, the voice of the master sounded behind him.

"Ann Anderson," he yelled, "stand on your seat."

With trembling limbs, Annie obeyed. At first she could scarcely stand because her knees were shaking beneath her. For some time her color kept changing between red and white. It was a terrible punishment to be exposed to the looks of all the boys and girls in the school. The elder of the two Bruces tried hard to make her see one of his vile faces. But she did not dare look away from the book she was holding upside down before her. This was the punishment for falling asleep, just as hell was the punishment for forgetting God. There she had to stand for a whole hour.

"*The devil catch you, Malison!*" and various other whispered phrases were murmured about the room. Annie was a favorite with most of the boys, and all the more because she was "the General's sweetheart," as they said. But these comments were all too faint to reach Annie's ears and offer her much comfort. Worst of all, from her position high above the class, she had to witness every detail of the master's cruelty when his temper broke forth more violently than it ever had before.

A small class of mere children, with the Truffey orphans among them, had been given to the care of one of the bigger boys while the master was busy with another class. All at once a noise in the younger children's class attracted the master's attention. He turned and saw one of the Truffeys hit another boy in the face.

He strode upon him at once. Asking not a single question as to the reason he struck him, he grabbed the boy by the neck, stuck it between his knees, and began to lash him with stinging blows. In his agony the little fellow managed to twist his head to one side and get a mouthful of the master's leg, crunching his teeth together in a manner Juno herself would have been proud of in her former days.

The master caught him up and threw him on the floor. There the child lay motionless.

Alarmed and cooled off as a result, Malison slowly lifted him up. When the boy recovered consciousness, it was discovered that his leg was hurt. It appeared afterward that the kneecap was greatly injured. Moaning with pain, he was sent home on the back of a big parish scholar.

Annie stared at all this with horror. The feeling that God was angry with her grew and grew, and for a time Murdoch Malison became the exact idea of God in her mind.

The master still looked uneasy and nervous about what he had done. He threw the tawse into his desk and beat no one else that day. Indeed, only half an hour of school time was left. The moment it was over, he set off at a rapid pace for the old grandfather's cottage.

What went on there was never known. The other Truffey came to school the next day as usual and told the boys that his brother was in bed. In that bed he lay for many weeks, and the master paid him many visits. This did much with the townsfolk to wipe away any blame. They spoke of the affair as an unfortunate accident, and pitied the schoolmaster even more than they did the victim.

When finally the poor boy was able to leave his bed, it became apparent that he would be a cripple for the rest of his life.

CHAPTER TWENTY-FOUR

MR. COWIE AGAIN

When Annie descended from her hateful position just before the final prayer, it was with a deep sense of condem-
nation. Even the attentions Alec tried to give her as soon as they
were out of school could not help. The thought that God was
against her took the heart out of everything. Nothing else was
worth anything till something was done about that. As soon as
Alec left her, she walked straight to Mr. Cowie's door.

She was admitted at once and shown into the library where
the clergyman sat before the red glow of the fireplace. "Well,
Annie, my dear," he said, "I am glad to see you. How does the
boat get on?"

Touched by his kindness, Annie burst into tears. Mr. Cowie
was distressed. He drew her to him, laid his cheek against hers,
and said tenderly. "What's the matter with my little daughter?"

After some hopeless attempts at speech, Annie finally suc-
ceeded in giving the following account of the matter, much interrupted by sobs and new outbursts of weeping.

"You see, sir, I went last night to the Missionary kirk to hear
Mr. Brown. And he preached a grand sermon. But I haven't been
able to stand myself since then. For I'm one of the wicked that
God hates, and I'll never get to heaven, for I can't help forgetting

Him sometimes. And the wicked'll be turned into hell and all the nations that forget God. And I can't stand it."

A quiet anger rose in the heart of the good man against the overly spiritual and pious who had thus terrified and bewildered that precious being, a small child. He thought for a moment and then gave in to his common sense.

"You haven't forgotten your father, have you, Annie?" he began.

"I think about him most every day," she answered.

"But there comes a day now and then when you don't think much about him, doesn't there?"

"Yes, sir."

"Do you think he would be angry with his child because she was so much taken up with her books or her play—"

"I never play with anything, sir."

"Well, with learning poems and songs to recite to Alec Forbes and Willie Macwha? Do you think he would be angry that you didn't think about him every day, especially when you can't see him?"

"Indeed no, sir. He wouldn't be so hard on me as that."

"What do you think he would say?"

"If Mr. Bruce were to get after me for it, my father would say, 'Let the lassie alone. She'll think about me another day—there's time enough.' "

"Well, don't you think your Father in heaven would say the same?"

"Maybe He might, sir. But, you see, my father was my own father, and would make the best of me."

"And is God not kinder than your father?"

"He couldn't be that, sir. And besides, there's what the Scripture says about God."

"That he sent his very own Son to die for us."

"Ay—for those who are chosen, sir, but not the rest," returned the little theologian.

This was gradually becoming more than poor Mr. Cowie knew how to deal with! He was not well-equipped to counter such arguments. And there were the girl's eyes, blue and hazy with tearful questions, looking up at him hungrily.

"Annie, my child," he said finally, "don't trouble your head about predestination or whether you are one of God's elect and all that. No mortal man can get to the bottom of all that theology anyway. Go home, say your prayers, and remember that God is better than your own father no matter what any preacher may tell you. There's a sixpence for you."

His kind heart was grieved that he had no more comfort to give her. But I happen to think the sixpence had more reality in it than any theological answer he might have offered. For was it not the symbol and sign of love?

However Annie drew back from the gift.

"No, thank you, sir," she said. "I couldn't take it."

"Won't you take it to please an old man, child?"

"Indeed I will, sir, if that would please you. I would do a lot more than that for you."

Again the tears filled her blue eyes as she held out her hand—receiving in it a shilling which Mr. Cowie had substituted for the sixpence.

"It's a shilling, sir!" she said, looking up at him with the coin lying on her open palm.

"Well, why not? Isn't a shilling a sixpence?"

"Ay, sir. It's two of them."

"Well, Annie," said the old man, "when God offers us a sixpence, it may turn out to be two. Good night, my child."

Annie was not completely satisfied, yet she went away comforted. After such a day of agony, Mr. Cowie's kiss greatly restored her spirits. It had something in it which was not in Mr. Brown's sermon. And yet if she had gone to Mr. Brown, she would have found him kind also—very kind, but solemnly and piously kind, with religious tenderness, not human love.

But despite the comfort Mr. Cowie had given her, Annie's perplexity remained. There was only one other man who knew about such secret things, she thought, and that man was Thomas Crann. Thomas was a rather dreadful man, with his cold eyes, high shoulders, and wheezing asthmatic breathing, and Annie could not help being a little afraid of him. But she would endure anything if she could get rid of the sadness that lay upon her heart.

So she plucked up her courage, and decided to set off for the house of the huge religious man that very evening, as soon as he would be home from his work.

She went home and ate a bit of oatcake with a mug of blue milk. Then she went up to her garret and waited drearily for the time to pass. But she did not try to pray.

THOMAS CRANN

It was very dark by the time she left the house, for the night was drizzly. But Annie knew the windings of Glamerton almost as well as the way up her attic stair.

Thomas's door was half open and a light was shining from the kitchen. She knocked timidly. Her knock was too gentle and was not heard inside. But as Thomas's housekeeper Jean was passing the door a moment later, she saw Annie standing alone just outside. She stopped with a start.

"The Lord preserve us, lassie!" she cried.

"Jean, what are you swearing at?" cried Thomas from the next room.

"At Annie Anderson," answered Jean.

"Why are you swearing at her? What does the child want?"

"What do you want, Annie?"

"I want to see Thomas, if you please," answered Annie.

"She wants to see you, Thomas," shouted Jean, then saying in a low voice, "He's deaf as a doornail, Annie."

"Tell her to come in," called Thomas.

"He's telling you to come in, Annie," said Jean. "Go in there," she directed, leading Annie across the kitchen and opening the door of the next room where Thomas sat. Annie entered and stood before the chair where sat the ungentle but not unkind stonemason.

"Well, lassie," he said, "what do you want with me?"

Annie burst into tears.

"What's the matter, my child?"

"I was at the Missionary kirk last night," faltered Annie.

"Ay! And the sermon took a grip of you?"

"But I can't help forgetting Him, Thomas."

"But you must try and not forget Him, lassie."

"I do. But it's hard work, and almost impossible."

"To the old Adam impossible, but to the young Christian a weary watch."

"A person might have a chance then?" asked Annie with a hopeful sound in her voice, "even if she did forget Him sometimes?"

"No doubt, lassie. The nations that forget God are them that don't care, that never bother their hearts about Him. If you *want* to remember him, and you *try* to walk in the light, that's a different matter."

"So if you try to remember Him, that's as good *as* thinking about Him."

Thomas had to reflect a moment. Even his religious brain, which had a stock answer for every possible objection any atheist in Scotland might propose, was momentarily stumped about how to answer the tiny maiden.

"As long as you be one of God's chosen," he answered at length.

Alas, Annie's troubles returned over her like a giant wave!

"But how's a person to know whether she *be* one of God's chosen?" she asked in almost a forlorn wail.

"That's a hard question. But it's not necessary for you to know that just yet."

"But I can't let it alone! I've got to know. Could *you* let it alone, Thomas?"

"You have me there, lassie. No, I couldn't let it alone. And I plagued the Lord night and day till He let me know."

"I tried hard last night," said Annie, "but the rats were too many for me."

"Satan has many wiles," said the mason thoughtfully.

"Do you think they weren't rats?" asked Annie.

"Oh, no doubt, I dare say."

"Because if I thought they were only devils, I wouldn't be afraid of them."

"It's much the same whatever you call them, if they keep you from God's throne of grace."

"What am I to do then, Thomas?"

"You must just trust the Lord, lassie, and keep after Him like the poor widow did with the unjust judge. And when the Lord hears you, you'll know you're one of the elect, for it's only His own elect that the Lord does hear. Eh, lassie! It's little you know about praying and not fainting."

Alas for the parables if Thomas was to have his way with them! Annie's only reply to his bewildering words was a fixed gaze. "Ay, lassie," he went on, "say what they like, it's my firm belief that there can be but one way of coming to the knowledge of the secret of whether you be one of the chosen."

"And what's that?" asked Annie, whose whole life seemed to hang upon the answer he would give.

"To get a sight of the face of God. It's my own belief that no man can get a glimpse of the face of God but one of the chosen. I'm not saying that a man's not one of the elect that hasn't had that favor vouchsafed to him, but I do say that he can't *know* his election without that. Try to get a sight of the face of God, lassie, then you'll be at peace."

"What is it like, Thomas?" said Annie eagerly.

"The Holy Spirit will tell you, and when He does, you'll know it."

Teacher and scholar were silent. As much as she wanted to, Annie could find no practical help in the big man's words. There was nothing for her to do in them. Annie was the first to break the silence.

"Am I to go home now, Thomas?"

"Ay, go home, lassie, to your prayers. I'll go with you," he added, rising.

"No, I could go home blindfolded."

But Thomas was already half out the door. As they stepped from the kitchen into the cold night, he clasped her soft little hand in his great calloused one, and Annie trotted home by his side. As soon as they entered the shop, instead of turning to leave, Thomas went up to the counter and asked for an ounce of tobacco, as if his appearance with Annie was merely accidental. With perfect appreciation of his Scottish caution, Annie ran through the gap in the counter without another word.

She was comforted and so tired that she fell asleep at her prayers by her bedside. Presently she awoke in terror. It was Pussy, however, that had waked her, as she knew by the green eyes. Then she finished her prayers quickly, jumped into bed, and was soon fast asleep.

In her sleep she dreamed that she stood in the darkness in the midst of a huge field full of black pits full of terrible water. She was unable to move for fear of falling into one of the hundreds of holes. She tried hard to pray but could not. And she sank down to the ground in despair, overcome with the terrors of those frightful holes full of black water.

But then a hand came out of the darkness, laid hold of hers, and lifted her up and led her through the field and away from the bogs. She dimly saw the form that led her, and it was that of a man who walked looking down upon the ground. She tried to see his face but she could not, for he walked always a little in front of her. And he led her to the old farm, where her father came to the door to meet them. And he looked just the same as in the old happy days, only his face was strangely bright. And with the joy of seeing her father, she awoke to a gentle sorrow that she had never seen the face of her deliverer.

The next evening she wandered down to George Macwha's and found the two boys at work. She had no poetry to give them, no stories to tell, no answers to their questions as to where she had been the night before. She could only stand in silence and watch them, have the tool they needed ready, clear away their shavings from the busy plane, and lie in wait for any chance of putting her little strength to help. The skeleton of the boat grew beneath their hands. But it was on the workers and not on their work that her gaze was fixed.

Annie's heart was burning within her. She could hardly keep herself from throwing her arms about their necks and begging them to seek the face of God! Oh, if only she were sure that Alec and Curly were of God's chosen!

"What's come over Annie?" said the one to the other after she had gone.

CHAPTER TWENTY-SIX

THE SCHOOLMASTER'S NEW FRIEND

So time went slowly on, and Annie said her prayers, read her Bible, and tried not to forget God. If only she could have known that God never forgot her! Whether she forgot Him or not, He continued to give her sleep, friends, occasional happiness, and the light of life everywhere!

He was now leading on the blessed season of growth, when the earth would be almost heaven to those who had passed through the fierceness of the cold. The old and weary winter was slowly vanishing before the sweet approaches of the spring—a symbol of that eternal spring before whose slow footsteps death itself shall one day vanish.

By degrees school became less difficult for Annie. She grew more interested in her work. A taste for reading began to wake in her. Still she haunted George Macwha's shop where the boat soon began to reveal the full grace of its form.

As I said, reading became a delight to her, and Mr. Cowie threw open his library. She brought home every new book she borrowed with a sense of richness I can hardly describe. Now that the days were growing longer she had plenty of time to read. Although her guardians made critical remarks about her idleness, they imposed very few restrictions on her. With the fear of James Dow before their eyes, they let her alone.

As to her ever doing anything to help out in the store, she was far too much an alien to be allowed even the lowest of duties in that sacred Temple of Mammon. So she read anything she could get her hands on. And as often as she found anything particularly interesting, she would take the book to the boat, where the boys were always ready to listen to whatever she brought them.

At the school, the master's behavior was gradually changed as a result of the last outbreak of his fury. One midday in spring, just as the last of a hail shower was passing away and one thin sunbeam was struggling out, the schoolroom door opened. In came Andrew Truffey for the first time since the incident, with a smile on his worn face. He swung himself along on a crutch. He looked long and deathly, for he had grown several inches while lying in bed, and if possible was even more gaunt than before.

The master rose hurriedly from his desk and walked forward to meet him.

A deep stillness fell upon all the scholars. They dropped their work and gazed at the meeting between the two. The master held out his hand. With awkwardness and difficulty, still trying to manage the crutch, Andrew presented his own hand. But the crutch slipped and he staggered. He would surely have fallen, but the master caught him in his arms and carried him to his old seat beside his brother.

"Thank you, sir," said the boy with another smile. His sad suffering was easy to see through his thin features and pale eyes. It was all the master's fault—as Mr. Malison knew better than anybody.

"Look at the master," whispered Curly to Alec. "He's crying."

For Mr. Malison had returned to his seat and had laid his head down on the desk to hide his emotion.

"Hold your tongue, Curly," returned Alec. "Don't look at him. He's sorry for poor Truffey."

Everyone behaved with marked respect toward the master

that day. And from that moment on Truffey was in universal favor.

I should say again that Mr. Malison was not a *bad* man. It was only that his view of right fell in with a natural fierceness. Along with that, the church had come along and wrongly taught him that everyone in the world—his pupils among them—was hopelessly bad, and that the only thing he could do to help their sinful condition was whip them, to teach them of God's justice. The Catechism itself taught: "Every sin deserveth God's wrath and curse both in this life and that which is to come." The master, therefore, considered himself to be God's helper in carrying out that truth with every blow he inflicted on his pupils.

He probably did not think it out in exactly this manner. But these were the principles he acted upon. And with all his brutality, he was never as guilty of such cruelty as some schoolmasters of the same period were. Nor were the boys ever guilty of such cruelty to their fellows as was excused by many schools of the time in England.

Gradually punishment in the classroom became less and less frequent, and even when the whip was used, the blows became less severe. And the discipline of the school did not suffer as a result. If you want to make a hard-mouthed horse more obedient to the rein, you must *relax* the pressure and friction of the bit, not increase it.

But the amazing thing to see was how Andrew Truffey haunted the steps of the master and followed him about—in and out of school. There was no hour of a day off from school in which Truffey could not tell where Mr. Malison was about town. If one caught sight of Andrew hobbling down a street or leaning against a building, he could be sure the master would pass within a few minutes.

And this haunting of little Truffey worked on the master's conscience, and his better nature gradually began to reveal itself. For imagine what it would be like to have a visible sin of your own, in the shape of a lame-legged little boy, peeping at you round every corner!

He learned to love the boy. And so appeared the deeper truth of divine vengeance against sin—repentance and love flowing out of the heart of the wrongdoer. Ah, how different is God's way from human vengeance!

CHAPTER TWENTY-SEVEN

THE BONNIE ANNIE

At length the boat was calked, tarred, and painted.

One evening as Annie entered the workshop, she heard Curly cry, "Here she is, Alec!" and Alec answered, "Let her come. I'm just done."

Alec stood at the end of the boat with a paintbrush in his hand. When Annie came near, she discovered to her surprise, and of course to her delight, that he was finishing off the last E of "T-H-E B-O-N-N-I-E A-N-N-I-E."

"There," he said. "That's her name. How do you like it, Annie?"

Annie was much too pleased to reply. She looked at it for a while with a flush on her face. Then turning away she went to her usual seat on the pile of shavings.

How much that one winter, with its dragons and heroes, its boat-building and its poetry, its discomforts at home and consolations abroad, its threats of future loss and comforts of present hope, had done to make the wild country child into a thoughtful little woman.

Now who should come into the shop at that moment but Thomas Crann—the very man of all men not to be desired on this occasion.

"Ay, ay! Alec," said Thomas. "So your boat's built at last."

He stood looking thoughtfully at it for a moment, with admiration in his eye, and then said, "If you had her out on a lake, do you think you would jump over the side if the Savior told you to, Alec Forbes?"

"Ay, would I, if I were completely sure He wanted me to."

"You would stand and argue with Him, no doubt?"

"I'd be behooved to be sure it was really Him, you know, and that He did in fact call me."

"Oh, ay, laddie! Well, I hope you would, Alec. I have good hopes for you, my man. But there may be such a thing as leaping into the sea out of the ark of salvation. And if you leap when He doesn't call you, or if you don't get a grip of His hand when He does, you're sure to drown, as sure as the swine that ran headlong in and perished in the water."

Alec hardly knew what he was talking about, but he listened in respectful silence. And when he was through, he concluded that enough religious words had been uttered over the boat to make her faithful and fortunate.

At length the day arrived when *The Bonnie Annie* was to be launched.

It was a bright Saturday afternoon in the month of May. A few early primroses were peeping from the hollows damp with moss and shadow along the banks. And the trees by the stream were green with small, young leaf. There was a light wind full of memories of past summers and promises for the new one at hand, one of those gentle winds that blow the eyes of the flowers open that the earth may look at the heaven. In the midst of this baby-waking world, the boat was to glide into her new life.

Alec got one of the men on the farm to yoke a horse to bring the boat to the river. With George's help she was soon placed in the cart, and Alec and Curly climbed in beside her. When they had got about halfway to the river, Alec said to Curly, "I wonder what's become of Annie? It would be a shame to launch the boat without her."

"I'll run and look for her, and you can look after the boat."

So saying, Curly bounded out of the cart. Away he ran over a field of potatoes as straight as the crow flies, while the cart went slowly on toward the Glamour.

"Where's Annie Anderson?" he cried as he burst into Robert Bruce's shop.

"What's *your* business with her?" asked Bruce, though from his tone it was clear he didn't really want an answer.

"Alec wants her."

"Well he can keep wanting her," retorted Bruce, shutting his jaws with a snap and grinning a mean grin toward Curly.

Curly left the shop at once and went around the house into the back yard. There he found Annie walking up and down with the Bruce's baby in her arms. She looked very tired. It was the first time she had had to carry the baby, and she was terribly fatigued. Till now Mrs. Bruce had had the assistance of a ragged child whose father owed them money for groceries. Since he could not pay, they had taken the work of his daughter instead. She had at last slaved out the debt and had gone back to school. The sun was hot, the baby was heavy, and Annie's arms and back ached with the new assignment. She was all but crying when Curly darted to the gate, his face red from the run and his eyes sparkling with excitement.

"Come, Annie," he cried. "We're going to launch the boat!"

"I can't, Curly. I have the baby to mind."

"Take the baby to its mother."

"I don't dare."

"Lay it down on the table and run."

"No, Curly. I couldn't do that. Poor little creature!"

"Is the beastie heavy?" asked Curly, with deceitful interest.

"Dreadful."

"Let me try."

"You'll drop her."

"Indeed I won't. I'm not so weak as that! Give me a hold of her."

Annie yielded her burden. But no sooner had Curly possession of the baby than he ran off toward a huge sugar cask. The great barrel had been made into a reservoir, for it stood under a spout, and was at that moment about half full of rainwater.

First Curly made sure that Mrs. Bruce would see him from the kitchen. Then he climbed a big stone that was sitting beside the barrel, and pretended to lower the baby into the water.

Almost at once he received such a box on the ear that, if he hadn't been expecting it, he would in reality have dropped the child into the cask. The next moment the baby was in its mother's arms, and Curly was sitting at the foot of the barrel, holding his head and pretending to cry. The angry mother sped into the house with her rescued child.

No sooner had she disappeared than Curly was on his feet running back to Annie, who had been watching his behavior in utter bewilderment. She could no longer resist his pleading. Off she ran with him to the banks of the Glamour. They soon came upon Alec and the man in the very act of putting the boat on the bank, where they had already shovelled out a groove from the dirt, so that she might glide in more gradually.

"Hurrah! There's Annie!" cried Alec. "Come on, Annie. Here's a glass of whisky I got from my mother to christen the boat. Fling it at her name."

Annie did as she was told, to the perfect satisfaction of all present. Particularly pleased was the tall thin farm servant who had helped move the boat. When Alec's back was turned, the man swallowed the whisky and substituted brown Glamour water, which no doubt did equally well for the purpose of the ceremony. Then with a gentle push from all, *The Bonnie Annie* slid into the Glamour where she lay afloat in contented grace.

"Isn't she bonnie?" cried Annie, clapping her hands in delight.

And indeed she was, in her green and white paint, lying like a giant water beetle ready to scamper over the smooth surface. Alec sprang on board, nearly upsetting the tiny craft. Then he grabbed a tiny bush on the bank to steady it while Curly handed in Annie, who sat down in the back. Curly then got in himself and he and Alec each seized an oar.

Out into the river they went!

But with their inexperience they didn't get along too quickly at first. They knew nothing about boating, and the river was shallow and so full of stones that in some places it was impossible to row. They looked almost like they were just sitting floating in a tub. Alec's arms were stronger than Curly's, so for a time they did nothing but go round and round in a circle.

At last they gave up, and just let *The Bonnie Annie* float in the stream, and gradually the current began to take them down river. They took care to keep her off the rocks, and past them went the banks—steep and stony but green with moss where little trickling streams found their way into the channel. Then they came to a place where the shore was low, covered with lovely grass full of daisies and buttercups, with a willow tree rising just at the river's bank, with low boughs hanging down to the water.

A little while ago they had skated down this frozen surface and had seen a snowy land shooting past them. Now with an unfelt gliding they floated down, and the green meadows dreamed away as if they would skim past them forever. Suddenly as they rounded the corner of a rock, a great roar of falling water burst on their ears and they looked at each other in dismay.

"The sluice is up!" cried Alec. "Grab your oar, Curly."

Along this part of the bank, some twenty feet above them, ran a mill-stream. The water from the stream ran the machinery of a mill as it turned the mill's various water-wheels. Then as it left the mill, the stream went through a wooden sluice, which could be open or shut depending on how much water there was and whether the owner of the mill needed more water or not. Leaving the sluice, the water from the mill-stream shot into the Glamour, creating—if there was enough water—a small waterfall right into the river.

Now because of the recent spring rains, there was a great deal of water, and the sluice was wide open. The extra water rushed from the stream into the Glamour in a huge, foaming waterfall. Annie could see that the boys were uneasy, and became very frightened. She closed her eyes and sat still.

Louder and louder grew the raging of the waters till the sound seemed to fall in a solid thunder on her brain. The boys tried hard to row against the current of the river, but without success. Slowly and surely the current carried them along toward the very center of the boiling waterfall.

Finally the boat drifted under the fall, rear end first. A torrent of water struck Annie and poured into the boat as if it would beat the bottom out of it. Annie was tossed about in fierce white waters and ceased to know anything.

When she came to herself she was in a strange bed, with Mrs. Forbes bending anxiously over her. She tried to get up, but Mrs. Forbes told her to lie still, which indeed Annie found much more pleasant.

As soon as they had gotten under the fall, the boat had filled with water, floundered, and immediately turned over. Alec and Curly could swim like otters and were out of the pool at once. Alec made a plunge into the deep water to grab Annie, but had missed her. The moment he got his breath he swam again into the boiling pool, dived, and got hold of her. But the water was beating down on him so hard from the waterfall that he could not pull her out, for here the water was very deep. But he refused to let go of his hold on Annie, so both of them were in danger of being drowned.

In the meantime, Curly had scrambled onto the shore, climbed up the bank to the mill-stream, and managed to turn the crank to shut down the sluice. In a moment the tumult of the waterfall stopped and Alec and Annie were in quiet water. Alec got her on the bank, apparently dead, and then carried her home to his mother in terror. She immediately put one or two very strong-smelling things under Annie's nose, and presently was successful in awakening the soaking girl.

As soon as Annie had opened her eyes, Alec and Curly hurried off to rescue their boat. They met the owner of the mill in an awful rage. For turning off the sluice had dammed up the water of the stream, which had then backed up into his mill. All the extra water had set off his machinery crazily, breaking one old millstone and putting the miller and his men in great danger, in addition to stopping the progress of their work for several hours.

"You ill-designed villains!" he cried at them. "What made you close the sluice? I'll teach you to mind what you're about. Devil take you rascals!"

He seized one of the boys in each of his muscular hands.

"Annie Anderson was drowning under the fall," said Curly.

"The Lord preserve us!" cried the miller, letting go his hold. "How was that? Did she fall in?"

The boys told him the whole story.

In a few minutes more the fall was again turned off, and the miller was helping them get their boat out. *The Bonnie Annie* was found not to be injured. Only the oars and cushions had floated down the river and were never seen again. The boys went home, and the miller again turned on the fall by opening the sluice, and went back to his work.

Alec had a terrible scolding from his mother for getting Annie into such mischief. She did not like the girl's being so much with her son, but she thought to herself that before long he would go away to college and forget her. In the meantime she was very kind to Annie, and kept her in her home until she had recovered, in order to excuse her absence. The Bruces were, of course, highly offended. Mrs. Bruce solemnly declared that judgment had fallen upon Annie for Willie Macwha's treatment of her baby.

"If I hadn't just gotten a glimpse of him in time, he would have drowned the bonny infant before my very eyes!"

The first voyage of *The Bonnie Annie* may seem like a bad beginning. But I am not sure that many things that end well have not had such bad beginnings. Alec and Curly walked about for a few days with rather quiet expressions. But as soon as the boat was refitted, they got George Macwha to go with them, and under his instructions they made rapid progress in learning to row and guide their craft.

The boat was eventually fitted with a rudder. And with Annie again as their companion, she had several lessons in steering, and soon became very proficient. Many a moonlight row they now had on the Glamour. And many a night after Curly and Annie had gone home, Alec would again unmoor the boat and float down the water alone—not always sure that he wasn't dreaming himself.

CHAPTER
TWENTY-EIGHT

CHANGES

The season went on. Like a great flower afloat in space, the world kept opening its thousandfold blossoms.

Hail and sleet were things lost in the distance of the year. The butterflies, with wings looking as if all the flower painters of fairyland had wiped their brushes upon them in artistic sport, came forth in the freedom of their wills and the faithful ignorance of their minds. The birds, the poets of the animal creation, awoke to utter their own joy and wake a similar joy in others of God's children. Then the birds grew silent, because their history had laid hold upon them, compelling them to turn their words into deeds, keep eggs warm and hunt for worms. The butterflies died of old age and delight. The green life of the earth rushed up in grain to be ready for the time of need.

The summer gradually turned to fall. The grain grew ripe and therefore weary, hung its head, died, and was laid aside for a life beyond its own. The keen sharp mornings and nights of autumn came back as they had come so many thousand times before, and made human arms and legs strong and human hearts sad and longing. Winter would soon be near enough to stretch out a long forefinger once more, and touch with the first frosty shiver some little child that loved summer and shrank from the cold.

My story must already have shown that, although several years younger than Alec, Annie had more character than he. Alec had not yet begun to look the realities of life in the face. The very nobility and fearlessness of his nature kept him from looking within himself and asking what things mean and where they are leading. Full of life and restless impulses to activity, all that had been required of him as yet was that his actions should be innocent, and even if mischievous, then usually harmless—unless he was taking action against injustice.

But now there began growing in Alec, though it was still just a vague sense in his mind, that he could be doing better, that it might be time for the mischief of boyhood to give way to thoughts of growing toward manhood. Perhaps the maturity brought about by the building and care of the boat had its share in this deepening growth within him.

Therefore, once the autumn harvest was past and school begun again, Alec began to work better and more diligently. Mr. Malison saw the change and acknowledged it. This increased Alec's feelings of affection for the master. During the following winter he made three times the scholastic progress than he had ever made in any year before.

With the passing of the sea of summer, and the coming again of the cold winds, ghostlike mists, and damps and shiverings of winter, Nature went again to sleep. The boat was carefully laid up across the rafters of the barn at Howglen, well wrapped in a tarp. It was buried up in the air, and the Glamour on which it had floated so gayly would soon be buried under the ice. Summer alone could bring them together again—the one from the dry gloom of the barn, the other from the hidden cold of its wintry sleep.

Meanwhile, Mrs. Forbes was somewhat troubled in her mind as to what should be done with Alec, and she talked several times to the schoolmaster about him. She was of higher birth socially than her late husband, and for that reason had the ambition that her son should be well educated. She was less concerned that he prepare for some profession as that he simply obtain an education. She hoped that he would continue to be interested in the farm, for it had been in her husband's family

148

for hundreds of years, and she did not want to see it pass into the hands of strangers. And Alec himself also had a strong attachment to the ancestral soil.

His increased diligence with his schoolwork, along with continued encouragement from Mr. Malison, strengthened Mrs. Forbes' feeling that Alec ought to go to college. He would be no worse a farmer for having earned a degree at the University.

So it was decided that the following winter he would go to the city. This decision spurred Alec on all the more. He gave his studies even more earnest attention, and now, rather than being the schoolmaster's adversary, he became his most dedicated pupil and assistant.

And thus it was, after another round of the seasons—several months before his sixteenth birthday—that Alec found himself, toward the end of October, on his way to the city and the University where his future lay.

CHAPTER
TWENTY-NINE

THE WINTER IN GLAMERTON

In Glamerton the winter passed very much like former winters to all but three—Mrs. Forbes, Annie Anderson, and Willie Macwha. To these the loss of Alec was dreary. So they were compelled to draw closer.

At school, Curly assumed the protectorship of Annie, which had naturally fallen upon him. Though there was now hardly any reason for its use. And Mrs. Forbes, finding herself lonely in her parlor during the long dark afternoons and evenings, got into the habit of sending Mary at least three times a week to fetch Annie. This practice was not agreeable to the Bruces. But the creditor named after the king waited until the time came for his revenge. And Mrs. Forbes had no idea how offended he was with her invitations.

The parlor at Howglen was to Annie a little heaven hollowed out of the winter. The warm drawn curtains, the blazing fire— it was indeed a contrast to the dreary shop and the rat-haunted garret.

After tea they took turns working and reading. There were more books in the house than was usual even in the home of a gentleman farmer like Alec's father. There were several of Sir Walter Scott's novels, besides some travel books and a little Scottish history. In poetry, however, Annie had to hunt for books for herself, and continued occasionally to visit Mr. Cowie.

The bond between the lady and the lass grew stronger every day. Mrs. Forbes enjoyed having a girl to love besides her son. As a result, Annie was surrounded by many wholesome influences. It was a time when she was growing fast and needed a woman like Mrs. Forbes. Thus the relationship had its full effect both upon her mind and her body.

One result was that Annie began to show a quiet grace in her habits and the way she walked. Mrs. Forbes came to her aid with dresses of her own, which they altered and remade together to fit Annie. This caused even further resentment by the Bruces, who continued to use Annie's money in their bank account but spent nothing at all on her to make her life comfortable. Indeed, they would have let her clothes become nothing but shabby rags if they didn't feel she should at least be decent on Sundays for church.

Now that she was warmly and decently dressed, thanks to Mrs. Forbes, she began to feel and look more like the lady-child of twelve that she really was. No doubt the contrast was very painful to her when she returned from Mrs. Forbes' warm parlor to sleep in her own attic, with the snow on the roof, thin covers on the beds, and rats in the floor. It is wonderful how one gets through what one cannot avoid.

Robert Bruce was making money, but not so fast as he wished. This led to a certain change in the Bruces' habits with important results for Annie. Bruce had long been active in the parish Presbyterian church. But, as I have said, although he was making haste to be rich, he was not succeeding fast enough in his own eyes. So he began thinking about the Missionary church, and how it was getting rather large and successful. If he were to leave his former church and join the Missionaries, it might result in more business coming to him from its members.

A month or two before this time the Missionaries had chosen a very able man for their new pastor. The man had gathered about him a large congregation of the lower classes of Glamerton, and Bruce had learned with some uneasiness that many of his customers were to be found in the Missionary kirk. There was a grocer among the Missionaries, and he feared this man might draw some of his customers away from him. Should he join the congregation, he would keep his regulars and have a chance to gain new customers as well. He might even be able to pull some of the other man's business to his own shop!

So he took a week to think about it. Then he went to hear Mr. Turnbull alone, in order that the change might not seem too sudden. And then the following Sunday he and his entire family were seated in a pew under the balcony. His presence added greatly to the prestige of the place in the eyes of his poorer Missionary customers.

Annie found the service even more boring than good Mr. Cowie's. And it lasted forty-five minutes longer! Yet the honest heart of the maiden did her best to listen and try to recognize the truth when she heard it. The young Bruces would gladly have gone to sleep. But they were kept sitting straight and awake by constant jabs of the parental elbow, and the regular administration of the unfailing peppermint candies. To Annie, however, no such ministry was given. It would have been a downright waste, Mrs. Bruce thought to herself, seeing she was perfectly able to keep awake without it.

One bright frosty morning the sermon appeared to have no relation to anything around them, but only the covenant made with Abraham. Annie tried to amuse herself and keep from shivering with the cold by gazing at one brilliant sunstreak on the wall. As she did she found her eyes drawn toward a very peculiar face on the other side of the church. At first she thought the woman was watching the same sunbeam as she was, and she wondered whether she too was hoping for a bowl of hot broth after the service—broth being the Sunday fare with the Bruces. But then Annie realized that the woman was completely blind. Though it was one of the ugliest of faces, over it flowed the light of an inner glow.

When the service was over, almost before the words of the benediction had left the minister's lips, the people hurried out of the church as if they could not possibly endure one word more. But Annie stood staring at the blind woman. She followed the woman out into the open air, and saw her standing by the door, turning her sightless face on all sides as if waiting for someone. Annie watched her, then saw that she was murmuring, "The child's forgotten me!" She walked up to her and said gently, "If you'll tell me where you live, I'll take you home."

"What do they call *you* child?" returned the blind woman in a gruff voice.

"Annie Anderson," answered Annie.

"Oh, ay! I thought as much. I know about you. Give me a hold of your hand. I live in that wee house down at the bridge, between the dam and the Glamour, you know. You'll keep me away from the stones?"

"Ay, I will," answered Annie with confidence.

"I could go alone, but I'm growing old now, and I'm just rather afraid of falling."

"What made you think it was I? I never spoke to you before," said Annie as they walked on together.

"Just half guessing, you know. You see, I know all the children and young folks that come to our church already. And I heard that Master Bruce was come. So when a lassie spoke to me that I never heard before, I just kind of thought it might be you."

The woman held Annie's hand and yielded like a child to her guidance as they went. It was a new delight to Annie to have someone whom she, a child, could help and be like a mother to—fulfilling a woman's highest calling, that of ministering. So it was with something like a sacred pride that she led her safely through the snowy streets and down the steep path that led from the level of the bridge, with its three stone arches, to the little meadow where her cottage stood.

The woman's name was Tibbie Dyster, and as soon as they entered her cottage, she was entirely at ease. The first thing she did was lift the kettle from the fire and feel the fire with her hands to see what its condition was. She would not allow Annie to touch it—she could not trust the creature that had nothing but eyes to guide her with such a delicate affair. The very hands looked like blind eyes trying to see, as they went wandering over the top of the pieces of live peat. She rearranged them, put on some fresh pieces, blew a little at them without doing the fire much good, was satisfied, coughed, and then sank in a chair.

Her room was very bare. But it was as clean as it was possible for a room to be. Her bed was against one of the walls, and this small one-room cottage was her whole habitation.

Annie looked all about, but saw no signs of any dinner for Tibbie. This reminded her that her own chances for having any were rapidly shrinking.

"I must go home," she said with a sigh.

"Ay, lassie. They'll be waiting their dinner for you."

"No fear of that," answered Annie with another sigh. "I doubt there'll be much of the broth left when I get home."

"Well, then stay, child, and take a cup of tea with me. It's all I have to offer you. Will you stay?"

"Won't I be in your way?"

"No, no. No fear of that. You can read to me a bit afterward."

"Ay, will I."

So Annie stayed all the afternoon with Tibbie, and went home with the Bruces after the evening service.

It quickly grew into a regular habit for Annie to take Tibbie home from church—a habit the Bruces could hardly have objected to. And indeed, they didn't mind, for it saved the broth so they could all have a little more, and Annie's absense was an added Sabbath blessing.

Much as she was neglected at home, Annie was steadily gaining a good reputation in the town. Old men said she was a *gude bairn* and old women said she was a *douce lassie*, while others simply expressed disapproval of the Bruces for "letting her run about like a beggar," when everyone knew "whose bull Rob Bruce was plowing with."

But Robert Bruce nevertheless grew and prospered all day by the use of Annie's money, all the time dreaming that he was nearly as important a man as the ancient king of old.

Chapter Thirty

ALEC'S HOMECOMING

Winter began to withdraw its ghostly troops and Glamerton began to grow warmer.

Annie, who had been very happy all that season, began to be aware of something more within her. A flutter barely recognizeable, as of the wings of awakening delight, now stirred her heart occasionally with a sensation of physical presence and motion. She would find herself giving a skip as she walked along, and now and then humming a bit of a song. A hidden well was throbbing in her soul. Its waters had been frozen by the winter. Now the spring, which sets all things springing, had made it flow and grow, soon to break forth bubbling. But her joy was gentle, for even when she was merriest, it was in a sober and maidenly fashion. She had already walked with Sorrow and was not afraid.

Robert Bruce's last strategical move against the community had been very successful, even in his own eyes. Profits were up, and he was enough satisfied with himself that he could afford to be in good humor with other people. Even Annie came in for her share with an occasional smile. She knew him too well to have any respect for him, but it was nice not to have to dread a critical word every time she met him. This comfort, however, stood on a sandy foundation.

At length, one bright day toward the end of March, Alec came home after his first term at college. He seemed the same cheery, active youth as before. The only visible difference in him was that he had grown considerably and that he wore a coat. There was a certain slight change in his tone and manner, a hint of polish, which most of the men and women who saw him considered an improvement.

In order to prepare for the mathematical studies of the following year, Alec went to the school in the morning on most days, for he knew Mr. Malison could give him the assistance he needed. The first time he made his appearance, a momentary silence as of death spread throughout the classroom to welcome him. But an uproar soon arose and discipline was for a moment thrown to the wind.

Annie sat still, staring at her book, turning white and red one after the other. But he took no notice of her, and she tried to be glad of it. When school was over, however, he came up to her in the street and addressed her kindly.

But the delicate little maiden felt that a hidden change had passed over the old companion and friend. True, the change was only a breath—a mere shadow. Yet it revealed a gulf between them. Alec had become a *young gentleman*, and her heart sank within her. Her friend was lost, and a shape was going about *looking* like the old Alec who had carried her in his arms through the flooded street. But alas! it was no longer him, and Annie went to her garret that night sad.

Mrs. Forbes never asked her to the house now, and it was good for Annie that her friendship with Tibbie Dyster had begun.

Yet as the days went by and she saw Alec day after day at school, the old colors began to revive out of the faded picture. And when the spring got a little warmer, the boat was got out. Alec could not go rowing in *The Bonnie Annie* without thinking of its godmother and inviting her to join them.

Indeed, Curly would not have let him forget her. He felt that she was a bond between him and Alec. And he loved Alec all the more devotedly now that the difference between their social positions had begun to show itself. The dedication of the schoolboy to his childhood superior had now begun to change into something like the devotion of a clansman to his chief. And every once in a while an odd laugh between Annie and Curly would reveal the fact that they were both watching for some word of reaction or smile from Alec, whom they both looked up to.

In due time the harvest came. Annie haunted the fields as surely as the crane would fly south when the summer was over. She watched all the fields around Glamerton; she knew how each was growing in relation to the sun and which would first be ripe for cutting and reaping. And the very day that the sickle was put in, Annie was there to see and share in the joy.

She became one of the company of reapers, gatherers, binders, and stookers, all who were assembled to collect the living gold of the earth from the early fields of the farm of Howglen. Sometimes her thoughts went sadly back to the old days when Dowie was master of the field on the other side of the valley, and she was Dowie's little mistress. Not that she met with anything but kindness from Mrs. Forbes' workers—only it was not the same kindness she had had from Dowie.

But the pleasure of being once more near Alec almost made up for every loss. And he was quite friendly, although, she had to confess, not quite so friendly as of old. But that did not matter, she tried to assure herself.

The laborers all knew her well, and made sure that she should have the portion of their food her assistance had earned. She never refused anything that was offered her except money. That she had taken only once in her life—from Mr. Cowie, whom she continued to love all the more dearly, although she no longer attended his church.

Again the harvest was safely stored away, and the sad old age of the year sank through the rains and frosts to his grave.

The winter came and Alec went.

He had not been gone a week when Mrs. Forbes' invitations began again. And, as if to make up for the neglect of the summer, they were more frequent than before. No time was so happy for Annie as the time she spent with Alec's mother. And this winter she began to make some return for the lady's kindness in the way of helping with small portions of the work of the household.

CHAPTER THIRTY-ONE

TIBBIE'S COTTAGE

In addition to the time she spent at Howglen, Annie's visits to Tibbie Dyster increased as well, and she began reading regularly to the blind woman.

One Saturday evening, after she had been reading for some time, the latch of Tibbie's door was lifted and in walked Robert Bruce. He stared when he saw Annie, for he thought she was at Howglen. Then he said in a sharp tone. "You're everywhere at once, Annie Anderson. A downright runabout!"

"Let the child be, Master Bruce," said Tibbie gruffly. "She's doing the Lord's will, whether you may think so or not. She's visiting them that's in the prisonhouse of the dark."

"I'm not saying anything," said Bruce defensively.

"You are saying, Rob Bruce. You're offending one of His little ones. You should take hold of the millstone."

"Hoot, toot, Tibbie. I was only wishing that she would keep a small part of her ministry for her own home and those there who do so much for her. There's my wife and me just martyrs to that shop, with no one to help us. And there's the baby in need of some ministration now and then."

A grim squeezing of her mouth was Tibbie's only reply. She did not choose to tell Robert Bruce that although she was blind—

and possibly because she was blind—she heard more gossip than anyone else in Glamerton. His appeal to her sympathy had no effect on her. She knew his financial standing well enough, as well as how Annie was treated. Finding she made no reply, Bruce turned to Annie.

"You're not needed here any longer, Annie. I have a word or two to say to Tibbie. Go home and learn your lessons for tomorrow."

"It's Saturday night," answered Annie.

"But you have your lessons to learn for Monday."

"Ay. But I have a book or two to take home to Mistress Forbes. I think I'll stay there and come to church with her in the morning."

Now even though all that Bruce wanted was to get rid of her, he went on opposing her. Common-minded people feel that they must always take exception with others. Somehow agreement is seen with them as a sign of weakness.

"It's not safe for you to be about in the dark."

"I know the road to Mrs. Forbes' like the back of my hand."

"No doubt," he answered with a sneer. "And there's dogs about," he added.

As gentle as she was, by this time Annie was getting a little angry.

"The Lord'll take care of me from the dark and the dogs and the rest of you, Mr. Bruce," she said.

Bidding Tibbie a good night, she picked up her books and departed, trembling lest some unseen dog should attack her as she went.

As soon as she was gone, Bruce tried to make himself agreeable by retelling all the bits of gossip to Tibbie he could think of. All the while he kept peering about the room from door to chimney, turning every which way and surveying all he saw. From the changes in his voice Tibbie could tell what he was doing.

"So your old landlord's dead, Tibbie?" he said at last.

"Ay, and an honest man he was. He always had a kind word for a poor body."

"Ay, no doubt. But what would you say if I told you I had bought your little house and was your new landlord, Tibbie?"

"I would say that the doorsill needs mending to keep the snow out from under it, and the poor place is in sore need of new thatch on the roof."

"Well, that's very reasonable, no doubt, if all is as you say."

"What do you mean by that?"

"All I mean is that you're not altogether like other folk. I don't mean any offense, you know, Tibbie. But you don't have the sight of your eyes."

"Maybe I don't have the feeling of my old bones either, Master Bruce? Maybe I'm too blind to have rheumatism, or to smell the old wet thatch when there's been a scattering of snow or a drop of rain!"

"I didn't want to anger you, Tibbie. All that deserves attention. It would be a shame to let an old person like you—"

"Not that old, Mr. Bruce."

"Well, you're not too young not to need to be well taken care of—are you, Tibbie?"

Tibbie grunted.

"Well, it comes to the point that the house is in some need of doctoring."

"Indeed, it is," added Tibbie. "It needs a new door."

"No doubt you're right, Tibbie. But seeing that I have to spend so much for repairs, I'll have no choice but to add another threepence onto the rent."

"Another threepence, Robert Bruce! 'Tis all I'm able to do to pay my sixpence! An old blind woman like me doesn't fall in with sixpence that easily. And you would raise it in one fell swoop to nine!"

"You do a heap of wool-spinning, Tibbie, with those long fingers of yours. No one in Glamerton spins like you."

"Maybe ay and maybe no. But it's not much that comes to. I wouldn't spin so well if it weren't that the Almighty put some sight into the points of my fingers 'cause there was none left in my eyes. And if you make another threepence out of that, you'll be turning the weather that He sent to run my mill into your dam, and I wouldn't doubt that it will play ill with your waterwheels."

"Hoot, toot, Tibbie. It hurts my heart to appear so hard-hearted. But business is business, as they say."

"I have no doubt you don't want to *appear* so. But do you know that I make so little by the spinning that the church gives me a shilling a week to make up with? And if it weren't for kind friends, 'tis a poor enough living I would have in dour weather like this. Don't you imagine, Mr. Bruce, that I have any money put away, except sevenpence in a stocking. And if you raise my rent it would have to come from my tea or something else I would hate to miss."

"Well, that may be very true," said Bruce, "but I would have increased expenses, as I say. Wouldn't the church give you the other threepence?"

"Do you think I would take it from the church to put it into your till?"

"Well, I want to be as kind to you as I can, Tibbie. Let's just agree on sevenpence then, and we'll be done arguing over it."

"I tell you, Robert Bruce, rather than pay you one penny more than the sixpence, I'll go out in the snow and let the Lord look after me."

Robert Bruce went away and did not purchase the cottage. It had just come on the market at a low price. He had intended Tibbie to believe, as she did, that he had already bought it. And if she had agreed to pay even the sevenpence, he would have gone immediately to buy it.

CHAPTER
THIRTY-TWO

A TALK WITH TIBBIE

When Alec next visited home for the summer and saw Annie and Curly, he did not speak to them quite as heartily as on his former return. He had made new friends in the city, and his mind was full of them.

As they were making their way toward her cottage one afternoon, Tibbie brought him up in the conversation. "He's a fine lad, that Alec Forbes."

"Ay, he is," answered Annie sadly.

The old woman caught the tone.

"I doubt," she said, "that he'll get any good at that college."

"Why not?" returned Annie. "I was at school with him and never found anything to find fault with."

"Oh no, lassie. I mean to find no fault with him. His father was a douce man, and a God-fearing man, though he made few words about it. I think we're sometimes too hard on them that promises little, but maybe *does* more. You remember what you read to me before we came out together, about the lad that said to his father, *I won't go*, but then afterward he repented and went."

"Ay."

"Well, I just hope young Alec Forbes turns out to do the will of his Father in the end."

They walked over the bridge hand in hand, and round to the end and down the steep hill to the cottage below.

"Now," said Tibbie after they had arrived, "you'll just read a chapter to me, lassie, before you go home and I go to my bed. Blindness is a painful way to save candles."

She forgot that it was summer, and that in those northern regions the night has no time to gather before the sun is flashing again in the east.

The chapter happened to be the one where Jesus cured a man blind from his birth. When she had finished, Annie asked, "Might He not cure you, Tibbie, if you asked Him?"

"Ay, He might, and He will," answered Tibbie. "I'm only biding His time. But I'm thinking He'll cure me better than He cured the blind man. He'll just take the body off of me altogether and then I'll see, not with eyes like yours, but with my whole spiritual body. I wish Mr. Turnbull would take it into his head to preach about that sometime before my time comes, which won't be that long, I'm thinking. The wheels'll be stopping at my door before long."

"What makes you think that, Tibbie? There's no sign of death about you," protested Annie.

"Well, you see, I can't well say. Blind folk somehow know more than other folk about things that the sight of the eye has little to do with. But never mind. I'm willing to wait in the dark as long as He likes."

When their talk was over, Annie went home to her garret.

It was a remarkable experience she enjoyed in the changes that came to her with the seasons. The winter with its frost and bitter winds brought her a home at Howglen with kind Mrs. Forbes. The summer, whose airs were warm, liquid kisses, took it away and gave her the face of nature instead of the face of a human mother. In place of the snug little room in Howglen—in which she often heard the rain and hail storming outside—she now had the attic room with its cold bed and through whose roof the winds easily found their way. But the winds were warmer now, and through the skylight came the sunbeams to lighten up the room. The light enabled her to read there, but it also showed all the rat holes and wretchedness of decay.

There was comfort out of doors in the daytime—in the sky and the fields and all the goings-on of life. And this night, after her talk with Tibbie, Annie did not mind so much going back to the garret. Nor did she lie awake wondering what was becoming of Alec.

She dreamed instead that she saw the Son of Man. There was a veil over His face like the veil that Moses wore in the scripture she had recently read to Tibbie. But the face was so bright that it almost melted the veil away. And what she saw made her love that face more than the presence of Alec, more that the kindness of Mrs. Forbes or Dowie, and even more than the memory of her father.

CHAPTER THIRTY-THREE

ANNIE'S KITTEN

During all this time Annie had scarcely seen a thing of her aunt, Margaret Anderson. Hence, on one of the beautiful afternoons of that unusually fine summer, Annie took a longing to see her old aunt and set out to see her. It was a walk of two miles through farms and fields. She went along the road slowly, enjoying the few wild flowers and other sights, so that it was almost evening before she reached the house.

"Preserve us! Annie Anderson, what brings you here this time of night?" exclaimed her aunt.

"It's a long time since I saw you, Auntie, and I wanted to visit you."

"Well, come into the house. You're growing into a queen!"

Margaret had no use for children—thoughtless creatures, always wanting other folk to do everything for them. But growth was a curative process in her mind, and when a girl began to look like a woman, she regarded it almost as a sign of conversion. So she led Annie into the presence of her uncle, a little old man, worn and bent, with gray hair peeping out from under a Highland bonnet.

"This is my brother James's child," she told him.

The old man received Annie kindly, and made her sit down

beside him, talking to her as if she had been quite a child. Her great-aunt was confined to her bed with rheumatism. Supper was being prepared and Annie was not sorry to be invited to have a share, for during the summer her meals were scanty enough. While they ate, the old man kept helping her to the best, talking to her all the time.

"Will you not come and stay with me, Annie?" he said.

"No, no," interrupted Margaret. "She's at the school, you know, Uncle, and we mustn't interfere with her schooling. How does that lying Robert Bruce treat you, child?"

"Oh, I just never mind him," answered Annie.

"Well, it's all he deserves from you. But if I were you, I would let him know that if he plants your corn, you have a right to more than the scraps."

"I don't know what you mean," said Annie.

"Well, you may just as well know. Robert Bruce has two hundred pounds of your own, lassie. And if he doesn't treat you well, you can just tell him that I told you so."

This piece of news did not have the overpowering effect on Annie her aunt had expected. The money seemed in her eyes a limitless fortune. But then Bruce had it. She might as well think of robbing a bear of her cubs as getting any money from Bruce. Besides, what could she do with it if she had it? She had not yet learned to love money for its own sake. When she rose to go home, she felt little richer than when she had entered, except for the kind words of John Peterson.

"It's too late for you to go home alone, dawtie," said the old man.

"I'm not that scared," answered Annie.

"Well, if you walk with Him, the dark'll be light about you," he said. "Be a good lass, and run home as fast as you can. Good night to you, dawtie."

Rejoicing as if she had found her long-lost home, Annie went out into the twilight feeling it impossible anything should frighten her. But when she came to the part of the road bordered with trees, she could not help thinking she saw a figure just within the wood, and her imagination quickly fancied it a wild dog.

Slowly she kept on, hoping to slip by unnoticed. As she reached a gate leading into the wood, a dark figure suddenly bounded over it and came straight toward her. To her relief it went on two legs instead of four. And when it came still nearer she recognized it.

She stopped and cried out joyfully, "Curly!"—for it was her old champion's helper.

"Annie!" was the equally joyful response.

"I thought you were a wild beast!" said Annie.

"I hate to think I scared you. But how are you, Annie? And how's Blister Bruce?" Curly was dreadfully prolific in nicknames.

Annie had not seen him for six months. He had continued to show himself so full of mischief, though of an innocent sort, that his father thought it best to send him to a neighboring town to learn the trade of a saddler.

This was his first visit home during that time.

"You're some grown, Annie," he said.

"So are you, Curly," answered Annie.

"And how's Alec?"

"Very well, though I don't see him too often."

Much talk followed as they walked together toward Glamerton. At length Curly asked, "And how's the rats?"

"Well and thriving."

"Well, just put your hand in my coat pocket and see what I have brought you."

Knowing Curly's bent for tricks, Annie refused. "It's a wild beast," said Curly.

So saying, he pulled out of his pocket the most delicately-colored little kitten.

"Did you bring this all the way for me, Curly?"

"Ay, did I. You see, I don't like rats either. But you must keep it out of their way for a few weeks or they'll tear her to bits. But she'll soon be a match for them."

Annie took the kitten home, and it shared her bed that night.

"What's that meowing sound?" asked Bruce the next morning, the moment he rose from morning prayers on his knees.

"It's my kitten," said Annie. "I'll let you see it."

"We have too many mouths in the house already," said Bruce

as she returned with the little kitten peering from between her arms. "We have no room for more. Here, Rob, take the creature and put a bag around its neck and a stone in the bag and throw it into the river."

Not waiting for a discussion, Annie darted from the house with the kitten. Rob bolted after her, delighted with his father's order. But instead of finding her at the door as he had expected, he saw her already a long way up the street, flying like the wind.

He set off after her in keen pursuit. He was now a great lumbering boy. He had better wind than Annie, but she was a faster runner. She took the direct road toward Howglen and Rob kept floundering after her. Before she reached the footbridge she was out of breath and now he was gaining quickly on her.

Just as she turned the corner of the road, leading up on the other side of the water, she met Alec. Unable to utter a word, she smiled but passed at a half run without speaking. There was no need for Alec to ask the cause of her pale, fearful face, for there was young Bruce at her heels. Alec collared him instantly.

"What are you up to?" he demanded.

"Nothing," answered the panting pursuer.

"If you're after nothing, you'll find that nearer home," retorted Alec, twisting him round in that direction and giving him a shove to send him on his way. "If I hear of you troubling Annie Anderson again, I'll take a piece out of your skin the next time I lay my hands on you!"

Rob obeyed like a frightened dog, while Annie kept on to Howglen as if her enemy were still on her track. Rushing into the parlor, she fell on the floor before Mrs. Forbes. The kitten sprang out of her arms and ran under the sofa.

"Ma'am," she gasped at length, "please take care of my kitten. They want to drown it! But it's my own. Curly gave it to me."

Mrs. Forbes comforted her and readily took on the assignment. Annie was very late for school that day, for Mrs. Forbes made her sit down to another good breakfast before she went. Fortunately, Mr. Malison was in a good mood and said nothing. It is hardly surprising that Rob Bruce looked devils at her. I do not know what he told his father. But whatever it was, it was all written down in Bruce's mental books against Alexander Forbes of Howglen.

Mrs. Forbes' heart grieved her when she found out what persecution her little friend was exposed to at the Bruces'. But she did not see how she could help the situation. She was herself in the power of Bruce too, so protest from her would be worth little. She made up her mind to be kinder to her than ever the following winter when Alec was back at the University. For the present she just said to Annie when she left, "Be sure to come when you find yourself in any trouble."

CHAPTER THIRTY-FOUR

THE FIVE-POUND
NOTE

A spirit of prophecy, whether from the Lord or not, spread throughout Glamerton this summer. Those who read their Bibles took to reading nothing but the prophecies. And every man took to interpreting the shadowy glimpses presented into the future. Whatever was known, whether about ancient Assyria or modern Tahiti, found its theoretical place. And of course the Church of Rome, the Church of England, and the Church of Scotland all occupied positions of prominence as well.

Thomas Crann and his minister, Mr. Turnbull, were ready to fly at any man or woman of Glamerton with terrible denunciations of the wrath of the Almighty for their sins. To them Glamerton was the center of creation, providence, and revelation. All the evildoers of the place feared Thomas. They called him a wheezing old hypocrite, and would walk a good distance out of their way to avoid him.

In the midst of this commotion, the good Paster Cowie died. He had taken no particular interest in what was going on. Ever since Annie had come asking his counsel, he had been thinking in a deeper way than he had ever thought before about his own relationship to God. Now he had carried his thoughts into another world.

Except for his own daughters, there was no one who mourned so deeply the loss of Mr. Cowie as Annie Anderson. She had left his church and gone to the Missionaries, but she could never forget his kisses, or his gentle words, or his shilling. By them Mr. Cowie had given her a more trusting notion of God and His tenderness than she could have found in a hundred sermons put together. What greater gift could a man give?

When she had entered his room for the last time and found him in his bed supported with pillows behind him, he stretched out his arms to her feebly, held her close to him, and wept.

"I am going to die, Annie," he said.

"And go to heaven, sir, to the face of God," returned Annie, with tears streaming silently down her face.

"I hope so, Annie."

"If God loves you half as much as I do, sir, you'll be well off in heaven. And He must love you more than me. For God is love itself."

"Sometimes I don't know what God thinks of me anymore, Annie. But if I ever do get there, I'll tell Him about you and ask Him to give you more help than I was able to give you."

Love and death makes us all children.

Annie had no answer but what lay in her tears.

He reached to a table beside the bed. "Here, Annie," said the dying man, "here's my Bible that I wish I'd made more use of myself. Promise me that if you ever have a house of your own, you'll read out of that book every day. I want you to have it, and not to forget me, as I shall never forget you."

"I will, sir," said Annie earnestly.

"You will find a new five-pound note between the pages. Take it for my sake."

"Yes, sir," answered Annie, feeling this was no time for objecting to anything.

"Goodbye, Annie. I can't speak anymore."

He drew her to him and kissed her for the last time. Then he turned over, and Annie went home weeping, with the great Bible in her arms.

Without thinking in her grief, she ran into the shop.

"What have you got there, lassie?" demanded Bruce, in a tone that seemed to accuse her of stealing it.

"Mr. Cowie gave me this Bible. He's dying himself and doesn't want it any longer," answered Annie.

"Let me look at it."

Annie hesitated, but gave it to him.

"It's a fine book, with a pretty binding. We'll just lay it upon the room table, and we'll have worship out of it sometimes."

"I—I want it myself," objected Annie in dismay. She did not think of the money at the moment. She had better reasons than that for not wanting to give up the book.

"You can use it when you want. Surely that's enough."

Annie could hardly think that much comfort. The door to *the room* was always kept locked, and Mrs. Bruce would have boxed her ears if she caught her trying to find a way in. To be put there meant not to have it at all!

Before the next Sunday Mr. Cowie was dead.

By this time Robert Bruce had become a great man in the community—in his own judgment at least—and certainly one of the fashionable and leading members of the Missionary kirk. It so happened that after the next Sunday evening's service a special prayer meeting was set to be held. Robert Bruce remained to join in intercession for the wicked town and its wicked neighborhood. He even "engaged in prayer" for the first time in public since joining the Missionaries, astonishing some of the older members by his gift of devotion.

He had been officially received into the church as a member only a week or two before. There had been one or two murmurs against his reception. But nothing was specifically known against him. And since he had learned many of the phrases and words and expressions currently circulating in the Missionary community, he was able to satisfy them that he was indeed saved according to the terms they set down. No doubt his wealth had something to do with the ease of his acceptance. Probably they thought if the gospel moved mightily in this new disciple, more of his money might eventually be used for good missionary purposes. And now he had been asked to pray, and had prayed with much emotion. To be sure, Tibbie Dyster did sniff in disdain during his performance, which was her way of silently expressing her disapproval.

When the meeting was over, Robert Bruce, Thomas Crann, and James Johnstone, who was one of the deacons, walked away together. Very little conversation took place between them, for no subject but a religious one would have been admissible. But Bruce was so pleased with himself to find that he could pray in public before the judges of the Missionary cause, that he thought he might like to try it again, and further increase his standing among the leaders of the congregation. He also thought of the grand Bible lying upstairs on his table that he might impress these men with.

"Come in, sirs," he said as they reached his door, "and take part in our family worship with us. We have devotions, every morning and night, you know."

Neither of the men was particularly interested, yet both agreed. He led them upstairs, unlocked the musty room, and then proceeded to gather his family together, calling them one by one.

"Mother," he cried from the top of the stair.

"Yes, Father," answered Mrs. Bruce, who had remained at home with the others because of colds.

"Come to worship.—Robert!"

"Ay, Father."

"Come to worship.—Johnnie!"

And so he went through the family roll call. When all had entered and seated themselves, the head of the house went slowly to the side table, took from it reverently the study Bible of the minister who had died only that week, sat down by the window, laid the book on his knees, and solemnly opened it.

Now a five-pound note is not thick enough to make a big Bible open between the pages where it is laid. But the note might very well have been laid in a place where the Bible was in the habit of being opened for a favorite passage. And in this case, the instant the pages fell open, there was the small fortune staring out at him.

Without an instant's hesitation, Robert snatched it, slipped it away, crumpled it up in his hand, and read out the twenty-third psalm as if nothing out of the ordinary had taken place. He heard not a word of the passage himself, however, for his brain was spinning over the new-found wealth.

Finding the twenty-third too short for the respectability of worship, he went on with the twenty-fourth, turning the page with thumb and forefinger, while the rest of his fingers clasped the bill tight in his palm, and reading as he turned, "He that hath clean hands and a pure heart—"

As soon as he had finished this psalm, he closed the book with a snap. Then in a solemn tone, thinking to please his guest, he said, "Thomas Crann, will you engage in prayer?"

"Pray yourself," answered Thomas gruffly. So Robert rose, knelt down, and did pray himself.

But instead of leaning forward in his chair and closing his eyes as he knelt, Thomas glanced around sharply at Bruce. He had seen him take something from the Bible and crumple it up in his hand. He would have thought nothing of it had it not been for the surprised expression of happy greed which had come over Bruce's face in the act. He had always been a little suspicious of Bruce, and he wanted to know more.

He saw Bruce take advantage of the kneeling position to stuff something into his pocket.

When worship was over, Bruce did not ask them to stay for supper. Prayers did not involve expense; supper did.

Thomas went home thinking. He had many prayers yet to pray before his heart would be quiet in sleep. Especially there was Alec to be prayed for, because he could not help worrying about the lad's spiritual condition when away at the college. And his dawtie Annie. And in truth the whole town of Glamerton, and the surrounding countryside—and Scotland, and the whole world.

Indeed, sometimes Thomas went even further than that in his prayers. It is not reported of him that he ever actually prayed for the devil. Yet he did something like it once or twice when he prayed for "the whole universe of God, and the beings in it, up and down, that we know so little about."

CHAPTER
THIRTY-FIVE

THOMAS'S SUSPICION

The summer shone on and the grain grew green and bonnie. Summer flowed into autumn. The green grain turned pale at last before the gaze of the sun. The life within had done its best and now shrank back to the earth.

Anxious farmers watched their fields and joyfully noted every shade of progress. All day the sun shone strong, and all night the moon leaned down from heaven to see how things were going and to keep the work gently moving. At length the new revelation of ancient life was complete, and the grain stood in living gold, and men began to put it to the sickle because the time of harvest was come.

Both master and boys in the schoolroom longed for the harvest holiday. The boys thought with delight of having nothing to do on those glorious hot days but to gather blueberries or lie on the grass or swim in the Glamour and dry themselves in the sun ten times a day. For the master, however, the reasons were different. He planned to take a holiday away from Glamerton.

At length the slow hour arrived, and the twelve o'clock of the final Saturday came. Almost the moment the *amen* of the final prayer was out of the master's mouth, the first boys were shouting jubilantly in the open air. Truffey, who was always the last, was crutching it out with the rest when he heard the master's voice calling him back. He obeyed it.

"Ask your grandfather, Andrew, if he will allow you to go down to the seaside with me for two or three weeks," said Mr. Malison.

"Yes, sir," Truffey meant to say, but the only thing to come out of his mouth was an unearthly screech of delight. Then he went off in a series of bounds worthy of a kangaroo, lasting all the way to his grandfather's and taking him there in half the usual time.

And the master and Truffey did go down to the sea together. The master borrowed a buggy and hired a horse and driver. They all three sat in the space meant for two. To Truffey a lame leg was hardly to be compared with the glorious happiness of that day! Was he not the master's friend from now on? And was he not riding with him in a buggy? Supreme happiness! Truffey was prouder than ever a boy of Glamerton had been.

About this time Tibbie caught a bad cold and cough and for two weeks was confined to bed. Annie became her constant companion.

"I told you I would have the light before long," she said the first time Annie came to her.

"Hoots, Tibbie! It's only a cold," said Annie. "Don't be downhearted."

"Downhearted! How could I be downhearted within sight of the New Jerusalem?"

"But, Tibbie," protested Annie, "however willing you may be to go, we're not so willing to lose you."

"You'll be better off without me, lass."

Annie's quiet squeeze of her hands was Annie's only argument against the words. Annie waited on Tibbie day and night. And that year, for the first time since she had come to Glamerton, the harvest began without her. But when Tibbie got a little better, Annie ran out now and then to see what progress the reapers were making.

One bright morning Tibbie said, "Now, child, I am feeling much better today. You just run out into the fields, and don't let me see you before dinnertime."

At Howglen there happened to be a field of oats not far from the house, the reaping of which was to begin that day. It was a warm, glorious morning, full of sunshine. So after a few stooks had been set up, Alec went out, lay down by some sheaves, and watched. He fell into a doze, and at length the sun rose till the stook could shelter him no more.

Suddenly a shadow came over him to shade his eyes. When he looked up, he could see nothing but an apron held up— hiding both the sun and the face of the helper.

"Who's there?" he asked.

"It's me—Annie Anderson," came the voice from behind the apron.

"Don't bother me, Annie," he said. "I don't want the shade."

Annie dropped her arms and turned away in silence. If Alec could have seen her face, he would have been sorry he had refused her service. She vanished in a moment, he moved back under the shade of the stook, and fell fast asleep again.

Annie walked away, a deep pain in her heart keeping her from returning to watch the workers in the field. She wandered away, thinking how greatly things had changed since the happy old times. She walked toward a little old cottage where some of the farm workers lived. She knew Thomas Crann was at work there, and she found him busy spreading the outside of it with plaster.

"You're busy working, Thomas," said Annie just for the sake of something to say.

"Ay, just helping to make a hypocrite," answered Thomas, with a nod and a smile as he threw a trowelful of the morter against the wall.

"What do you mean by that?" asked Annie.

"If you knew this place as well as I do, you wouldn't need to ask that question. It should have been torn down completely a century ago it's so old and rotten inside. And here we are putting a clean face on it."

"It *looks* good enough."

"I told you I was making a hypocrite," chuckled Thomas. "You remember what Jesus said about whitewashed tombs and the like?"

"Ay."

Thomas went on whitening his "hypocrite" in silence for a few moments. Then he said, "Where did Robert Bruce get that grand Bible, Annie, do you know?"

"That's my Bible, Thomas. Old Mr. Cowie gave it to me when he was lying close to death."

"Hmm. And why didn't you take it and put it in your own room?"

"Mister Bruce took it and laid it in his room as soon as I brought it home, and wouldn't let me keep it for myself."

"Did Master Cowie say anything to you about anything that was in it?"

"Ay, he did. He spoke of a five-pound note he had put in it. But when I looked for it, I couldn't find it."

"When did you look for it?"

"I forgot it for two or three days—maybe a week."

"Do you remember that Sunday night that two of us came home with Bruce and had worship with him and you?"

"Ay, well enough. It was the first time he read out of my Bible."

"Was it before or after that when you looked for the money?"

"It was the next day. For the sight of the Bible reminded me of it. I ought not to have thought of it on the Sabbath, but it came of itself. I didn't look for it till the Monday morning before they were up. The room was still unlocked. I reckon Mr. Cowie forgot to put it in after all."

"Hmm! hmm! Ay! ay! Well, sometimes riches take to themselves wings and fly away, and so we mustn't set our hearts on them. The worst bank a man can lay up his own money in is his own heart."

Annie had soon forgot her own troubles in Thomas's presence, for in his own way he helped to be a shelter to her. He was certainly not felt to be such by all he encountered. For his ambition was to rouse men from the sleep of sin, to set them face to face with the terrors of the Ten Commandments and Mount Sinai, and to shake them over the mouth of the pit till they were all choked with the fumes of the brimstone of hell. But to Annie and Tibbie, at least, Thomas showed a gentler side.

"How's Tibbie today?" he asked.

"A wee bit better," answered Annie.

"She's a good honest woman who has the glory of God in her heart," Thomas reflected, then went on with his work.

Annie did not return to the harvest field again that day. She did not want to go near Alec again. She lingered a while longer with Thomas, then wandered slowly across some fields of barley stubble. The fresh young clover was already spreading its soft green up through the dirt. She then went over the Glamour by the bridge with the three arches, down the path at the other end, over the single great stone that crossed the dyer's dam, and so back to Tibbie's cottage.

Had Annie been Robert Bruce's own daughter, she would have had to mind the baby, do part of the housework, and probably attend to the shop during meals. But Robert Bruce thought Annie knew about the investment of her money. Therefore he allowed her near complete freedom of action since he assumed she knew she was paying her own way.

But in reality Annie never thought about the matter and simply did as she pleased. Though most of the townspeople knew that her money sat in Bruce's bank account, in tight-lipped Scottish fashion, none of her Glamerton friends had given her any information about her little fortune. And she had hardly given another thought to her aunt's one reference to the fact. Had Bruce known how ignorant she really was about it, he would never have allowed her such liberty, and would have given her constant work to do.

Thomas did not doubt for a moment that Robert Bruce had stolen the five-pound note. But he did not see what he ought to do about it. The thing would be hard to prove. And if such a man would steal, he would lie to cover up his theft.

But he bitterly regretted that such a dishonest man should have found his way into their church congregation.

CHAPTER
THIRTY-SIX

RAIN

A t length the oats and wheat and barley were gathered in all over the valley of the two rivers. The master returned from the seacoast, bringing Truffey back radiant with life. Nothing could lengthen his shrunken leg, but in the other and the crutch together he had more than the function of the two.

The master was his idol. And the master was a happier man. He had been loving and helping. And the love and help had turned into a great joy, whose tide washed from his heart the bitterness of his remembered sin. When we love God and man truly, all the guilt and oppression of past sin will be swept away.

So the earth and all that was in it did the master good. And when the children gathered again in his classroom on the Monday morning to end the holiday, the master's prayer was different from what it used to be, and the work was not so bad as before, and school was not so hateful as they had expected.

The light grew shorter and shorter. A few rough, rainy days stripped the trees of all their leaves. But then the sun shone out again and made lovely weather, though it was plain to all the senses that autumn was drawing to a close.

There had been numerous prophetic utterances declared against Glamerton and the harvest. But they had all proved themselves false. Never had a better harvest been gathered. Yet still the passion for prophetic warnings throughout the whole district continued.

A week or two after the resumption of school, the sky grew gloomy, and a thick, small, steady rain brought the dreariest weather in the world. There was no wind, and miles and miles of mist were gathered in the air. After a day or two the heavens grew lighter but the rain fell as steadily as before, and in heavier drops. Still there was little rise in the rivers, the Glamour or the Wan Water.

On Saturday afternoon, weary of some attempts to study his Greek and Latin in preparation for the coming session, Alec went out for a walk. He wandered along the bank, with the rain above and the wet grass below. He stood for a moment gazing at the muddy Glamour which was now full in its bank.

"If this keeps up, we'll have a flood," remarked Alec to himself when he saw how the water was beginning to invade the trees on the steep banks below.

That evening, in the schoolmaster's house, little Truffey sat triumphantly at the tea table. The master had been so pleased with an exercise which the lad had written for him that he had taken the boy home to tea with him, dried him off at his fire, and given him as much buttered toast as he could eat. Oh, how Truffy loved his master!

"Truffey," said Mr. Malison, after a long pause, during which he had been staring into the fire, "how's your leg?"

"Quite well, thank you, sir," answered Truffey, putting out the foot of his good leg toward the fire. "There isn't anything the matter with it."

"I mean the other leg, Truffey—the one that I—that I—hurt."

"Perfectly well, sir. It's hardly worth asking about. I wonder why you take such pains with me, sir, when I was such a mischievous nickum."

The master could not reply.

He was more grateful for Truffey's generous forgiveness than he would have been for the richest estate in all of Scotland. Such forgiveness gives us back ourselves—clean and happy. And for what can we be more grateful?

"It's time to go home, Andrew Truffey. Put on my cloak—there. And keep out of the puddles as much as you can."

"I'll put the small foot in them," answered Truffey cheerfully, holding up the end of his crutch as he stretched it forward to make one bound out of the door. For he delighted in showing off his agility to the master.

When Alec looked out of his window the next morning, he saw a broad yellow expanse below. The Glamour was rolling, a mighty river, through the land. A wild waste of foamy water, it swept along the fields which had only recently been covered with golden grain. But he had seen the river this high before. And all the grain was safely in the barns.

All night Tibbie Dyster had lain awake in her lonely cottage, listening to the rising water. She was still not completely recovered from her cold, and was now all the more convinced that the Lord was going to let her see His face.

On Sunday morning, Bruce walked to the chapel with only Annie at his side. But the moment he stepped through the door, Annie darted off to see Tibbie. He made his way to his chosen pew near the front, angry at Annie and ashamed to show it thus empty to the eyes of his brethren. But there were many pews half empty that morning.

The rain eased a little in the afternoon, and so the church was crowded in the evening. The faces of the congregation were expectant, for Mr. Turnbull always tried to give his sermons added clout by bringing Nature in to help him make his point.

The Bible verse he had chosen was, "But as the days of Noah were, so shall the coming of the Son of Man be." When in the middle of his sermon a flash of lightning cracked, followed by an instant explosion of thunder and burst of rain as if a waterspout had broken over their heads, most of those present jumped an inch out of their seats.

Was this the way the judgments that had been predicted were going to come upon them—with a second flood about to sweep them all from the earth? They all stared at the minister as if they were paying attention to every word he uttered about the flood of Noah. But in reality they were much too frightened at the little flood in the valley of the two rivers of Strathglamour!

When the service was over, they rushed out of the church.

Robert Bruce was the first to step outside, nearly up to his ankles in water.

"The Lord preserve us!" he exclaimed. "There's sugar in the cellar we must save! Children, run home yourselves! I can't wait for you!"

At that moment Annie was slipping past him to run back to Tibbie. He made a pounce on her and grabbed her by the shoulder.

"No more of this, Annie," he ordered. "Come home and don't be running about nobody knows where."

"Everybody knows where," returned Annie. "I'm only going to stay with Tibbie Dyster, poor blind woman!"

"Let the blind sleep with the blind, and come home with me," said Robert, misquoting at least two verses of Scripture in one breath and pulling Annie away with him.

Angry and disappointed, Annie made no further resistance. And how the rain did pour as they went home! They were all wet to the skin in a moment, except Mr. Bruce, who had a fine umbrella. As to the thought of sharing it, he reasoned that his Sabbath clothes were more expensive than those of the children.

By the time they reached home, Annie had made up her mind about what to do. Instead of going all the way up to her room, she waited on the landing, listening for all the footsteps to stop. The rain poured down on the roof with such a noise that she found it difficult to be sure. There was no use changing her clothes only to get them wet again. At length when she was satisfied that everyone was in their own rooms, she stole out of the house as quietly as a kitten and was quickly out of sight. Not a creature was to be seen. The gutters were all running over with water, and the streets had become riverbeds. But through it all she dashed without fear to Tibbie's cottage.

"Tibbie!" she cried as she entered, "there's going to be a terrible flood."

"Let it come!" cried Tibbie. "The little house is built on a rock, and the rains may fall and the winds may blow, and the floods may beat against the house, but it won't fall. It can't fall, for it's founded on a rock."

Perhaps Tibbie's mind was wandering a little, for when Annie arrived she found Tibbie's face red and her hands moving restlessly. But Annie thought no more about the rising waters of the Glamour now that she was there with Tibbie.

"What kept you so long, lassie?" said Tibbie after a moment's silence.

Annie told her the whole story as she arranged the peats on the fire.

"And did you have no supper?"

"No. I don't need any."

"Take off your wet clothes then, and come to your bed."

Annie crept into the bed beside her—not even dry then, for she had to keep on her last garment. Tibbie was restless and kept moaning, so that neither of them could get much sleep.

The water kept sweeping on faster, rising higher up the rocky mound on which the cottage stood. The old woman and the young girl lay inside and listened, fearless.

CHAPTER THIRTY-SEVEN

THE FLOOD

A lec too lay awake and listened to the untiring rain. In the morning he rose and looked out of the window. The Glamour spread out and rushed on like a torrent of ocean. He dressed himself and went down to its edge. Past him came trees torn up by the roots; sheaves went floating by, then a cart with a drowned horse.

Truffey went stumping through the rain and the streams to the morning school. He would liked to have waited on the bridge which he had to cross to look at the water. But the master would be there, and Truffey would not be late. When Mr. Malison arrived, Truffey was standing in the rain waiting for him. Not another student was there. The master sent him home. And Truffey went back to the bridge over the Glamour and stood there watching the awful river.

Mr. Malison sped away westward toward the Wan Water. Its waters had never within memory overflowed the ridge between it and the town. But now, people said, if it rose even another foot, it would go over the ridge and begin flowing into Glamerton itself. Then the two rivers would merge into one, with the town right in the middle of them! So instead of going to school, all the boys, along with many inhabitants of the town, had gone to look, and there the schoolmaster followed them.

But while the excited crowd of his townsmen stood in the middle of a field watching the progress of the river, Robert Bruce was busy in his cellar making final preparations to get everything as high as possible in case the river did invade his shop. As soon as he had finished his task, he hurried off to join the watchers of the water.

James Johnstone's workshop was not far from the Glamour. When he went into the shop that Monday morning and found half of it under water, he realized there could be no work done that day. He therefore continued on toward the bridge to watch the flood.

As he came near the bridge, he saw the small, crippled Truffey leaning over the edge with a horror-stricken face. The next moment the boy bounded across the bridge to the other side.

When James reached the bridge he could see nothing to immediately explain the terror on Truffey's pale face, nor to explain where he had run off to. But being shortsighted and curious, he set off after Truffey as fast as he could go.

Alec had been on his way toward the mill, and saw two men on the edge of the brown torrent, the miller and Thomas Crann. Thomas had been up all night, wandering along the shore of the Wan Water, sorely troubled about Glamerton and its spiritually careless people who had ignored the prophetic utterances that had been spoken. Toward morning he had crossed the Glamour and had wandered up the side of the water. He had come upon the miller, worrying about his mill, which was now in the middle of the torrent.

Alec joined the two and their talk continued. But it was soon interrupted by Truffey. He was attempting to run toward them across the field. But despite frantic efforts, his crutch sunk so deep into the muddy ground that he had to stop with nearly every step. He tried to shout, but they could hear nothing more than what sounded like the screech of a hoarse chicken.

Finally Alec noticed him, and started off to meet him. But just as he reached him, Truffey's crutch broke in the earth, and he fell and lay unable to speak a word.

In another minute Thomas Crann walked up.

"Annie Anderson!" panted out Truffey at length.

"What about her?" said both Thomas and Alec in alarm.

"Tibbie Dyster!" sobbed Truffey in reply.

"Here's James Johnstone!" said Thomas. "He'll tell us about it."

Johnstone came up to Thomas's anxious questioning. But neither knew more than the other. Truffey was again trying to speak.

"They'll all be drowned! They can't get out!"

Thomas and Alec turned and stared at each other.

"The boat!" gasped Thomas.

Alec made no reply. That was a terrible river to look at. And the boat was so small.

"Can you guide it in such water, Alec?" asked Thomas.

Still Alec made no reply. He was afraid.

"Alec!" shouted Thomas, "we can't let the women drown!"

The blood shot into Alec's face. He turned and ran.

"Come on, Thomas!" cried Alec over his shoulder, already across three or four ridges of the field. "I can't carry the boat alone."

Thomas followed as fast as he could. But before he reached the barn he met Alec and one of the farm servants with the boat on their shoulders.

It was but a short way to the water. They had her afloat in a few minutes, below the footbridge. At the edge the water was still as a pond.

Alec seized the oars and the men shoved him off.

"Pray, Alec!" shouted Thomas.

"I haven't time. Pray yourself!" shouted Alec in reply, and gave a stroke with the oars that shot him far out toward the current of the river. The moment Thomas saw the boat being grabbed by the current, he turned his back on the river, fell on his knees in the grass, and cried out to the Lord in agony.

Johnstone and the farm lad who had helped with the boat ran down the riverside. Truffey had tied his crutch with a piece of rope and now started for the bridge again. Thomas remained kneeling in prayer.

Alec did not find it so hard as he had expected to keep the

boat from capsizing. But the speed with which he flew past the banks was frightening. The cottage lay on the other side of the Glamour, lower down. All he had to do was keep the front of the boat pointed downstream and gradually work his way across the current.

Tibbie's cottage lay between the channel of the river and the stream through the mill. During the night the waters had risen so high that the two were now one and the cottage was completely surrounded by swirling water, which was already beating against the stone walls of the house itself.

Alec would hardly have known where to guide his tiny craft, the look of everything was so changed by the floodwaters. But he knew where Tibbie's cottage stood in relation to the bridge. It was now crowded with people, anxiously watching as Alec sped toward the doomed little house.

As he approached, Alec could see that the water was already halfway up the door. He decided to aim his boat right through the doorway, yet was doubtful whether it was wide enough to let him through. But he had no other choice. If he could not get his boat inside the flooded house, the current would sweep him instantly past it and there would be no hope of his rowing upstream to make a second run at it. There was no dry ground anywhere around the place, and no other possible way for Annie and Tibbie to escape except by boat.

He hoped the boat would slip right through the doorway. If that failed, he would then be in danger himself. But there was no use worrying further until he had to.

As he came near the cottage, he grabbed the oars firmly in his hands to guide him. He took a few vigorous pulls, made a good aim straight for the door, then drew in the oars, bent his head forward, and prepared for the shock of hitting the house.

Crash went *The Bonnie Annie!* The door of Tibbie's cottage burst open, the sides of the boat rammed against the door posts, and the beam above the door fell down on Alec's shoulders.

But now I will tell you how the night had passed with Tibbie and Annie.

CHAPTER
THIRTY-EIGHT

RESCUE AND LOSS

Tibbie's moaning grew gentler and less frequent. Finally both women fell into a troubled slumber. Annie awoke at the sound of Tibbie's voice. She was talking in her sleep.

"Don't wake Him," she said, "don't wake Him. He's too tired and sleepy. Let the wind blow, lads. Do you think He can't see when His eyes are closed? If the wind meddles with you, He'll soon let it know it's in the wrong."

A pause followed. It was clear that she was in a dreamboat with Jesus in the back asleep. The sounds of the water outside had stolen through her ears and made a picture in her brain. Suddenly she cried out, "I told you so! I told you so! Look at it! The waves are going down as if they were little pups!"

She woke with her own cry—weeping.

"I thought I had the sight of my eyes," she said, sobbing, "and the Lord was blind with sleep."

"Do you hear the water?" said Annie.

"Who cares for *that* water," she answered in a tone of contempt. "Do you think He can't manage *it!*"

But there was a noise in the room beside them, and Annie heard it. The water was lapping at the foot of the bed.

"The water's in the house!" cried Annie in terror, jumping up.

"Lie still, child," said Tibbie with authority. "If the water's in the house, then there's no way for us to get out. The house is safe. The water will fall before morning. Lie still."

Annie lay down again and in a few minutes more she was asleep again. Tibbie slept too.

But Annie woke from a terrible dream—that a dead man was chasing her and had laid a cold hand upon her. The dream was gone, but the cold hand remained.

"Tibbie!" she cried. "The water's in the bed!"

"What's that you say, lassie?" returned Tibbie, waking up.

"The water's in the bed!"

"Well, lie still. We can't sweep it out."

It was pitch dark. Annie, who lay in front, stretched her arm over the side. It sunk to the elbow. In a moment more the mattress beneath her was like a full sponge. She lay in silent terror, longing for the dawn.

"I'm terrible cold," said Tibbie.

Annie tried to answer her, but the words would not leave her throat.

Still the water rose. Now they were lying half-covered with it. Tibbie broke out singing. Annie had never heard her sing, and it was not very musical. *Savior, through the desert lead us. Without thee we cannot go.*

"Are you awake, lassie?"

"Ay," answered Annie.

"I'm terrible cold, and the water's up to my throat. I can't move. I'm so cold. I've never felt water so cold."

"I'll help you to sit up a bit. You'll have dreadful rheumatism after this, Tibbie," said Annie. She got up on her knees in the bed and tried to lift Tibbie's head and shoulders and draw her up in the bed.

But the task was beyond her strength. She could not move the helpless weight. In her despair she let Tibbie's head fall back with a dull splash upon the pillow.

Seeing that all she could do was sit and support her, she got out of bed and waded across the floor to try to find her clothes. But they were gone. The chair they were on had floated away.

She returned to the bed, got behind Tibbie, lifted her head on her knees and sat.

A horribly dreary time followed.

The water crept up and up. Tibbie moaned a little, and then lay silent for a long time, drawing slow and feeble breaths. Annie was almost dead with cold.

Suddenly in the midst of the darkness, Tibbie cried out, "I see light! I see light!"

A strange sound in her throat followed. Then she was quite still. Annie's mind began to wander. Something struck her gently on the arm and kept bobbing against her. She put out her hand to feel what it was. It was round and soft. She said to herself, "It's only somebody's head that the water's torn off," and she put her hand under Tibbie again.

In the morning she found it was a drowned hen that had floated in through one of the broken windows.

At first she saw motion rather than light. The only thing she saw of the dawn was the yellow flood that filled the floor. There it lay swirling all about.

The light grew. She strained her eyes to see Tibbie's face. At last she saw that the water was over her mouth where she lay in bed. Her face looked like the face of her father in his coffin. She knew that Tibbie was dead. Nevertheless she tried to lift her head out of the water, but she could not.

So she crept out from under her with painful effort, and stood up in the bed. The water almost reached her knees. The table was floating near the bed. If the water rose much higher she would have to try to get outside and onto the roof of the cottage. She got hold of the table, scrambled onto it, and sat with her legs in the water. The table went floating about the room, and Annie dreamed she was having a row in *The Bonnie Annie* with Alec and Curly. In the motions of the water, she had passed close to the window and Truffey had seen her from the bridge above.

Suddenly she was wide awake! She jumped in terror from her dream at the terrible *crash*. The door burst open! She thought the cottage was falling, and that she was about to die!

In shot the sharp front of *The Bonnie Annie*, and in glided the stooped-down form of Alec Forbes. Annie gave a loud wailing cry, and forgot everything.

In the next instant she was in Alec's arms. In another moment, wrapped in his coat, she was lying in the bottom of the boat.

Alec was now as cool as any hero should be, for he was doing his duty. He looked all about for Tibbie. At length he saw her drowned in her bed.

"I wish I had been in time," he said.

But what was to be done next? He had to go down the river. Yet they would reach the bridge in two minutes after leaving the cottage and be smashed to bits against it!

He would have to shoot for the middle arch, for that was the highest, and hope there was room underneath it for the boat to squeeze through! Still the risk was a terrible one. The water had risen to within a few feet of the peak of the arch, and the current was swift and torturous. Even if he should escape being dashed against the bridge, and even if he managed to get in a straight line for the high arch, what if the boat could not clear under it? The boat would splinter apart and he and Annie would surely drown!

But when Alec shot *The Bonnie Annie* again through the door of the cottage, the high arch was nowhere to be seen. The entire bridge had disappeared!

The boat flew down the open river like an arrow, with nothing in its way.

CHAPTER THIRTY-NINE

THE FALL OF THE GLAMOUR BRIDGE

Approaching the cottage down the current, Alec had not been aware that the wooden bridge upstream had given way just moments after he had entered the water with his boat. The entire bridge floated down the river after him, but nearer the shore. As he turned to row into the cottage, on it came and swept past him toward the other bridge.

The stone bridge was full of spectators, eagerly watching the boat. For Truffey had told everyone of the attempted rescue. When news of the situation reached the Wan Water, those who had been watching it were now hurrying toward the bridge of the Glamour.

The moment Alec disappeared into the cottage, some of the spectators caught sight of the huge beams of the wooden bridge coming rapidly down the river straight for them. Already there was fear for the safety of the stone bridge for the tremendous weight of water rushing against it. And now that they saw this ram coming down the stream, a panic arose. Cries and shouts of terror were heard as everyone scattered to escape the bridge. A general rush left the bridge empty just at the moment when the heavy floating mass struck one of the main piers.

But there was one in the crowd much too absorbed in watching the cottage to pay any heed to the cries and warnings and commotion about him. This was Andrew Truffey. Leaning wearily on the edge of the bridge with his broken crutch at his side, he was watching anxiously through the cottage window.

Even when the floating beams from upstream struck the pillar of stone beneath him, and as the mass under his feet trembled, he still kept staring at the cottage. Not till he felt the bridge begin to sway did he have an inkling of his danger. Then he sprang up and made for the street. Half of the bridge crumbled away behind him, and vanished in a seething yellow-brown hole.

At this moment the first of the crowd that had been watching the Wan Water reached the foot of the bridge. Among them was the schoolmaster. Truffey was making desperate efforts to struggle across the remaining portion of the bridge to reach the bank. His mended crutch had given way and he was hopping wildly along.

Murdoch Malison saw him, and rushed upon the falling bridge. He reached the cripple, caught him up in his strong arms, turned back toward the shore, and was halfway back to the street when—with a swing and a sweep and a great splash—the remaining half of the bridge reeled and fell into the current and vanished.

Murdoch Malison and Andrew Truffey left the world in each other's arms. Their bodies were never found.

A moment after the fall of the bridge, Robert Bruce, gazing with the rest at the raging torrent, saw *The Bonnie Annie* go darting past. Alec was in his shirt sleeves, facing down the river, holding on to the two oars. But Bruce did not see Annie in the bottom of the boat.

"I wonder how old Margaret is," he murmured to his wife the moment he reached home.

But his wife could not tell him. Then he turned to his children.

"Annie Anderson's drowned," he said. "Ay, she's drowned," he continued, as they stared at him with frightened faces. "The Almighty's taken out His anger on her for her disobedience, and for breaking the Sabbath. See what you'll come to, children, if you take up with loons and don't mind what's said to you."

Mrs. Bruce cried a little. Robert would have set out at once to see Margaret Anderson, for uppermost in his mind was what action this might prompt her to make concerning Annie's money. He wanted to be prompt in putting in his own claim. But Margaret would have to wait. There was no possibility of crossing the Wan Water.

Fortunately for Thomas Crann, James Johnstone reached the bridge just before the alarm rose and sped to the nearest side, which was the one away from Glamerton. So having seen the boat go past with Alec still safe in it, he was able to set off with the good news for Thomas. After searching for him at the miller's and at Howglen, he found him where he had left him, still on his knees in the grass.

"Alec's safe, man!" he cried. Thomas fell on his face and gave humble thanks.

Down the Glamour and down the Wan Water—for the two rivers were now one—the terrible current bore *The Bonnie Annie*.

Alec could find nowhere to land until they came to a small village several miles away. The river was now flowing into the streets of it. He rowed hard, got out of the main current, and rowed up to the door of a public inn.

The fat kind-hearted lady had certainly expected no guests that day. In a few minutes Annie was in a hot bath, and before an hour had passed, was asleep in a dry bed upstairs, breathing peacefully. Alec got his boat into the coachhouse, rented a horse from the landlord, and rode home to his mother.

She had heard only a confused story about all that had happened. She had been dreadfully worried about him when he made his appearance. As soon as she learned that he had rescued Annie and where he had left her, she had one of her horses hitched to her buggy, and drove immediately to see her.

From the moment the bridge fell the flood began to subside.

Tibbie's cottage did not fall. Those who entered the next day found her body lying in the wet bed, its face still shining from the light which had broken upon her spirit as the windows were opened for it to pass into the next life.

"She sees now!" said Thomas Crann to James Johnstone as they walked together at her funeral. "The Lord sent that flood to wash the scales from her eyes."

Mrs. Forbes brought Annie home to Howglen as soon as she was able to be moved.

A week later Alec left for the city again, to begin his third winter session at the University.

CHAPTER FORTY

THE COMING OF WOMANHOOD

For several months Annie lay in her own little room at Howglen.

Mrs. Forbes was dreadfully anxious about her. She often feared that her son's heroism had only prolonged the process of dying, and that despite his efforts, that awful night might eventually take its toll.

At length on a morning in February, the first wave of the feebly returning tide of life visited her heart. She looked out her window and saw the country wrapped in a sheet of snow. A thrill of gladness, too pleasant to be borne without tears, made her close her eyes. It was not gladness for any specific reason, but the essential gladness of *being* that made her weep. There lay the world, white over green. And here she lay, faint and alive.

As the spring advanced, her strength increased till she became able to move about the house again. Nothing was said of her returning to the Bruces. What Robert Bruce's reaction was to the news that she was alive after all, I will not venture to speculate. But suffice it to say that they were not more desirous of having her than Mrs. Forbes was of parting with her.

If there had ever been any danger of anyone falling in love with Annie, there was much more now. As her health had returned, it became evident that a change had passed upon her. She had always been a womanly child. Now, at fifteen, she was a childlike woman.

Her eyes had grown deeper and the outlines of her form more graceful. A flush as of sunrise dawned oftener over the white roses of her cheeks. She had not grown much taller, but her shape produced the impression of tallness. When Thomas Crann saw her after her illness, he held her at arm's length and gazed at her.

"Eh! lassie," he said, "you're a grown woman! You'll have a bigger heart to love the Lord with. You'll be going back to Robert Bruce before long, I'm thinking."

"I don't know. The mistress has said nothing about it. And I'm in no hurry, I can tell you that, Thomas. It's a fine thing to have thick pure white milk for your porridge instead of sky-blue water with a spoonful of milk thrown into every cupful," said Annie with a smile.

Under the genial influences of home tenderness and early womanhood, a little spring of gentle humor had begun to flow softly through the quiet fields of Annie's childlike nature.

The mason gazed at her doubtfully. Annie saw his look, and took his great hand in her two little ones. She looked full into his cold, gray eyes, and asked, still smiling, "Eh, Thomas, would you have a person never poke fun of something?"

"We don't hear that the Savior himself ever so much as smiled," he returned.

"Well, that would have been little wonder with all the burdens He had upon Him. But I'm not sure that He didn't. I'm thinking that if one of the children that He took upon His knees had held up his little toy horse with a broken leg, and had prayed Him to work a miracle and mend the leg, He would have smiled or maybe laughed a bit, I dare say, and then would have fixed it some way to please the little one. And if I were on His knee, I would rather have had the mending of His own two hands on my toy, with a knife to help them maybe, than twenty miracles upon it."

Thomas gazed at her for a moment in silence. Then with a slow shake of the head, and a full smile on his rugged face, he said, "You're a curious creature, Annie. I don't rightly know what to make of you sometimes. You're like a tiny child and a grandmother both in one. But I'm thinking that between the two, you're mostly in the right."

That spring a great pleasure dawned for Annie.

Not long after this conversation with Thomas Crann, James Dow came to visit. He had a long interview with Mrs. Forbes, but Annie did not learn the result of it for some time later. One of Mrs. Forbes' farm servants who had been at Howglen for some years was planning to leave. She had asked Dow whether he knew of anyone to take his place. He offered himself, and they arranged everything for his taking the position as her foreman, the post he had occupied with James Anderson.

Few things could have pleased Mrs. Forbes more, for James Dow was recognized throughout the country as one of the best of possible foremans. He had a great reputation for saving his employers much expense. Mrs. Forbes had lately found it more and more difficult to meet her current expenses, for Alec's financial needs at the college were greater every year. She had been forced to delay the last half-yearly payment of Bruce's interest. She was still annoyed when she remembered the expression on his weasel-like face when she told him that it would be more convenient to pay the money a month late. That month had passed, and still another, before she had been able to pay him. And now another installment would soon again be due!

She hoped that with James Dow's management things would go better.

CHAPTER
FORTY-ONE

ALEC'S ILLNESS

In late February, about a month before the end of the session, Mrs. Forbes received a letter. The postmark was from the city; the address given was of the house where Alec lived. The handwriting, however, she did not recognize. She opened it and read as follows:

My Dear Madam,

> *Please excuse my writing to you like this unbidden. I am employed at the college where your son Alec is a student, and, in fact, we have for the past year shared rooms in the same boarding house, and have become close friends. Though I am a great deal older than your son, I have come to admire him greatly, and, if I am not being too bold to say so, have come to love him as if he were my own.*
>
> *I must now, however, take upon myself the unpleasant task of informing you that your Alec has become deathly ill. It is pleurisy, I think. I have made arrangements for him to see a doctor, but I thought you should know that his condition is serious.*
>
> *I am, dear madam, your obedient servant,*
>
> C. Cupples.

Mrs. Forbes dropped the letter, her face white.

"What is it?" asked Annie.

Her voice seemed to bring her to herself, and Mrs. Forbes

rose at once. "I must go to the city immediately, Annie," she said. "Alec needs me."

She went into her room, but scarcely had begun to gather her things together when the front door burst open. In walked Alec, pale and trembling, almost too ill even to be questioned.

Both women rushed to him. His breathing was short.

"Mr. Cupples made me come, Mother," he gasped out. "As soon as he posted his letter he thought better of it. He put me on the next coach. If I hadn't come at once, I would have been laid up there and unable to move."

He nearly collapsed in his mother's arms. She led him to the sofa and made him lie down. Annie was sent for the doctor. He came and bled Alec at the arm, and sent him to bed.

Annie's heart swelled till she could hardly bear the aching of it to see him so worn and ill. She went to her room, put on her bonnet and cloak, and with her few things in her hand, was leaving the house when Mrs. Forbes caught sight of her as she came out of Alec's room.

"Annie, what are you doing, child! You're not going to leave me?"

"I thought you wouldn't want me here anymore, now that Alec is home."

"You silly child!"

Annie ran back to her room, hardly able to contain all her mixed emotions.

Now came a wonderful time of ministry for Annie. Up till now she had looked up to Alec as a great, strong creature. Suddenly they had changed places. The strong eighteen-year-old youth was weak and defenseless. The gentle girl opened her heart to shelter him. A new tenderness took possession of her, and all the tenderness of her tender nature gathered about her fallen hero.

Both Annie and Mrs. Forbes took their turns in the sick chamber, watching beside the half-conscious lad. Annie's feelings spread their roots deeper and wider. It seemed to the girl that she had loved him so always, only she had not thought about it. He had fought for her at school. He had saved her life from the greedy waters of the Glamour at the risk of his own. How could she not love him?

Never had she had happier hours than those in which it seemed only the stars and the angels were awake beside herself. And if she grew sleepy while watching him at night, she would kneel down and pray to God to keep her awake that no harm should come to Alec. Then she would wonder if even the angels could do without sleep always, or whether they sometimes lie down on the warm fields of heaven between their own shadowy wings. She would wonder next if it would be safe for God to close His eyes for one minute—safe for the world, she meant. Then she would nod, and wake up with a start, flutter silently to her feet and go peep at the slumberer.

Sometimes in those terrible hours after midnight that belong neither to the night nor the day, the terrors of the darkness would seize upon her, and she would sit trembling. But the lightest movement of the sleeper would rouse her. And a glance at the place where he lay would send away all her fears.

CHAPTER FORTY-TWO

MR. CUPPLES
IN HOWGLEN

M r. Cupples wrote to Mrs. Forbes two or three times to ask about Alec's health. But he received no satisfactory answer, and had grown anxious about him. The very day the term was ended, therefore, he resolved that he would go in person and visit his young friend.

He arrived in Glamerton late and tired. He entered the first shop he came to, and asked about where there might be a cheap room to rent. For he said to himself that even the least expensive inn was no doubt more than he could afford.

Robert Bruce scrutinized him keenly from under his eyebrows, debating within himself whether the man was respectable—that is, whether he could pay. Mr. Cupples was a strange looking man, an odd blend of scholar and vagrant. He might have been almost any age between twenty five and fifty. He was a little man, who wore a long, black coat much too large for him, and dirty gray trousers. He had no shirt collar visible, although a loose rusty stock revealed the whole of his brown neck. His hair was long, thin, and light, mingled with gray, and his ears stood far out from his large head. His eyes were rather large, bright and blue. He was altogether one of the strangest of the men to be found about the college. But since moving into the boarding house where Mr. Cupples occupied the garret, Alec had found him more knowledgeable in Greek, Latin, and mathematics than anyone else he knew in the city. The student had applied often to the little man for assistance, and the two had become fast friends.

Bruce eyed him cautiously, and was slow with an answer.

"Are you deaf, man?" demanded Cupples.

"Go on your way," said Bruce, irritated. "We want no tramps in this town."

"Well, perhaps I am a tramp," returned Cupples. "But I have read of several tramps that were respectable enough. If you won't give me anything in this shop—even information—at least will you sell me an ounce of tobacco?"

"I'll sell it if you can pay for it."

"There you are," said Cupples, laying a penny on the counter. "And now will you tell me where I can get a respectable, decent place to lie down in? I'll want it for a week, maybe more."

Before he finished the question, the door behind the counter opened and young Bruce entered. He had just returned the previous day from his first year in the city at the college. Mr. Cupples knew him well enough by sight, and they greeted each other.

"This gentleman is the librarian of our college, Father."

Bruce took off his hat. "I beg your pardon," he said. "I'm terribly shortsighted in the candlelight."

"I'm used to being mistaken," answered Cupples, beginning to perceive that he had gotten hold of a character. "Make no apologies, but just answer my question."

"Well, to tell you the truth, seeing you're a gentleman, we do have a room ourselves. But it's a garret room, and maybe—"

"Then I'll take it, whatever it be, if you don't want too much for it."

Mr. Cupples was partial to garrets. He could not be comfortable if any person was over his head. He could breathe, he said, when he got next to the stars.

"Well, you see, sir, your college is a great expense to humble folk like ourselves, and we have to make it up the best we can."

"No doubt. How much do you want for the week?"

"Would you think five shillings too much?"

"Indeed, I would."

"Well, we'll say three then—for *you*, sir."

"I won't give you more than half a crown."

"Hoot, sir. That's too little."

"Then I'll look further," said Mr. Cupples, moving toward the door.

"No, no, sir. You'll do no such thing. Do you think I would let the librarian of my son's own college go out my door at this time of night? You may have it at your price. You'll have your tea and sugar and some pieces of cheese from me included, you know?"

"Of course—of course. And if you could get me some tea at once, I should be obliged to you. I am very tired."

"Mother," cried Bruce through the house door. When she came he held a brief whispering with the partner of his throne.

"So your name's Bruce, is it?" resumed Cupples, as the shop-keeper returned to the counter.

"Robert Bruce, at your service."

"It's a grand name," remarked Cupples.

"Indeed it is, and I have a right to bear it."

"You're a descendant of the king?"

"The very king himself, sir."

After a private talk, Mr. and Mrs. Bruce came to the conclusion that it might be useful, for Rob's sake, to treat the librarian with more than usual consideration. For that reason, Mrs. Bruce invited him to come down and have his tea in *the room* after he was well settled.

Mr. Cupples came down the stairs before it was quite ready, entered the empty room, and looked about. The only thing that attracted his attention was a handsomely bound Bible. He picked it up, thinking to get a laugh or two from the births of the famous Bruces. But the only inscription he could find beyond the name of *John Cowie* was the following in pencil: "*Super Davidis Psalmum tertium vicesimum, syngrapham pecuniariam centum solidos valentem, quae, me mortuo, a Annie Anderson, mihi dilecta, sit, posui.*"

205

Then came some figures, and then the date, with the initials J.C.

"It's a grand Bible," he said as Mrs. Bruce entered.

"Ay, it is. It belonged to our parish minister."

Nothing more was said about it, for Mr. Cupples was hungry.

After a long sleep in the morning, Mr. Cupples called on Mrs. Forbes. By this time Alec was sufficiently better that the two had a joyful reunion, and much happy talk followed. Mrs. Forbes' initial reaction to the man was like that of most people. Annie liked the old man immediately.

"Annie Anderson," he said when they met. "I've surely heard that name before. Well, I won't forget your name again even if I do forget where it was I first heard it."

He called on Alec every day. Mrs. Forbes gradually began to understand him better. When he was not with Alec, Mr. Cupples walked throughout the town and countryside. Before the week was over, there was hardly a man or woman about Glamerton whom he had not spoken with. On the next to last day of his intended stay, Mrs. Forbes at last consented to allow him to sit up the night with Alec, with the result that both the women were able to sleep. In the morning he found a bed ready for him. The end of it was that he did not go back to Mr. Bruce's again except to pay his bill. And he did not leave Howglen for many weeks.

One lovely morning when the sun shone into the house and the deep blue sky rose above the earth, Alec opened his eyes and suddenly became aware that life was good and the world was beautiful. Cupples propped him up with pillows and opened the window that the warm air might flow in upon him.

He smiled and lay with his eyes closed, looking so happy that Cupples thought he must be praying. But he was only blessed. So easily can God make a man happy!

The past had dropped from him like a wild and weary dream. One of God's singing prophets was pouring out a jubilant melody outside his window. The lark thought nobody was listening, but God heard in heaven, and the young man heard on the earth. He would be God's child from this moment on, for one bunch of the sun's rays was enough to be happy upon!

His mother entered and saw the beauty on her son's worn face. She saw the noble, watching love in his friend's eye. And her own face filled with light as she stood silently looking at the two. Annie entered and gazed for a moment, then fled to her own room and burst into tears.

She *had* seen the face of God! And that face was Love—love like a mother's, only deeper, tenderer, lovelier, stronger. She could not recall what she had seen or how she had known it. But in that moment she suddenly realized that she had seen His face, and that it was infinitely beautiful.

He has been with me all the time, she thought. *He gave me my father, and sent Brownie to take care of me, and Dowie, and Thomas Crann, and Mr. Cowie, and Mrs. Forbes, and Alec. And He sent the cat when I prayed to Him about the rats. And He's been with me—I don't know how long. And He's with me now. And I have seen His face. And I'll see His face again. And I'll try hard to be good. It's so wonderful, for God's just . . . nothing but Love himself!*

CHAPTER
FORTY-THREE

ANNIE RETURNS TO GLAMERTON

W ithin another few weeks Annie began to realize that it was time for her to go. She had two major reasons. First, with Alec so greatly improved, there was no longer as much need of her help. Second, she was finding in herself certain feelings which she did not know what to do with.

"Annie's coming back to you in a day or two, Mr. Bruce," said Mrs. Forbes when she called in the shop to pay some of her interest. "She's been with me a long time. But you know she was ill after the flood, and besides I could not bear to part with her."

"Well, mem," answered Bruce, "we'll be very happy to have her home again, as soon as you have had all the use you want of her."

He had never used such a friendly tone before, either to Mrs. Forbes or with regard to Annie. Something had clearly changed in the Bruces' thinking. But Mrs. Forbes took no notice of it.

Both Mr. and Mrs. Bruce received the girl so kindly that she did not know what to make of it. Mr. Bruce especially was all sugar and butter—spoiled butter, to be sure. When she went up to her old rat-haunted room, her astonishment was doubled. The holes in the floor and roof had been mended, the skylight was as clean as glass a hundred years old could be, a square of carpet lay in the middle of the floor, and curtains hung from the bed-posts. Her first thought was that these luxuries had been purchased for Mr. Cupples during his stay in her room. But she could not understand why they had been left for her.

And the consideration shown upon her return continued. All the former discomforts stopped. The baby had become a sweet-tempered little girl. Johnnie was at school all day. And Robert was decently well-behaved, though still a sulky college youth. He looked down on Annie, but was at least civil. He was a good student, and had use of *the room* for a study.

Fifty pounds would have been, in the eyes of scheming Robert Bruce the elder, a sum well worth marrying to obtain. But two hundred! No sacrifice would be too great to get one's clutches upon such a fortune!

Thus in the course of time, Robert Bruce had told his heir of his designs for Annie, that she should become Mrs. Robert Bruce, Jr. His son, however, had said he was not interested, and refused to help toward his father's goal. Nothing for the moment was said about Annie's money.

But now that young Rob was almost seventeen, he began to notice that Annie had grown very pretty. It might be a nice thing to fall in love with her after all, he thought. She must have money. Why else would his father have been so interested in his marrying her?

Annie suspected nothing until one day she chanced to hear the elder say to the younger, "Don't push her. Just go into the shop and get a piece of the red sugar-candy and give it to her next time you see her alone. The likes of her knows what that means. And if she takes if from you, you may have the run of the candy drawer! It's worthwhile, you know. Those that won't sow, won't reap."

From that moment Annie was on her guard.

In the meantime, Alec got on better and better, went out with Mr. Cupples in the carriage, ate to make up for his months of inactivity, drank water and milk and tea like a hippopotamus, and was rapidly recovering his former strength.

One evening over their supper, Alec was for the twentieth time trying to talk Mr. Cupples out of leaving. At length he said, "Alec, I'll stay with you till the next session on one condition."

"What is that, Mr. Cupples?" said Mrs. Forbes. "I would be delighted to know it."

"You see, mem, this young rascal here didn't finish his classes at the end of last session. Now for such as him, there's an examination at the beginning of the next. If they don't take it and pass it, they have to go through all their classes over again—if they want their degree. And that's a terrible loss of time. Now, if Alec'll work like a man, I'll stay and help him all I can. By the time the session's ready to begin, he'll be caught back up with the rest."

That very day Alec started up again with his studies, with Mr. Cupples as his mentor. They worked gradually up to it until he was able to study hard for four hours a day.

The rest of each summer day they spent in wandering about or lying in the grass, for it was hot and dry. Then came all the pleasures of the harvest. And when the evenings grew cool, there were many books as companions.

Mr. Cupples missed Annie once she left Howglen. He went often to see her, taking what books he could for her to borrow. With one or another of these books, she would often wander along the banks of the clear, brown Glamour, now reading a page or two, sometimes sitting down on the grass beside the shadowy pools. Even her new love did not more than occasionally ruffle the flow of her inward river. She had long cherished a deeper love, which kept it very calm.

Her stillness was always wandering into prayer. But never did she offer up a request which joined Alec's fate with her own. Though sometimes she would find herself holding up her heart like an empty cup.

One day she thought she heard Mr. Cupples walking up the stairs toward her garret room. She jumped up and ran down with a smile on her face, which fell off like a withered leaf when she saw it was but Robert the student. He took her smile as meant for him, and approached her demanding a kiss.

An ordinary Scottish maiden of Annie's rank would have answered such a request from a man she did not like with a blow on the side of the head, delivered with force! But Annie was too proud even to struggle. She stood like a marble statue while Rob kissed her. But she could not help wiping her lips afterward. The youth walked away more unsettled than if she had protested angrily.

Annie rushed back to her room, sat down, and cried.

That same evening, without saying a word to anyone, she set out for Clippenstrae, on the opposite bank of the Wan Water. It was a gorgeous evening. The sun was going down in purple and crimson, divided by light bars of gold. A faint rose mist hung its veil over the hills about the sunset. The air was soft and the light sobered with a sense of the coming twilight.

When she reached her aunt's, she found that God had directed her footsteps there. Her aunt came from the bedroom just as she entered, and Annie knew at once by her face that death was in the house. Her aunt's expression brought to her mind her father's sad departure. Her great-uncle, the little gray-haired old farmer in the Highland bonnet, lay dying. He has had nothing to do with our story, except that once he made our Annie feel that she had a home. And to give that feeling to another is worth living for.

Auntie Meg's grief was plainly visible. She led the way into the deathroom, and Annie followed. By the bedside sat an old woman with more wrinkles in her face than moons in her life. She was perfectly calm, and looked like she was herself already half across the river, watching a friend as he passed her toward the opposite bank. The old man lay with his eyes closed.

"You're come in time," said Auntie Meg. She leaned down and whispered to the old woman—"my brother James's child."

"Ay, you're come in time, lassie," responded the great-aunt kindly, and said no more.

The dying man heard the words, opened his eyes, glanced once at Annie, and closed them again.

"Is that one of the angels come?" he asked, for his wits had gone a little way before.

"No, it's Annie Anderson, James Anderson's lass."

"I'm glad to see you, dawtie," he said, still without opening his eyes. "I've wanted to see more of you, for you're just such a child as I would have liked to have myself if it had pleased the Lord. You're a douce, God-fearing lassie, and He'll take care of His own."

His mind began to wander again.

"Margaret," he said, "are my eyes closed, for I think I see angels?"

"Ay, they are."

"Well, that's very well. I'll have a sleep now."

He was silent for some time.

Then he returned to his fancy that Annie was the first of the angels come to carry away his soul. He began to murmur brokenly, "Be careful how you handle it, for it's weak and not too clean. I know myself there's a spot over the heart of it which came from a mean word I said to a child for stealing from me once. But they did steal a lot that year. And there's another spot on the right hand which came of a good bargain I made with old John Thompson over a horse. And that spot would never come out with all the soap and water in the world, for I'd already done the deed and had his money. But hoots! I'm ranting! It's on the hand of my soul, where soap and water can never come. Lord, make it clean, and I'll give it all back when I see him in thy kingdom. And I'll beg his forgiveness too. But I didn't cheat him altogether. I only took more than I would have given for the colt myself."

He went on this way, with wandering thoughts that in their wildest whimsies were yet tending homeward. Even when his words were too soft to hear, they were yet busy with the wisest of mortal business—repentance.

By degrees he fell in a slumber. And from that, about midnight, he drifted into the deepest sleep of all, which is really a coming awake.

CHAPTER
FORTY-FOUR

—

ANNIE AND CURLY

The next morning Annie set out to walk home. She could not feel oppressed or sorrowful at such a death, and she walked up the river to the churchyard where her father lay.

The Wan Water was shallow and full of dancing talk about all the things that were deep secrets when its banks were full. She went a long way along the river, then crossed some fields and came to the churchyard. She did not know her father's grave, for no stone marked the spot where he sank in this broken earthly sea. She lingered a little, then set out on her slow return.

Sitting down to rest about halfway home, she sang a song which she had found in her father's old songbook. She had said it once to Alec and Curly, but they did not care much for it. She had not thought of it again till now.

> "Ane by ane they gang awa'
> The gatherer gathers great an' sma'.
> Ane by ane maks ane an' a'.
>
> "Aye whan ane is ta'en frae ane,
> Ane on earth is left alane,
> Twa in heaven are knit again.

213

"Whan God's hairst is in or lang,
Golden-heidit, ripe, an' thrang,
*Syne begins a better sang."**

She looked up, and saw Curly walking through the wide, shallow river to where she sat.

"I knew you a mile off, Annie," he said.

"I'm glad to see you, Curly."

"I wonder if you'll be as glad to see me the next time, Annie."

Then for the first time Annie realized that Curly looked serious and nervous.

"Why do you say that, Curly?"

"I hardly know what I'm saying, Annie. They say truth always finds a way to get out. But I wish it would without having to say it."

"What can be the matter, Curly?" Annie was growing frightened. "It must be bad news you have to tell me, or you wouldn't look like that."

"I don't doubt it'll be worse news to them that it's news to."

"You're speaking in riddles, Curly."

He tried to laugh, but did not succeed. He just stood before her with his eyes looking down at the ground. Annie waited in silence.

"Annie, when we were at the school together, I would have given you anything," he burst out at last. "And now I've given you my heart in the bargain."

"Oh, Curly," murmured Annie, and said no more. She felt as if her heart would break.

"I liked you at the school, Annie. But now there's nothing in the world for me but you."

Annie rose gently, and walked close to him. She laid a hand

---

*One by one they go away.
The gatherer gathers great and small.
One by one makes one and all.

And when one is taken from one,
One on earth is left alone,
Two in heaven are knit again.

When God's harvest is in before long,
Golden-headed, ripe, in full throng,
Then begins a better song.

on his arm and said, "I'm sorry, Curly."

He half turned his back, and was silent a moment. Then he said in a trembling voice, "Don't distress yourself. But I couldn't help myself. I had to tell you, Annie."

"But what'll you do, Curly?" asked Annie in a tone full of compassion.

"God knows. I'll just have to wrestle through it. I reckon I'll go back to the pig-skin saddle I was working on," said Curly, with a smile at the bitterness of his fate.

"It's not that I don't like you a heap, Curly. You know that. I would do anything for you that I could do. You have been the best friend in the world a body could have."

Suddenly Annie burst out crying.

"Don't cry. The Lord preserve us! Don't cry, Annie. I won't say another word about it. I'm not worth you crying over. Why, that's almost as good as if you loved me," said Curly in a voice ready to break.

"It's a sad thing that things won't go right!" said Annie, at last succeeding to stop her tears. "It's my fault, Curly."

"Deil a bit of it!" cried Curly, "And I beg your pardon for bringing him into it. Your fault! I was a fool. But maybe," he added, "might I not have a chance with you—someday? Far away, you know, Annie?"

"No, Curly," she said softly. "I'm sorry."

His face grew red.

"You're not going to marry that lick-the-dirt Bruce's son!"

"I won't marry anybody I don't like, Curly."

"You don't like him, I hope to God."

"I can't stand him."

"Well, maybe—who knows. I won't despair."

"Curly, Curly. I must be honest with you as you were with me. When once a body's seen one, she can't see another, you know. Who could have been at the school as I was so long, and then be rescued out of the water, you know, and not—"

She stopped herself, fearing she'd said too much. But Curly knew her meaning instantly, and his face brightened almost as if she'd pledged her love to him.

"But you hold your tongue, Curly!" she went on quickly. "It's not many lasses would have told you such a thing. You're the only one who has my secret. Keep it, Curly."

"I'll keep it like death itself," said Curly. "But would you just let me kiss your hand, and I'll go back to my work content."

Wisely done or not, it was truth and tenderness that made her offer her lips instead. He turned in silence, comforted for the time, and began to walk back toward the river.

"Curly!" cried Annie, and he came back.

"I think I see Rob Bruce coming," she said. "He's probably come to Clippenstrae to ask about me. Don't let him come farther. He's an uncivil fellow."

"If he gets by me, he'll have to have feathers," retorted Curly, and walked toward the village. He was glad to have someone to take his emotions out on.

Annie watched, and saw the young men meet.

Curly spoke first as he came up to Bruce. "A fine day, Robbie," he said.

Bruce made no reply, for things had changed since school days and he thought rather highly of himself. But it was an unwise moment to carry a high chin to Willie Macwha, for Curly was out of temper with the whole world except Annie Anderson.

"I said it was a fine day!" he repeated loudly. "And it is the custom in this country to give an answer when you're spoken to in a gentlemanly way."

"I do not consider you a gentleman."

"That's just what the bonnie lassie yonder said about you when she asked me not to let you come a step nearer to her."

Curly found it at the moment particularly agreeable to quarrel. He had always disliked Bruce.

"I have as much right to walk here as you or anyone else," challenged Bruce.

"And Annie Anderson has a right not to be disturbed when her poor uncle is lying waiting for his coffin in the house yonder."

"I'm her cousin."

"And it's small comfort any of your family every brought her. Cousin or not, you'll not go near her."

"I'll go where I please," answered Bruce, moving to pass.

Curly moved right in front of him. "I'll see the devil take you!" shouted Bruce.

"Maybe you may, being likely to arrive at the spot first."

Bruce swore, and tried to shove Curly out of his way. But the sensation he instantly felt in his nose astonished him, and the blood beginning to flow humbled him at once. He grabbed his handkerchief and put it to his face. Then he turned and walked back to Glamerton. Curly followed him at a safe distance, and then went to his own father's shop for a visit.

Had Annie returned to the garret over Robert Bruce's shop after this incident, she would not have found the holes in the floor and roof reopened. But she *would* have found that the carpet and curtains were gone. However, she did not return that night, but turned back to Clippenstrae instead.

Before week's end the report went through Glamerton that she and Willie Macwha were *courting*.

CHAPTER FORTY-FIVE

THE DECEPTION

The interest in prophecy had left with the passing of the flood the previous winter. The people of Glamerton had no capacity for spiritual excitement left. As a result, the congregations in the churches began to dwindle. No longer feeling anxious about impending doom, few people were interested in being chastised week after week about their sins.

In addition, the newness of Mr. Turnbull's style had worn off, and he was not preaching with the same fervor as before. Even his strongest supporters in the Missionary Church admitted that he had "lost his anointing."

Thomas Crann's conclusion was that some evil had gotten into the camp to defile the ranks of the faithful, and that this was the cause of so many losing interest. And who else could it be but the money-loving, mammon-worshiping Robert Bruce? But he did not see what could be done. He had been guilty of no open, visible sin.

Having been in and around Glamerton and Howglen now for some months, Mr. Cupples had become rather well acquainted with most of the men of the place, including James Dow, whom he often saw about the farm, and Thomas Crann. And surprisingly, Crann and Cupples, so different and peculiar each in their own way, had become rather good friends.

Thus it was that one day Thomas Crann came upon Alec and Mr. Cupples in the harvest field. Having finished their studies for the day, they were out for a walk when Thomas approached. After a few minutes of friendly talk, Alec returned to the house. Cupples and Crann continued on through the field together, and before he knew it, Thomas was telling him the whole story of Annie's five-pound note along with his concern for the Missionary Church. As he spoke, Cupples found a half-forgotten dream coming back upon him. All at once light flashed into his brain.

"And so I don't see what I am to do," Thomas was saying. "I can't prove anything against the man. But in my own mind, knowing his nature, I'm certain that it was the lassie's money he took out of the Bible."

"What if I could put the proof in your hands?" asked Cupples. "You?"

"Ay, me, Thomas Crann, unless I'm badly mistaken. Or maybe you wouldn't take proof from such a sinner as me against such a saint as Bruce."

"If you can direct me to the purification of our small temple, I'll listen humbly. I only wish you would repent and be one of us."

"I'll wait until you've gotten rid of Bruce, anyway. I care little for all your small separatist churches. You're all so divided from each other it's a wonder you don't pray for a darkening of the sun that you might do without the common daylight. But I do think it's a shame for such a sneak to be in the company of honest folk. You'll hear from me in a day or two."

Cupples had remembered the inscription inside the big Bible, which, according to Thomas Crann, Mr. Cowie had given to Annie. Mr. Cupples now went to James Dow.

"Did Annie ever tell you about a Bible Mr. Cowie gave her, James?"

"Ay, she did."

"Could you get hold of it?"

"I don't know. The creature's laid his own claws upon it. It's too bad Annie's out of the house now, or she could take it herself."

"If it's truly her own, she still might. Aren't you a kind of guardian to her?"

"I have made myself that, in a way. But Bruce would be looked upon as her legal guardian, for she's still but a lass of sixteen."

"Do you have hold of the money?"

"He has it, but I made him sign a lawyer's paper about it."

"Well, just go and demand the Bible, along with the rest of Annie's property. You know she's had trouble about her chest and can't get it from him. And if he makes any difficulty, just drop a hint of going to the lawyer about it. The likes of him's as afraid of a lawyer as a cat is of cold water. But we must get the Bible."

Dow was a peaceable man. He did not like the idea. But for Annie's sake he finally agreed.

So after his day's work, which was hard enough at this season of the year, James Dow put on his blue Sunday coat and set off to the town. He found Robert Bruce dickering with a country girl over some butter. He wanted to give her less than a fair price, and was complaining that the butter had a bad taste. Listening to Bruce try to make a shrewd deal by cheating the farm girl roused Dow's anger.

"I won't give you more than fivepence.—How are you today, Mr. Dow?—I tell you, this butter has the taste of turnips."

"How can that be, Mr. Bruce?" the girl said. "There are no turnips this time of year, but plenty of grass, which is all my cows eat."

"It's not for me to say how it can be. That's not my business.—Now, Mr. Dow?" he said, turning away from the girl for a moment.

The love of Bruce's life was in driving hard bargains. And he greatly disliked any interruption of the process. So he turned to James, hoping to get rid of him quickly so he could go on dickering with the girl. He wanted her butter, for it was indeed of a fine quality. And he would pay her price in the end if he had to, but not until he had made every attempt to get it for less.

"Now, Mr. Dow?" he repeated.

"My business'll keep," replied Dow.

"But you see I'm busy tonight."

"Well, I don't want to hurry you. But I wonder why you would buy butter that is bad, even to please such a bonnie lass."

"Some folk like the taste of turnips in their butter, though I don't myself," answered Bruce. "But the fact is that turnips are not a favorite in the marketplace with most folks, so that brings the price down."

"Turnips is neither here nor there," retorted the girl. She picked up her basket and turned to leave the shop.

"Wait a minute, my lass," cried Bruce. "My wife would like to see you. Just go into the house there with your basket and see what she thinks of your butter. I may be wrong, you know."

So saying, he opened the inner door and ushered the young woman into the kitchen.

"Now, Mr. Dow?" he said once more. "Is it a bit of tobacco you're wanting?"

"It's Annie Anderson's chest and belongings."

"I'm surprised at you, James Dow. There's the lassie's room up the stairs, fit for any princess whenever she wants to come back to it. I can't imagine what's come over her, to leave us again without a word. But she always was a riotious lassie."

"You lie, Rob Bruce!" exclaimed Dow, surprised by his own outburst. "Don't you dare say such a thing to me!"

Bruce remained calm. "Don't lose your temper, Mr. Dow."

"Just give me the child's things, or I'll go to them that will."

"Who might that be, Mr. Dow?" asked Bruce, wanting to know how far Dow was prepared to go.

"You have no right to keep that lassie's clothes, as if she owed you anything for rent."

"Have *you* any right to take them away? How do I know what will come of them?"

"Well then, I'll just be off to Mr. Gibb the lawyer, and we'll see what can be done there. It's well known all over Glamerton, Mr. Bruce, how you and your family treated that orphan lassie. And so on my way I'll go into every shop down the street and tell them where I'm going and why."

Bruce dreaded profit-shrinking gossip about himself above anything else.

"Hoots! James Dow, you don't know a joke when you hear one. I was never a man to oppose anything unreasonable. I just didn't want it said about us that we drove the poor lassie out of the house, and then threw her things after her."

"The one you *have* done, for you certainly drove her away! The other you'll not have the chance to do, for I'll take them. And I'll tell you what folk will say if you don't give me her things. They'll say that you both drove her away and kept her duds. I'll see that everyone in town knows it. They'll say that—*and more besides*."

Bruce understood that he referred to Annie's money. His reason for refusing to give up her box had been to hold on to the chance of persuading her to return to live in his house for as long as possible. For once she had moved out completely, her friends could well demand the interest in cash money. Up till now he had only had to pay the interest in food and shelter, though that had come to little enough.

"Mother!" he cried, "put up Miss Anderson's clothes in her box to be taken out tomorrow morning."

"I'll take them with me now," said Dow.

"You can't. You have no cart."

"You get them ready and I'll fetch a wheelbarrow," said James, leaving the shop.

He borrowed a wheelborrow from Thomas Crann and found the box ready for him when he returned. The moment he lifted it, he was all but certain from the weight of the poor little property that the Bible was not there.

"You haven't put in Mr. Cowie's Bible."

"Mother! Did you put in the Bible?" cried Bruce, for the house door was open.

"Indeed no, Father. It's better where it is," said Mrs. Bruce from the kitchen in a shrill voice.

"You see, Mr. Dow, the Bible's lain so long there, that it's become like our own. And the lassie can't want it till she has a family to have worship with. And then she'll be welcome to take it."

"You go up the stairs for the book, or I'll go myself."

Bruce went and fetched it, with bad enough grace. With both

hands he handed the great book into the hands of James Dow.

That same night Mr. Cupples made a translation of the inscription and took it to Thomas Crann.

"Do you remember what Bruce read that night as you saw him take something out of the book?" he asked.

"Ay," answered Thomas. "He began with the twenty-third psalm, and went on to the next."

"Well, read that," said Mr. Cupples. "I found it written in hand on a blank leaf of the book."

Thomas read: *Over the twenty-third psalm of David I have laid a five-pound note for my dear Annie Anderson, after my death.*

Lifting his eyes, Thomas's face brightened as he stared at Mr. Cupples.

"But how could it be that Bruce didn't see this as well as you yourself?"

"Because it was written in Latin," replied Mr. Cupples.

"It must be a fine thing to be a scholar!" said Thomas with awe.

"Ay, sometimes. But can you tell me one more thing? What was the day of the month that you went home with your praying friend?"

"It was the night of our special prayer-meeting for the state of Glamerton. I can find out the date from the church books. But why that?"

"Go to the bank the man deals with, and ask whether a note of five pounds of a certain number was deposited the next day, and into whose account. That'll tell you everything."

For various reasons Thomas had to postpone any further action. And Robert went on buying and selling and making money, all the while unaware of the pit he had dug for himself.

CHAPTER FORTY-SIX

THE CHURCH
MEETING

The autumn months wore on. Alec's studies progressed. In October he and Mr. Cupples returned to their old quarters. Alec passed his examinations triumphantly. He entered into his fourth-year studies with greater diligence than ever, with an eye toward the medical profession.

Annie's great-aunt took to her bed for a while after her husband's funeral. Finding there was much to do about the place, Annie remained with Auntie Meg. She worked harder than she had ever worked before, blistered her hands, and browned her face and neck. Later in the month, she and her aunt together reaped the little field of oats, dug up the potatoes and covered them in a pit with a blanket of earth. Annie also helped look after the one cow and calf, fed the pigs and the poultry, and then went with a neighbor and his cart to dig their winter store of peats.

Before the winter came there was little left to be done. Annie saw by her aunt's looks that she was ready to be rid of her. With the simplicity that belonged to her childlike nature, the moment Alec was gone Annie said goodbye to Margaret at Clippenstrae and returned to Mrs. Forbes. The rainy, foggy, frosty, snowy months passed away much as they had done before, increasing even more the growth of Mrs. Forbes' love for the girl who was a child no longer.

Thomas Crann told no one of what he knew. His notion of discipline was severe, and he feared opposition if others knew of his plan ahead of time.

The time came for the regular business meeting of the Missionary Church. When all other matters of discussion had been finished, Thomas Crann rose from the rear of the assembly. An expectant silence fell.

"Brethren and officers of the church, I want to speak on a matter of discipline. We must work to discipline ourselves or the Spirit of God can't accomplish his purpose. For that reason I tell you, that on a certain Sabbath night last year, I went into Robert Bruce's house to have worship with him. When he opened the Bible, I saw him slip something out from between the pages and crinkle it up in his hand. Then he read the twenty-third psalm. I couldn't help watching and I saw him put whatever it was in his pocket. Afterward I found out that the book belonged to Annie Anderson and that old Mr. Cowie had given it to her upon his deathbed, and told her that he'd put a five-pound note between the pages for her to remember him by. Now what do you have to say to that, Robert Bruce?"

"It's a lie!" cried Robert, "made up between you and that ungrateful cousin of mine, James Anderson's lass, who I've cared for all these years like one of my own."

Bruce had been sitting trembling. But when Thomas asked him the question, thinking he had heard everything, he decided at once to meet the charge with a firm denial.

"You hear him deny it," resumed Thomas. "Well, I have seen the Bible myself, and there's this inscription written in poor old Mr. Cowie's hand: 'Over the twenty-third psalm of David, I have laid a five-pound note for my dear Annie Anderson, after my death!' Then followed the number of the bank note, which I can show them that wants to see. And I have the banker's word that on the next Monday morning, Bruce deposited into his account that very same five-pound note. What do you say to that, Robert Bruce?"

A silence followed. Thomas broke it himself with the words: "Do you not call that breaking the eighth commandment, Robert Bruce?"

But now Robert Bruce rose. Seriously and piously he spoke. "It is a sad thing among Christians, who call themselves a chosen priesthood, that a member of a church should meet with such an accusation as I have at the hands of Mr. Crann. To say nothing of his being such a hypocrite as to look around the room while on his knees in prayer, lying in wait to hurt a man when he pretended to be worshiping the Lord his Maker. But the worst of it is that he talks a thoughtless child, who has been the cause of much discomfort in our house, into joining in the plot. It is true that I took the bank note from the Bible, which was a very unsuitable place to put the unrighteous mammon. And it is true that I put it into the bank the next day—"

"What made you deny it, then?" interrupted Thomas.

"Wait a minute, Mr. Crann. You have been listened to without interruption, and I must have fair play, however falsely you may accuse me. I don't deny the fact that I took the note. But I deny the light of wickedness and thieving that Mr. Crann casts upon it. I saw that inscription and read it with my own eyes the very day the lassie brought home the book. I knew as well as Mr. Crann that the money was hers. But I said to myself, 'It'll turn the lassie's head, and she'll just throw it away on sweets and such,' for she was a greedy child. 'So I'll just put it into the bank with my own, and account for it afterward with the rest of her money.' "

He sat down and Mr. Turnbull rose.

"My Christian brethren," he said, "it seems to me that this is not the proper place to discuss such a question. It seems to me ill-judged of Mr. Crann to make such an accusation in public against Mr. Bruce, who, I must say, has met it with creditable self-restraint, and has answered it in a very satisfactory manner. Now let us sing the hundreth psalm in closing."

"I'm not finished, sir," exclaimed Thomas, forgetting his manners. "And where would be the place to discuss such a question but before a meeting of the church? Wasn't the church instituted for the sake of discipline? The Lord's withdrawn His pleasure from us, and the cause is sitting in the County Bank!"

"All this is nothing to the point," said Mr. Turnbull.

"It is very to the point," returned Thomas. "If Robert Bruce saw the inscription the day the lassie brought the Bible home, will he tell me how it was that he came to leave the note in the book till the Sabbath night?"

"I looked for it, but couldn't find it. I thought she had taken it out on her way home."

"Couldn't you find the twenty-third psalm? You found it well enough that Sabbath night! The book opened right to it!—But just one thing more. James Johnstone, will you just run over to my house and fetch the Bible.—Just have patience, all of you, till he comes back, and then we'll see how Mr. Bruce'll read the inscription. Mr. Bruce is a scholar, and he'll read the Latin to us."

By this time James Johnstone was across the street.

"There's some foul play in this!" cried Bruce. "My enemy has to send for an outlandish speech and a heathen tongue to ensnare one of the brethren!"

Silence followed as all sat expectantly. But they had to wait a full five minutes before they heard the footsteps of the returning weaver. In he ran with the large volume of the parish clergyman in both hands in front of him.

The book was laid out on the desk before Mr. Turnbull. Thomas called out from the back of the church, "Now, Robert Bruce, go up and find this inscription that you know so well about and read it to the church so that we can all see what a scholar we have among us."

But there was no movement nor voice.

"Mr. Bruce, we're waiting for you," he said. "Do not be afraid. You shall have justice."

A dead silence followed.

Presently some of those farthest back spoke in soft voices.

"He's not here."

"Not here!" cried Thomas.

They searched the whole place, but he was nowhere to be found.

227

"That would have been him when I heard the door bang," said one to another.

And so it was. Realizing that things had gone against him, he had slipped down in his pew, and crawled on his hands and knees to the door. In the candlelight of the meeting, Bruce had gone out of the church unseen.

A formal vote to expell Robert Bruce from the membership of the Missionary kirk was passed by a show of hands.

"Thomas Crann, will you engage in our closing prayer?" said Mr. Turnbull.

"Not tonight," answered Thomas. "I've done what was necessary to do, but I'm not in a right spirit to pray in public. I must get home to my own prayers. I have to ask the Lord to keep me from doing something myself that would make it necessary for you to dismiss me next. But if that time should ever come, I beg you not to spare me."

So after a short prayer by Mr. Turnbull, the meeting separated in a state of considerable excitement.

When Bruce was outside in the open air, he stood up and walked home. "Preserve us, Robert! what's come over you?" exclaimed his wife when she took one look at his face.

"I had such a headache, I was forced to come home early," he answered. "I don't think I'll be attending there any longer. They don't conduct things altogether to my liking."

Of the two, perhaps Thomas Crann was the more despressed in spirit as he walked home that night. He felt no happiness. He had promoted the fall of another man. Although the fall was a just one, he could not help feeling the reaction of a fellow human's humiliation. Now that the thing was done, the eternal brotherhood within his heart came forward, and Thomas pitied Bruce and mourned over him.

Most of the members of the Missionary Church stopped buying from Bruce's shop, and his weekly income was noticeably reduced. For a time he thought seriously of leaving the place and setting up his business in some distant village.

CHAPTER FORTY-SEVEN

ALEC'S PLANS

Alec wrote to his mother from the city requesting money to buy some better instruments. She replied sadly that she was unable to send it. She hinted that his education had cost more than she had expected. She was in debt to Robert Bruce for a hundred pounds and had recently been forced to be late with her interest payments. She told him too that, even with James Dow as manager, there seemed little hope the farm would ever make a profit to pay off the large amount his father had spent on it.

This letter stung Alec to the heart. It was bad enough that his mother should be in the power of such a man as Bruce. But that she should have to be late with her payments was even worse.

He wrote a humble letter to his mother, and worked harder still. Almost immediately he began to talk over with Mr. Cupples what might be the quickest way of his earning some money from his schooling, which would soon be complete. He would have his degree but no practical training, and the opportunities were limited. Yet he had to find some means, and quickly, to help with his mother's debts.

The very next week his landlady knocked on his door. She

knew his situation. "My cousin's here, Mr. Forbes," she told him, "Captain McTavish of the ship the *Seahorse*. He says that before long he'll be wanting a young doctor to go and keep the scurvy from his men while they're whale fishing. I thought of you and came up the stairs to see you. He says it'll be fifty pounds in your pouch for six months' work."

"Tell Captain McTavish I'll go," answered Alec, who did not hesitate a moment. He rose and followed her down the stairs.

He soon returned, his eyes flashing with delight. Adventure! And fifty pounds to send to his mother! The *Seahorse* may not be *The Bonnie Annie*, he thought, but it would take him across the real seas! When he heard from his mother, however, her enthusiasm was not as great as his. She had too much expense to oppose it, but she could hardly hide her worry. But Alec would return in the fall of the year, with enough to pay off half her debt, so he did not change his plans to go.

He passed all his examinations at the end of the session.

Mrs. Forbes did not know what to do about Annie. She could not bear the thought of turning her out this spring. She did not know where to send her, for she could not be in the same house with young Bruce. But even though she was seriously in debt, Mrs. Forbes was still of a higher class than most and clearly aware of the impossibility of any future between her own son and an orphan maiden. Despite Annie's charm and character, such a match would be unsuitable. And the mother felt it her duty to keep the two from having too much association with one another.

Alec arrived two days early and took away his mother's perplexity at once. If Annie were sent away from the house, he said, he would leave too. Mrs. Forbes agreed, thinking to herself that Alec's visit would be brief. She would not have to face a final decision until his return at the end of the year. So Annie remained where she was, much to her inward delight.

As Alec thought about his upcoming departure into a life and places unknown, he felt a desire to renew all his old friendships.

He took a day to see Curly and spent a pleasant afternoon talking about the old times and old stories and old friends. For the youth has a past just as does the man with the gray beard.

Curly told him of his encounter with young Bruce, but Annie's name never came up.

The next evening Alec went to see Thomas Crann. Thomas received him with a gruff form of tenderness.

"I'm right glad to see you," he said. "I'm glad with all your learning that you still remember an ignorant man like me. But, Alec, my man, there's some things I know better than you. Him that made the whales is better worth seeking than the whales themselves. Come down on your knees with me and I'll pray for you."

Alec agreed, and kneeled down. Thomas said: "O thou who made the whales to play in the great waters, be round about this youth, and when thou sees his ship go sailing into the far north, put down thy finger, O Lord, and strike a track before it through the hills of ice, that it may go through in safety, even as thy chosen people went through the Red Sea. For, Lord, we only want him home again in thy good time. But above all, O Lord, save him by thy grace and let him know the glory of God, even the light of thy face."

Alec rose with a serious face.

He even called on Robert Bruce, at his mother's request. He hated to do it, but he was surprised to find him pleasant. Bruce was friendly for two reasons—hope and fear. Alec was going away and might never return. That was the hope. For although Bruce had been the one to spread the rumor that Annie was engaged to Curly, he believed that Alec was the real obstacle to his plans. At the same time he was afraid of Alec. He was so cowardly himself that he thought Alec might take to physical violence if he offended him. Alec was now a great six-foot fellow and Bruce did not like to think what he might do if he was angered.

The day drew near. Alec had said goodbye to all his friends. He must go just as the spring was coming.

His mother kept her tears till after he was gone. Annie bade him farewell with a pale face and a smile that was sweet but not glad. She did not weep afterward. A gentle cold hand pressed her heart down, so that no blood reached her face and no water reached her eyes. She went about everything just as before, because it had to be done. But it seemed foolish to do anything. The spring might just as well stay away.

Mr. Cupples saw him on board at the harbor.

"You'll go see my mother?" said Alec as he was taking his farewell.

"Ay, I'll do that," replied Mr. Cupples. "You take care of your-self!"

So away went Alec northwards, over the blue-gray waters, doctor of the strong ship *Seahorse*.

CHAPTER
FORTY-EIGHT

ANNIE'S INTEREST

Two days after Alec's departure, Mr. Bruce called at Howglen to see Annie.

"How are you, Mistress Forbes? How are you, Miss Anderson? I was just coming over the water for a walk, and I thought I might as well bring the little bit of money that I owe you."

Annie's eyes opened wide. She did not know what he meant.

"It's been twelve months that you haven't had a bite or a drink under my humble roof. And since room and board was to make up for the interest, I must pay it to you now in cash since you wouldn't accept it in hospitality. So I've brought you the ten pounds."*

Annie could hardly believe her ears. Could she actually be the owner of such untold wealth? Bruce didn't give her time to say anything. Still holding the bunch of dirty one-pound notes in his hand, he went on.

---

*You might be interested to know how much the various sums of money spoken of in this story are worth today. Exact comparisons are impossible to make. But in comparing wages and buying power and the like, a pound in Annie and Alec's time was probably about the same as $75-$125 today. Annie's five-pound note would have been worth approximately $400-$500, these ten pounds around $1000, and her two-hundred pound inheritance sitting in Bruce's bank, some $20,000. Bruce was paying her five percent interest.

"But I'm thinking the best use you could put it to would be to let me put it with the rest of the principal. So I'll just take it to the bank as I go back. I cannot give you anything more for it, for that would be breaking the law against compound interest. But I can make it up to you in some other way, you know."

But Annie had been too delighted at the idea of having it to let the money go so easily.

"I have plenty of ways of spending it," she said, "without wasting it. And surely you can't expect me to let it sit in your bank without me earning any more interest from it? No, I think I'll just take it myself, Mr. Bruce, thank you."

She rose and took the bills from Bruce's unwilling hand. He had been about to put them back in his pocket when she rescued them. Pain was visible in his eyes, and Annie felt just the slightest tug of hesitation when he loosened his hold on the notes. All his energies were spent accumulating money, and there was no pain so severe to the man as letting it slip through his fingers. He went home feeling miserable and poverty-stricken.

Annie begged Mrs. Forbes to take the money, but she would not. She had said not a word to Annie about her own debt to Bruce. How Annie wished Tibbie Dyster were alive so she could give it to her! But she went instead to Thomas Crann, who helped her distribute the ten pounds among the poor of Glamerton.

After three months Bruce called again with two-and-a-half-pounds for the quarter's interest. Before the next period he had a meeting with James Dow. He told Dow that since he was now paying Annie's interest out in cash, the principal ought to be guaranteed to him for ten years. After consulting with Annie, James Dow agreed to a three-year loan, but he would not go beyond that. Papers were drawn up, and one quarter's more interest was placed in Annie's willing hand.

In the middle of the summer Mr. Cupples came for a visit. He ran about the fields like a child, gathered bunches of clover, made a great kite and romped over hill and dale with the children on his heels. He got out Alec's boat and capsized himself in the Glamour—fortunately, in shallow water. He was run away with by one of the plow horses in the attempt to ride him, and was laughed at and loved by everybody around Howglen.

CHAPTER FORTY-NINE

ROBERT BRUCE'S
INTEREST

The autumn drew nigh, and the two women of Howglen began watching the mail for the welcome letter announcing Alec's return from his sea voyage.

But the days went on and neither letter nor Alec came. All the while they imagined the *Seahorse* sailing homeward, she in fact lay frozen in a mass, trapped in a glacier of ice. The ship would not return this year, but would lay trapped in the wild waste of the arctic sea all winter long.

Their worries grew, turned into fear, and finally they were all but certain the *Seahorse* had sunk and Alec would never return. They continued to watch the shadows sadly. But at length the moment came when their eyes met and they burst into tears. Silence gradually closed in upon their days. Visions of horror tormented them. They heard Alec's voice calling for their help in their dreams, from the midst of angry winter storms. Sometimes they saw him plodding wearily home through huge snowdrifts. Mrs. Forbes forgot all about her debt, failed to pay Bruce his interest, and stopped caring what happened to her.

How often one trouble seems to come right on the heels of another.

One day, in the midst of their grief, Mrs. Forbes received a note from Robert Bruce telling her that he was at the point of leaving Glamerton to set up business in another town. He would be obliged, he said, for her to pay back the hundred pounds she owed him as soon as possible, along with the back interest she had failed to pay.

She wrote back and said to do such was impossible at present.

Within three days she received a formal request for the debt from a new lawyer. She paid no attention to it, wondering what would come next.

After about three months, a second formal application was made, on a legal form. In the month of May a third arrived, with the hint from the lawyer that his client was now prepared to begin foreclosure proceedings on her farm if she did not pay the full amount immediately.

At last Mrs. Forbes felt she must do something. She sent for James Dow and handed him the letter.

James took it and read it slowly. Then he stared at his mistress. He read it over again. At length, with a bewildered look, he said, "Give him the money. You must pay him, mem."

"But I can't. I haven't ten pounds!"

"The Lord preserve us! What's to be done? I've saved up about thirty pounds, but that wouldn't go far."

"No, no, James," returned Mrs. Forbes. "I am not going to take your money to pay Mr. Bruce."

"He's an awful creature."

"Well, I must see what can be done. I'll go and consult Mr. Gibb."

James left, dejected. Going out he met Annie. "Eh, Annie!" he said. "This has taken an awful turn!"

"What is it, Dooie?"

"The selfish Bruce is trying to destroy the mistress for a bit of money she owes him."

"He wouldn't dare!" exclaimed Annie.

"That man would do anything but lose money. Eh, lassie, if only we hadn't guaranteed him yours! I have no doubt that's why he wanted us to sign the papers for ten years, to put us out of reach of helping the mistress! He knew the term of her loan was coming up! He's a cunning scoundrel!"

"I'll go straight to him."

"He has your money for three years, Annie," said Dow. "He'll just laugh at you if you ask for some of it sooner."

"I must do what I can. But don't tell the mistress. She wouldn't like it."

"I'll hold my tongue," promised Dow.

When Annie entered Bruce's shop, the big spider was not busy with anyone, and was ready to devour her. He had been expecting her call, and put on his most gracious reception.

"How are you, Miss Anderson. I'm glad to see you. Come into the house."

"No, thank you. I want to speak with you, Mr. Bruce. What's all this about Mrs. Forbes and you?"

"Great folk like her mustn't ride over the top of poor people like me and think to take advantage of us, Miss Anderson."

"She's a widow, Mr. Bruce. She makes no claim to be great folk. What you're doing is not a Christian way of treating her."

"Folk have a right to their own. The money's mine and I must have it. There's nothing against that in the Ten Commandments. I can't turn my family into beggars just to hold up her big house. She must pay me or I'll foreclose on the house and take it."

"If you do, Mr. Bruce, you'll not have my money one minute after the three years is up. And I'm sorry we agreed to let you have it till then."

Now actually Bruce had altogether given up the notion of leaving Glamerton. His business was still successful enough even without the patronage of the Missionaries. He also had no intention of foreclosing on Mrs. Forbes' farm and possessions. He knew that would put him in a worse position with the public than any amount of quiet lying and stealing.

But he knew that Annie would be married someday, and then she would take her two-hundred pounds. Then he would be left without the capital necessary to carry on his business in the same expanded way as her money had allowed him—for he now supplied many of the little country shops as well as the people of Glamerton.

Therefore, his sly mind had hatched a scheme to twist the situation to his own advantage, for he knew exactly what Annie would do the moment she heard Mrs. Forbes was in need. Hence had come Bruce's threats against Alec's mother, and now here came his plan's success!

"You can have as much of my two hundred pounds to keep for yourself forever, Mr. Bruce," said Annie, "as much as it will take to clear Mrs. Forbes debt completely."

"Well, very well.—But you realize that your money's mine for another two-and-a-half-years anyway. That would only amount to losing her interest for two-and-a-half-years altogether. That won't do."

"What *will* do, Mr. Bruce?"

"I don't know. I want my own money."

"But you mustn't torment her, Mr. Bruce. You must know that."

"Well, Miss Anderson, I'm a reasonable man. I'm open to anything you might suggest in the way of a—shall we say, a settling of accounts."

"And just how would you propose to settle them, Mr. Bruce?"

"Well, there's the interest for two-and-a-half—call it three years—and what I could make on it—say eight percent—that's twenty-four pounds. Then there's her back interest, then there's the loss of the turnover, and then there's the loss of the money that you won't have to lend me. If you'll sign over a quittance for a hundred and fifty pounds, I'll give her a receipt showing her debt paid in full, though it'll be a sore loss to me."

"Anything you like," replied Annie.

Bruce immediately brought out the papers already drawn up by his lawyer. His plan had been thoroughly designed well in advance. He signed one of the papers, Annie the other.

"You'll remember," he added as she was leaving the shop, "that I have to pay you no interest now except on fifty pounds."

He had paid her nothing for the last six months at least.

He would not dared have taken advantage of the girl in this way if she had had any legal guardians, or if James Dow had possessed any legal power to protect her. Since he paid her only five percent interest, and had not even paid her that for the last two quarters, his computations were favorable to him to say the least. To cancel Mrs. Forbes' note of one hundred pounds in exchange for taking one hundred fifty pounds from Annie netted Bruce a handsome profit of fifty pounds. He took care to word the quittance so that if anything went wrong, he might still claim his hundred pounds from Mrs. Forbes.

Annie begged Bruce not to tell Mrs. Forbes. He was willing enough to agree. He did even more than that. He wrote to Mrs. Forbes and told her that, upon thinking the matter over, he had decided to drop further proceedings for the present.

He said nothing about her debt being cancelled in full, and all back interest paid.

When not long after that she took him a half-year's interest of four pounds, he took it in silence. The whole transaction was doubtful anyway, he told himself, and he had to take what he could get.

CHAPTER FIFTY

HOMECOMING

It was a dreary summer for everyone at Howglen. Why should the ripe grain wave joyous in the gold of the sunbeams when their dear Alec lay dead beneath frozen fields of ice? Yet the work of the world must go on. The grain must be taken in. Things must be bought and sold. Even those who mourned had to eat and drink.

So things went on of themselves, though no one at Howglen cared much for the work that summer. Annie grew paler, but continued to spread her kindness throughout the community. She told the friends she had befriended that she had no money for them now. She renewed her acquaintance with Peter Whaup the blacksmith by helping to minister to his wife who was ill. Her beauty, both inward and outward, was a quiet beauty, like the twilight, an inward, spiritual beauty. And her sorrow gave her a quiet grace, which was peacefully ripening into what is loveliest in ladyhood. She always looked like one waiting, or sometimes like one listening to melodies unheard.

The harvest came and was gathered.

One night toward the end of October, James Dow was walking by the side of his cart along a lonely country road. He was headed toward the nearest seaport for a load of coal. The moon was high and full. He approached a large stone beside the road in a desolate field. He drew near and could see an odd-looking figure seated on it. He was about to ask the person if he would like a lift, when the figure rose and cried out joyfully, "Jamie Dow!"

Dow staggered back. It was the voice of Alec Forbes!

He gasped for breath. All he could do for a moment was cry *whoa*! to his horse.

There stood Alec in rags, his face thin but brown—healthy, bold, and firm. He looked ten years older standing there in the moonlight.

"The Lord preserve us!" cried Dow, and could say no more.

"He has preserved me, you see, Jamie. How's my mother?"

"Just wonderful! She's just fine, Mr. Alec. The Lord preserve us! She's been terribly upset about you. You mustn't walk in on her tonight in her bed. The shock would kill her for joy."

"I'm awful tired, Jamie. Can you turn your cart around and take me home? I'll be worth a load of coal to my mother anyway. And then you can break the news to her."

Dow was already in the process of turning his horse. He helped Alec into the cart, covered him with his coat and some straw, and walked back along the road, half thinking himself in a dream. Alec fell fast asleep and did not wake up until the cart was standing still, about midnight, at his mother's door. He jumped up.

"Lie still, Mr. Alec," said Dow in a whisper. "The mistress'll be in bed. I'll go to her first."

Alec lay down again and Dow went to Mary's window on the other side to try to wake the maid. Just as he returned to the cart, they both heard Alec's mother's window open.

"Who's there?" she called.

"Nobody but me—James Dow," answered James. "I was half-way to Portlokie when I had an accident on the road. Bettie put her foot on a sharp stone and fell down and broke both her legs."

"How did she come home then?"

"She *had* to come home, mem."

"On broken legs! James Dow, what—"

"Just her knees, mem. I don't mean the bones, you know,

mem. Only the skin was broken. But she wasn't fit to go on. And so I brought her back."

"What's that in the cart? Is it anything dead?"

"No, mem. It's living enough! It's a stranger lad that I gave a lift to on the road. He's mighty tired."

But Dow's voice trembled, or something else revealed everything in an instant to the mother's heart.

She gave a great cry. Alec sprang from the cart, rushed into the house, and was in his mother's arms.

Annie was asleep in the next room. She half awoke with a sense of Alec's presence. She had heard his voice through the folds of sleep. And she half-dreamed that she was lying on the rug in front of the dining room fire with Alec and his mother at the table, as on that night when he brought her in from the snow hut. As she gradually came awake, she all at once knew that she was in her own bed and that Alec and his mother were talking in the next room.

She rose, but could hardly get dressed from trembling so violently. When she was dressed, she sat down on the edge of the bed to think.

CHAPTER
FIFTY-ONE

HOME LEAVING

Annie's joy at hearing Alec's voice was almost torture. But there was sadness in it too. For ever since she had believed Alec dead, she had been free to love him as much as she wanted. But Life had come in suddenly, and divided those whom death had joined. Now all at once he was a great way off, and the two were divided by the gulf of their birth. Alec would be a great gentleman some day, a landowner, a doctor. She would never be more than just a servant girl.

She did not even dare speak to him. The tide of her love had swelled so strong that she felt if she so much as looked once in Alec's face, it would break out in an agony of joy and betray her.

Not only this. What she had done about his mother's debt must come out and be discovered sooner or later. She could not stand the thought that he might feel obligated in some way to her.

All these things, and many more, worked in the sensitive maiden as she sat on her bed. The result was that as soon as she heard Alec and his mother go into the dining room, she put on her bonnet and cloak, stole like a shadow to the back door, and let herself out into the night.

She avoided the path and went through the hedge into a field of stubble at the back of the house. She walked across it, made her way to the turnpike road and the new bridge over the Glamour. She turned back many times to look at the window of the room where Alec was now talking with his widowed mother. Only when she reached a stand of trees which then blocked her view, did she finally begin to think of what she ought to do. She could think of nothing but to go to her aunt once more, and ask her to take her in for a few days. So she walked on through the sleeping town of Glamerton.

Not a soul was awake and the stillness was awful. In the middle of the large square of the little gray town, she stood and looked around her. All of one side lay in shade, the other three in moonlight. She walked on, passed over the western road and through the trees to the bridge over the Wan Water.

Everything stood so still in the moonlight! The smell from the withering fields, laid bare of the harvest and breathing out their damp odors, came to her mixed with the chill air from the dark hills around, already spiced with keen atoms of frost. She was not far from Clippenstrae. But she could not go there in the middle of the night, for her aunt would be frightened first, and angry next.

So she wandered up the stream to the old churchyard, and sat on one of the tombstones. It became very cold as the morning drew on. The moon went down. The stars grew dim. The river ran with a livelier murmur. And through all the fine stages of dawn she sat until the sun came forth rejoicing.

The long night was over. It had not been a weary one, for Annie had thoughts of her own to keep her company. Yet she was glad when the sun came.

She rose and walked through the long shadows of the graves down to the river which shone in the morning light like a flowing crystal of delicate brown. And then she walked on to Clippenstrae, where she found her aunt still in her nightcap. She was standing at the door, shading her eyes with her hand, as if looking for someone that might be crossing toward her from the east. She did not see Annie approaching from the north.

"What are you looking for, Auntie?"

"Nothing. Not for you anyway, lassie."

"Well, I'm come without being looked for. But you were look-ing for somebody, Auntie."

"No, I was only just looking."

Even Annie did not then know that it was the soul's hunger, the vague sense of a need which nothing but God can satisfy, that had sent her money-loving, poverty-stricken, lonely, grum-bling old aunt out staring toward the east. It is this formless idea of something at hand that keeps men and women always in search of something. How little they know that what they look for is in reality the God who made them, and who would live in their hearts!

"What do you want so early as this, Annie?"

"I would like you to take me in for a while," answered Annie.

"For an hour or two, certainly."

"For a week or two maybe?"

"Indeed not. I'll do nothing of the kind! Let them that made you proud keep you proud."

"I'm not so proud, Auntie. What makes you say that?"

"So proud that you wouldn't take a good offer of marriage when you had it. And then your grand rich friends throw you out when it suits them. I'm not going to take you in! There's the farmer Davie Gordon who needs a servant-lass. You can just go look for work like other folk."

"I'll go and see about it immediately. How far is it, Auntie?"

"Going and giving away your money to all the beggars about town as if it were dust, trying to act like a grand lady yourself! Never thinking about your own kin until you're in need yourself. You're not so grand, I can tell you! And then coming to poor folk like me to take you in!"

Auntie had been listening to evil gossiping tongues—so much easier to listen to than kind just tongues.

Annie had a difficult time keeping back her tears. She said nothing, tried to eat the porridge her aunt set before her, and then left. Before three hours were over she had been given charge of the dairy and cooking at the farm of Willowcraig for the next six months of coming winter and spring. Her spirits rose, and soon she was singing about the house.

When she did not appear at breakfast, and was still gone at

dinnertime, Mrs. Forbes set out with Alec to inquire about her. Not knowing where else to go first, they went to Robert Bruce.

He showed more surprise than pleasure at seeing Alec, smiling in his own unfriendly way.

"I thought you promised to bring me a barrel of whale-oil, Alec," was his only comment. "It would have cleared off a good piece of your mother's debt, you know, but I see you have come empty-handed."

Alec answered cheerily. "All in good time, Mr. Bruce. I do thank you for your patience with the debt, though."

"It can't last forever, you know," said Bruce, happy to still be able to bite, even though his poison was gone.

Alec made no reply.

"Have you seen Annie Anderson today, Mr. Bruce?" asked his mother.

"Indeed no, mem. She doesn't trouble herself with our company any more. We're not grand enough for her."

"Hasn't she been here today?" repeated Mrs. Forbes, with worry in her look and tone.

"Have you lost her, mem?" said Bruce. "That *is* a pity. She's probably run off with that vagabond Willie Macwha. He was in town last night. I saw him go by with Bobby Peterson."

They made him no reply. They did not go to George Macwha's, but set out for Clippenstrae. When they reached the cottage, they found Meg's nose high in the air.

"No, she's not here! Why should she be here? She has no claim upon me, although you decide to throw her out—after filling her up with notions that have just ruined her with pride."

"Indeed, I did not turn her out, Miss Anderson."

"Well, you should never have taken her in."

There was something in Margaret's manner that made them certain she knew where Annie was, but she refused to tell them a thing. And they had to depart having learned no more. Meg knew well enough that they would find out, but she found it pleasant to annoy Mrs. Forbes.

Indeed it was not many days before Mrs. Forbes did learn where Annie was. But she was so taken up with her son that the time passed quickly.

Alec had to go away once more to the great city. He had certain portions of study to finish at the university before he could obtain his physician's license. The good harvest would put a little money in his mother's hands, and the sooner he was able to practice medicine, the sooner he could relieve her of her debt.

The very day after he went, Mrs. Forbes drove to Willowcraig to see Annie. She found her dressed like all the other servants about the farmhouse. Annie was rather embarrassed at the sight of her friend. But Mrs. Forbes could easily see that nothing had come between their mutual love for each other.

She found that winter very dreary without Annie at Howglen.

CHAPTER FIFTY-TWO

ALEC FORBES
AND ANNIE

Annie spent the winter in housework, combined with the feeding of pigs and poultry and some milking of the cows. There was little real hardship in her life. She had plenty of wholesome food to eat, and she lay warm at night. The old farmer was kind to her because he liked her, and when his wife scolded her she never meant anything by it.

Annie remained peaceful about the future. When her work for the day was done, she would go out on long, lonely walks in the countryside.

One evening toward the end of April she went out to a certain meadow which was filled with wild flowers and singing birds. It had become one of her favorites. As she was climbing over a fence, a horseman came round the corner of the road. She saw at a glance that it was Alec. She stepped down beside the road.

Change had passed on them both since they had last seen each other. He was a full-grown man of twenty-two with a settled look. She was a lovely woman of nineteen, even more delicate and graceful than her childhood had promised.

As she got down from the fence, he got down from his horse.

Without a word on either side, their hands joined. Still they stood silent for a minute, Annie with her eyes on the ground, Alec gazing in her face, which was pale with more than its usual paleness.

"I saw Curly yesterday," said Alec finally, with what seemed to Annie a look of meaning.

Her face flushed red as fire. Could Curly have betrayed her secret?

She managed to stammer out as she dropped his hands, "Oh . . . did you?"

Silence fell again.

"We thought we would never see you again, Alec," she said at length.

"I thought so too," answered Alec, "when the great iceberg came down on us in the snowstorm and flung the ship onto the ice with her side crushed in. How I used to dream about the old school days, Annie, and finding you in my snow hut!"

But just then a figure came round the corner in search of Annie. "Annie, come home directly!" it cried. "You're wanted."

"I will come to see you again soon, Annie," said Alec. "But I must go away for a month or two first."

Annie replied with a smile and an outstretched hand—nothing more. She could wait well enough.

How lovely the flowers looked as she walked home. But the thought kept coming that Curly had told Alec something. Yet somehow she had become so beautiful before she reached the house that her aunt, who had come to see her, cried out, "Losh, lassie! What have you been about? Your face is all red!"

"That's easy enough to tell," said the farmer's wife. "She was just standing talking with a fine looking lad on a horse. But I won't have such doings about my house, I can tell you, lass."

Margaret Anderson flew into a passion and criticized her with many words. But Annie hardly heard them. Finally her aunt stopped and then left almost without a goodbye. But what did any of that matter? All Annie could think about was whether Curly had told Alec anything.

But all that Curly had said to his old friend was that Annie was not engaged to him.

So the days and nights passed. At the end of six months Annie hired on at the farm again for another term and gradually spring changed into summer. But still Alec did not come.

One evening, when a wind that seemed to smell of the roses of the sunset was blowing from the west and filling her rosy heart with joy, Annie sat down to read in an overgrown little garden near the house. It was a true country garden, containing the old-fashioned glories of sweet peas, larkspur, and poppies along with gooseberry and currant bushes, as well as potatoes and other vegetables. She sat with her back to a low stone wall, reading aloud the words from a sonnet by Milton, *Lady that in the prime of earliest youth*. As she finished it, a low voice said, almost in her ear, "That lady's you, Annie."

Alec was looking over the garden wall behind her.

"Alec!" she cried, startled. She jumped to her feet both shocked and delighted. "Don't say such a thing. Though I wish I was a little like her."

"Well, Annie," he said, "I think you're just like her. But come out with me. I have a story to tell you. Give me your hand and put your foot on the seat and I'll help you over."

She was over the wall in a moment, and they were soon seated under the trees of the meadow near where Annie had met him before. The brown twilight was coming on, and a warm sleepy hush filled the earth and air. It was broken only by the stream nearby, cantering away over its stones to join the Wan Water.

A long time went by without a word.

"They told me," said Alec at length, "that you and Curly were to be married."

"Alec!" exclaimed Annie, looking up in his face as if he had accused her of being untrue. But then she instantly dropped her eyes and said no more.

"I would have come looking for you the first day I returned if it hadn't been for that."

Annie's heart beat violently, but she said nothing. After a silence, Alec went on, "Did my mother ever tell you how the ship was lost?"

"No, Alec."

"It was a terrible, wind-blown snowstorm. We couldn't see more than a few yards ahead. The sails were down but we couldn't keep from drifting. All of a sudden a huge, ghastly thing came out of the evening and approached us like a ghost. It hit us and dashed us onto a floating field of ice. The ship was thrown onto its side and half-crushed, but, thank God, nobody was killed. It was an awful night, Annie, but I'm not going to tell you about it now.

"We made a rough barge out of the ship, and loaded it with provisions, and set out westward. We were carried west on the ice till we came near land. Then we launched our boat and got to the shore of Greenland. There we set out traveling southwards. Many of our men died, and I could do nothing to keep them alive. Every night as sure as I lay down in the snow to sleep, I dreamed I was at home. All the old stories came back to me. I woke once, thinking I was carrying you through the water in the street by the school and that you were crying on my face. And when I woke up, my face was wet. I think I'd been crying myself. All the old faces came around me every night. Thomas Crann and James Dow and my mother—sometimes one and sometimes another—but you were *always* there.

"One morning when I woke up, I was alone. I don't know how it happened. I think the men were nearly dazed with the terrible cold and the exhaustion of the walking, and I had slept so long they forgot about me. And what do you think was the first thought into my head when I came to myself in the terrible white desolation of cold and ice and snow?

"I wanted to run straight to you and lay my head upon your shoulder. For I had been dreaming all night that I was lying in my bed at home, terribly ill, and you were going about the room like an angel, with the glimmer of white wings about you, which I reckon was the snow coming through into my dream. And you would never come near me, and I couldn't speak to cry for you to come. At last, when my heart was ready to break because you wouldn't look at me, you turned with tears in your eyes, and came to the bedside and leaned over me, and—"

Alec's voice failed him.

"So you see it was no wonder that I wanted you when I found

myself all alone in the dreadful place, the very beauty of which was deadly.

"But that wasn't all. I was given more that day than I ever thought I'd get. Annie, I believe what Thomas Crann used to say must be true. I think a person may someday get a kind of a sight of the face of God. I was so miserable when I saw the men had left me behind that I sat down on a rock and stared at nothing. It was dreadful! And it grew worse and worse, till the only comfort I had was that I couldn't live much longer. And with that, the thought of God came into my head, and it seemed as if I had a right to call upon Him. I was so miserable."

Alec's voice again trailed away.

"And then a quietness came over me, like a warm breath of spring air." His voice became stronger as he went on with the story. "I don't know what it was, but it set me upon my feet, and I started to follow the rest. Snow had fallen so I could hardly see their tracks. I never did catch up with them, and I haven't heard from them since.

"The silence all around me had been fearful at first. But then, somehow or other—I can't explain it—the silence seemed to be God himself all about me. And I'll never forget Him after that, Annie."

She watched his face in wonder.

"I came upon tracks," Alec continued, "but they weren't from our own men. They had been made by some of the folk of the country. And they brought me where there was a schooner lying in the water ready to sail to Archangel. And here I am."

Could there have been a happier heart in all the world than Annie's? She was weeping as if her life would flow away in tears.

He stopped speaking, but she could not stop weeping. If she had tried to stop the tears, she would have been torn with sobs.

They sat silent for a long time. At length Alec spoke again.

"Annie, I don't deserve it—but *will* you be my wife someday?"

And all the answer Annie made was to lay her head on his chest and weep on.

CHAPTER FIFTY-THREE

ENDING FRAGMENTS

The farm of Howglen prospered. Alec never practiced further in the medical profession, but he did become a first-rate farmer. Within two years Annie and he were married, and began a new chapter of their history.

When Mrs. Forbes found that Alec and Annie were engaged, she discovered that in reality she had been wishing for it all along. She realized her earlier worries about their class differences had been entirely worldly.

Mr. Cupples came to see them every summer, and generally remained throughout the time of the harvest. He never married. But he wrote a good book.

Thomas Crann and Mr. Cupples had many long disputes, and did each other much good. Thomas grew gentler as he grew older. He learned to hope more for other people rather than merely preaching at them. And this caused him to hope more for himself too.

The first time Curly saw Annie after the wedding, he was astonished at his own presumption in ever thinking of marrying such a lady. When he was about thirty and had established a good saddlery business of his own, he married the daughter of Glamerton's clothier.

Margaret Anderson was taken good care of by Annie Forbes. But she kept herself clear of all sense of obligation since she never admitted any. In the end Robert Bruce was forced to refund Mrs. Forbes the interest he had taken from her and had to pay back the last fifty pounds he owed to Annie. He died worth a good deal of money anyway, which must have been some comfort to him on his deathbed.

His son, young Robert, is a minister, has married a rich wife, and is becoming so well known that he hopes to become Moderator of the Church Assembly someday. He never refers to his royal ancestor the king.